Advance Praise f[...]

"Sorrow and joy are at the wheel in a wild ride on the back roads of Iowa and beyond. Climb in, hang on, and hope."

Paul J. Willis, author of *Bright Shoots of Everlastingness: Essays on Faith and the American Wild*

"*Danny Gospel* lingers like a dream, as poignant as Danny's search for a normal, happy life, which is as elusive as it ought to be, as it must be."

Michael Larson, author of *What We Wish We Knew*

"*Danny Gospel* is as compelling and engrossing a read as I have had lately. Written in the tradition of Holy Fool stories, Danny will humble your heart and invite your soul to reconsider some of its assumptions."

Phyllis Tickle, author of *Shaping of a Life*

"The imagery and descriptions of nature within this work are rich and vivid. Athey is a true master of the English language. This novel is an instant classic."

Jess Moody, author of *Club Sandwich and A Drink at Joel's Place*

"If song is the doubling of prayer, as the saying goes, then Danny Gospel, in singing the story of a life, transmutes it into a prayer and draws the reader's life too into that full-voiced song and prayer charged with the power of praise and grace."

Seraphim Joseph Sigrist

"David Athey has written a Gospel novel, and not merely because of its title. It is a dreamlike and mystical narrative that takes us inside the mind and life of a Christian who has sought to seize the Kingdom in the midst of sorrows and failures. At a time when much so-called "Christian" fiction is obscenely sentimental, *Danny Gospel* is a bracing and honest book."

Ralph C. Wood, author of *Flannery O'Connor and t' Christ-Haunted*

"What is a song? It is a perfectly expressed emotion. It is words that dance. It is a place one returns to again and again, like a rhyme, like a home. It is a cry to heaven. *Danny Gospel* is a song. David Athey sings it."

Dale Ahlquist, President, American Chesterton Society

"We all know, whether we know it or not, what a good novel is: it's the one we don't want to stop reading, the one we don't want to end, and that is true of *Danny Gospel*. For those who love language this work is a feast. . . .

"Although there is a good deal of humor in it, one cannot read it without thinking deeply about life, faith and the struggle to believe in a saving God of power and love. *Danny Gospel* is the best American novel deliberately written from a Christian perspective."

Professor James B. Anderson, St. Cloud State University

"*Danny Gospel* is a tale charged with sorrow and suffering and hope and beauty. From the very first chapter, you will be whisked into a world of vivid detail, into a surreal existence in which every turned corner offers a sense of mystery. A cast of peculiar and diverse characters and a series of well integrated flashbacks help to unravel Danny's winding road to redemption."

Skylar H. Burris, Editor, *Ancient Paths Literary Magazine*

"Magical, mythical, profound, *Danny Gospel* takes us from the lost family farms of Iowa to the lost beaches of Florida and manages to cover everything: faith, doubt, kindness, cruelty, redemption and passion."

Faith Eidse, Ph.D., co-editor, *Unrooted Childhoods*

"The Great Old Truths don't change. But from generation to generation we need to hear them from new voices speaking in new ways. . . . This is a wonderful, valuable book, a joy to read, and a wonderful song to know our lives are part of."

Dr. Jack Hibbard, English Department, St. Cloud State University

Danny Gospel

a novel

David Athey

BETHANYHOUSE
Minneapolis, Minnesota

Published by Bethany House Publishers
11400 Hampshire Avenue South
Bloomington, Minnesota 55438

Bethany House Publishers is a division of
Baker Publishing Group, Grand Rapids, Michigan.

Printed in the United States of America

Library of Congress Cataloging-in-Publication Data

Athey, David.
   Danny Gospel / David Athey.
      p. cm.
   ISBN 978-0-7642-0444-9 (pbk.)
   I. Title.
   PS3601.T485D36   2008
   813'.6—dc22

                                      2007036281

To Kathleen Anderson, Dave Long, and everyone else who helped with this novel.

Thank you for believing.

—DA

chapter one

WE PLAYED OUR first concert by torchlight near the river. Free of charge, our old-fashioned act attracted a crowd to the hymns and spirituals that most people know by heart. "Amazing Grace," "Swing Low, Sweet Chariot," "Kum Ba Yah," "I'll Fly Away" . . .

My father, an ex-marine, was a Johnny Cash look-alike. He stood tall yet slumped in a black suit and wailed baritone. I stood next to him and added my ten-year-old voice to the cause. Grandmother, in a white Sunday dress, sat on a stool and strummed a sweet guitar. Jonathan wore jeans and a T-shirt and strutted with his banjo, grinning at the girls. Holly, our little tomboy princess, joyfully fiddled an old violin. And Mother, so mythological with her long black hair wisping to the ground, plucked the crowd skyward with her Celtic harp.

That summer of 1986, we performed free concerts all over Iowa—at fairs, festivals, and churches. And we became so famous that people began forgetting our family name. Everyone started calling us the Gospel Family.

On nights when there were no concerts, we gathered

on our porch and sang to the fireflies under the stars. And I believed the songs about the Promised Land were really about our farm.

Fifteen years later, the farm was just a memory and everyone in my family was dead, except for my brother, who rarely spoke to me. I was living in a trailer park in Iowa City and working as a mail carrier, delivering so much junk and so many bills. Every morning I met college girls traipsing off to class, the intelligence of God apparent in their walking, as if their graces could keep the world forever spinning in ecstasy. I was miserable, and went home after work and read books about hermits in the woods, monks in the cliffs, and warriors of prayer in the desert. One story that struck me was about a young man who wanted to shine. He sought out an elder who lifted his hands like tree branches to the sky, fingers glowing like candles. The elder challenged the young man, "Why not become all fire?"

I scribbled in the margin of the book: *God is light.*

Carrying the mail was relatively easy, and almost every day I was offered fresh baked goods—cookies, bars, brownies, and cupcakes—from apron-wearing ladies who greeted me at their doors. Because of so many sugars, I soon gained a grunting weight and had to put myself in serious training. Every night in my living room, I did hundreds of sit-ups and push-ups, followed by a strenuous reading of the lives of skinny, fiery lovers of God.

After showering, I'd collapse into bed and stare up at a mural of the Garden of Eden that I'd painted on the ceiling, the colors softly glowing in the dim light from a nearby streetlamp. I'd stare for hours and hours, wondering: why would anyone give up Paradise?

In the mornings, bleary-eyed, I'd crawl out of bed and deliver the mail. The junk and the bills. More junk and more bills. Even the greeting cards in their festive envelopes made me depressed. I forced smiles for the apron-wearing ladies and their gifts of baked goods, and they looked at me with pity, because it was obvious that I wasn't living a real life.

One clear windy day with red-orange autumn leaves swirling into the sky, Mrs. Henderson gave me a sprinkle cookie, and asked, "Danny, why don't you start another gospel band? Why not play with your brother?"

I answered, "I don't sing anymore. Thanks for the cookie. Here's your mail."

At the age of twenty-five, I felt lost and worthless, walking in circles, day after day, enduring the sweet old ladies, the traipsing college girls, and the whims of every sort of weather. I moped home after work, opened books about holiness, and then sweated through my exercises, making my body suffer. And I always prayed, deep into every night. Flat on my back in bed, with a luminous Adam and Eve looking down from the ceiling, I repeatedly asked for the same old thing: a normal happy life.

It didn't happen, and it didn't happen, until that morning in October 2001, when she appeared in my bedroom.

She was an average woman, perfectly lovely, dressed in white. She leaned down and kissed me lightly on the lips. Trembling, I wondered: is this normal and happy, or just a dream? The woman said something wonderful with her eyes. I reached up to touch her face. I whispered, "Are you—"

She disappeared from the room.

And I had to follow her.

I pulled on a pair of jeans, forgetting about shoes and a shirt, and rushed out into the sunrise. Where could the woman be hiding? She wasn't in my front yard. She wasn't in my backyard. Smiling, enjoying the chase, I climbed into my pickup and searched around the trailer park. Nothing. No sign of her. Yet I could still taste the kiss, and it felt stronger when I sped out to the shimmering cornfields, and I believed that my life was like a favorite book now turning to the happiest chapters. And I imagined a heavenly wedding, and everything in the world was like the first day of creation, as if every death specter that had plunged into me since baptism had been kissed clean away.

And then a hog truck appeared. The rig was covered with mud and filth, about to crash into me. A prayer for help arose in my heart but it couldn't get to my lips in time. Nevertheless, the hog truck swerved around me and into the ditch while I hit the brakes and skidded to a stop. I jumped out of my pickup and saw, through a cloud of golden dust, a herd of swine escaping from the back of the trucker's rig.

I called out to the driver, "C'mon, we can catch them."

"No," he said, not leaving his seat. "Let those pigs fly. The loss will be a good tax break."

"Don't be crazy," I said, pointing at the cornfield. "The herd could cause a lot of damage."

The truck driver lit a cigarette and added smoke to the cloud of dust. "Let those pigs fly," he said, "and mind your own business."

Driving away from the scene of the accident, something

told me that I should go into town and put on my uniform and report to the post office. Something told me that if I denied the kiss and the woman in white, then I could keep my job and salvage the life I'd been living.

"Salvage?" I whispered as I sped down the road. "What's left to salvage?"

Looking heavenward, I was startled to see so many birds. Above the yellow fields, the blue sky was filled with birds of many feathers, drifting and circling, inspiring me to sing my favorite spiritual: "*I got wings, you got wings. All of God's children got wings. When I get to heaven, gonna put on my wings. I'm gonna fly all over God's heaven.*"

Not paying attention to the earth, I plowed into a cornfield.

The truck was stuck, half buried, the stalks so thick and strong that my door wouldn't open. I had to squeeze through the window, my ears getting tickled by the ears of corn; and then I found myself face-to-face with a deer. The twelve-point buck was staring at my bare chest, as if thinking: man, are you okay?

I was better than okay. Because of the kiss, every nerve in my body was a solar flare. My heart was a pulsar.

"Mr. Deer," I said. "Would it be possible for you to run into town and find a tow-truck driver?"

The old buck leapt away, in the opposite direction of town.

Well, I thought. I better find a telephone.

That should have been a simple task: to walk barefoot to the nearest farmhouse and borrow a phone. And away I went, treading lightly on the gravel road between the fields.

Mile after long, lonely country mile, I searched for a house and saw nothing but corn.

When I was a little kid, even the larger farms had a sense of being part of a neighborhood, but now the land was looking more and more like an ocean of golden sprawl. I walked for at least an hour, eventually forgetting about finding a phone, thinking instead about trees, picnics in the shade, and old friends who understood what it meant to be a neighbor.

Finally, rising out of the sea of corporate corn, there appeared an island of perfect acres, a small farm consisting of bountiful patches of pumpkins and squash, an aspiring apple tree, and a wonderful scattering of yellow and orange chrysanthemums. Scratching around the flowers was a flock of cloud-white chickens.

I whispered, "Whoever lives here knows how to live."

I ambled up the dirt driveway to the farmhouse. On the porch was a solid-oak rocking chair, like the one my grandmother loved. Grammy Dorrie spent one hour each day on the porch, in every kind of weather, rhythmically watching the world.

One autumn afternoon, I stood beside her while she rocked, and I wondered if she saw something that my eyes couldn't see. I stood beside her for a long time, staring down the driveway.

Maybe she's waiting for Grandpa, I thought.

But I didn't say what I was thinking, because Grandma was a Baptist and Grandpa was in the grave, and Baptists don't believe in family visits from the grave.

Grammy took off her glasses, breathed deeply on the lenses, and cleaned them in the folds of her apron. She returned the glasses to her face and gazed longingly at the road.

And I left her alone with her secret.

Now on the morning of my kiss, at a farmhouse like my childhood home, the door opened and I turned from the rocking chair and saw an average, perfectly lovely woman. She was wearing a white peasant dress. Could it be? Was this her? The one I'd been searching for?

The woman said, "Hello. Where's your shirt?"

"I'm sorry. My truck broke down in the corn, and—"

"The corn stole your shirt?"

"Well, um, no. I guess I never put one on this morning. You see—"

"You're wounded," she said, staring at my chest.

"Yes. A long time ago."

The woman stood expectantly, waiting for me to explain how I got a scar over my heart in the shape of a cross. I just stood there, playing dumb, waiting for her to change the subject.

"Sorry to stare," she said. "I've never seen a scar like that."

"That's okay. May I please borrow your phone?"

The woman smirked warmly and handed me her cell phone. "Here. Call your therapist while I go find some flannel to cover you up."

"Thanks."

I sat in the rocking chair, leaned forward and back, took a deep breath, and dialed the gas station. "Grease, I need your help."

"Danny," he said, "where the heck are you? At the post office?"

"Listen," I said, rocking more quickly, "I'm out in the country. My pickup is stuck in a cornfield about a mile north of Saint Isidore's."

"Okay," Grease said, yawning, "here I come. You're lucky I'm not busy today."

"Thanks, Grease. I owe you."

"That's right. You never paid for your last tank of gas. What's with that? I thought mailmen were rich from stealing people's birthday cards."

"Shut up, Grease."

The woman returned with a man's shirt draped over her arm.

"My ex-fiancé, Ethan, never liked flannel. Or work boots. Or having to kill things. You should have seen Ethan the first time I butchered a chicken. He got the heaves and started flapping his arms. And he started clucking. Clucking! How crazy is that? Anyway, I'm Melissa."

I arose from the rocking chair. "I'm Danny."

"You look familiar," she said. "I've seen you somewhere. You were fully clothed."

"Maybe you saw me delivering the mail in town."

"No," she said, tapping her fingers against her thigh. "But I have seen you before. I'm positive."

"Well," I said, "thanks for letting me use your phone. And thanks for offering the flannel. I'm a big fan of flannel."

Melissa gave me the shirt and I gave her the cell phone. Our fingers lingered for an electric moment as we made the exchange, and I thought: hmm, could she be the one who kissed me?

Melissa was tall and strong. Her hair was short and

dark, and she spoke with a half-laughing voice. "This shirt was too big for Ethan. He had such narrow shoulders, and his arms were different lengths. And his poor head. It was asymmetrical! Our children would have been freaks. This farm would have become a circus."

I started to put on the shirt and hesitated because the fabric felt scratchy against my sunburned skin.

"Danny," she said, "if you're feeling shy, I can turn around while you get dressed."

"Okay. Thanks."

I struggled to pull the flannel over my flesh, but the shirt was too small. I couldn't even button a single button. So I said, "This isn't going to work," and gave the shirt back.

Melissa laughed. "Sorry, Danny. Ethan was one of the little people. Anyway, you wanna stay for lunch? I could butcher a chicken. Are you hungry? Would you like to have some lunch? Forgive me for blurting this out, but are you seeing anybody?"

"I am hungry, Melissa. And I would like to stay. But, truth be told, I saw somebody in my bedroom this morning."

Melissa raised an eyebrow. "This morning? You don't seem like that kind of a guy."

I thought: what kind of a guy am I? Why am I flirting with this woman who isn't the woman of my dreams?

"You're Danny Gospel," Melissa said. "Now I remember. I saw your family perform in Riverside Park. I was very moved by the music. Are you sure you can't stay for a while?"

I shook my head. "No. I can't stay."

Melissa shrugged. "Well, come visit again sometime. I'll butcher for you."

"Okay, that would be sweet," I said, and then hurried away from her farm.

The cool air, burning sun, and a swarm of mosquitoes fought over my skin while I jogged over the gravel. My bare feet were bleeding when I arrived at the cornfield where the pickup got stuck. Grease was standing there waiting, having already hoisted the Chevy. Good old Grease, with his big flat nose, pink ears, and great girth of gut. He was always dressed in dirty clothes, and he wore a dirty cap over his greasy comb-over. He was perhaps the dirtiest man on earth, but he'd been my good friend since childhood.

"This morning," he said, belching, "I was hung over from too many beers and three cans of beans. But at least I had the sense to put on a shirt and go to work."

I shrugged my red shoulders. "It's a long story."

Grease raised his unibrow. "Is there a woman in the story?"

"Yeah, buddy. I'm getting married."

Grease lowered his unibrow. "What?"

"I'm getting married. On Christmas Eve."

Grease snorted. "That's a fantasy."

"No, it's holy matrimony, and she already has a dress picked out."

Grease slapped his greasy thigh. "What did you do, order a woman from the Internet? I'm tempted to order one myself. I've been saving up."

"Hmm. Are you sure that's a good plan?"

"I'd love to buy a hot Italian, but I'd settle for a chilly Russian at half price."

"Grease, maybe you should pray about this."

"You know, Danny, a two-for-one Mormon special would be nice."

"Shut up, Grease."

We climbed into his truck, and he hauled my wreck away, down the gravel road. "Strangest thing," Grease said, rubbing a dirty hand across his stubble. "This is the second accident today. First one was a hog truck. Something weird is going on in the world."

A few minutes later, when we drove past Saint Isidore's Church, I could have sworn there were swine eyes peeking sheepishly through a stained-glass window.

That night, after showering and brushing my teeth, I put on my Sunday best and sat in a chair beside the bed. My neighbors turned up their TV. With guns and bombs and missiles, the McCuskeys' TV slaughtered soldiers and civilians all through the night, while I sat on the chair in my blue suit, waiting for my date.

Everyone knows the human heart keeps a sort of time with its beating, slow and steady, and sometimes more quickly, and always desiring to be stopped by a sudden moment of love breaking in, that grace-shocked moment outside of time that we all wish would last forever.

My heart did nothing special during that night of waiting, never stopping or skipping a beat, just slowly, slowly aching. In the light of late morning, with my face so tired of tears, I stood and went inside my closet, which doubles as a chapel. I lit a candle and contemplated the icons that I'd painted of my family.

Mother is white-robed and perched on a harp, her

black hair flowing in the wind like wings. She's about to fly away.

My father's icon shows him fishing in the far north. Something is pulling his canoe toward the sunrise. He's shining.

Grammy Dorrie is rocking on the porch, holding the family Bible. Musical notes flutter from the Scriptures. Grammy's wrinkled face is becoming smooth and child-like while she sings.

Holly, my little sister, was the hardest one to paint. Every time I held the brush, she was an angel in my mind, invisible, nothing but a perfect thought. Eventually, I was able to re-create the honeyed hair, the freckled face, her slim figure dancing on the water above where she'd drowned.

That's how I prayed in the closet. I stood for an hour with the images of my loved ones, remembering their suffering and hoping that I'd helped them.

I blew out the candle and came out of the closet-chapel, and felt the need to go for a drive. I telephoned Grease at the garage and asked, "Is the old Chevy running yet?"

"Well, sort of," Grease said, clanging a wrench against somebody's car. "You know, Danny, you ought to shoot that truck and put it out of its misery."

"Is it running?"

"It's limpin'."

"I'll be right over to pick it up."

"Okay, Danny. Are you wearing clothes today?"

"I'm wearing my blue suit."

Grease paused, knowing the last time I wore my suit was at a funeral; and then he spoke in a serious voice. "Has Rachel called you?"

"No, not yet."

"She calls every year, right?"

"Yeah. Rachel calls every year on our shared birthday. She always says she loves me."

"But that was back in September. When the—"

"It was a real busy day, Grease."

"And you've tried calling her?"

"A hundred times. There must be a problem with the phone company."

"Danny, you must be worried sick."

"Yeah, I am."

Twenty minutes later, I was driving the backfiring pickup around the university. And near the library, I pulled up behind a red Lumina at a stop sign. Inside the car was a woman with green hair. I waited patiently for several seconds, and I was just about to honk when I noticed that the woman's shoulders were shaking.

I jumped out of my truck and walked up to the Lumina. The woman lowered her window. "Auggh, this car! I've missed so many classes already, and today is the midterm exam."

Vehicles honked behind us, and I motioned for the drivers to pass by. The woman with the green hair watched them take the parking spots, her shoulders shaking as if her very life were breaking down.

"Hey," I said, "I have a friend who can fix your car. His shop is just a few blocks away."

The woman snapped at me. "There's no time for a tow truck! I need to be in class right now."

In a rage she turned the key. Nothing. She pounded the dashboard. "Auggh! This is driving me crazy!"

"Pull the lever for the hood," I said. "I'll see what I can do."

She nodded with angry politeness and pulled the lever. I reached under the hood and immediately felt an amazing amount of heat, an energy beyond the engine. *Vroom*, the dead Lumina fired up. I leapt away while the woman hit the gas and squealed toward the one remaining parking place.

I waved, wishing her well. And my fingers felt strange, but not burned. The thought crossed my mind that maybe I was like the elder whose prayerful fingers had become all fire.

"Oh, pshaw," I told myself. "The green-haired student was just playing a stupid trick on me. She's probably doing research on idiots."

And then I felt the need to go shopping.

At the corner of Dubuque Street and Iowa Avenue is dulcinea, a women's fine clothing store. Minding the store was Jane Jones, my first girlfriend. Jane was a devoted fan of the Gospel Family and often came with her parents to our concerts. Unlike most of the other girls that followed us, she ignored Jon and fell for me. Plain Jane, as she liked to be called, had shoulder-length brown hair, a pleasant face, and a sad smile.

"Danny, what are you doing here?"

I grinned. "Does dulcinea have any good bargains today?"

Plain Jane's eyes brimmed with concern. "I'm worried about you, Danny. Everyone is worried about you."

I reached over to a half-dressed mannequin and rattled the gold bracelet around its wrist. "Worried about me?

Why? I'm getting married on Christmas Eve. And today I'm buying a romantic gift for my lady."

Jane sighed, and I realized my stupidity. I shouldn't be prattling to a former girlfriend about the latest love of my life.

"Danny," she said, "my grandmother called this morning."

"Your grammy is great, one of the nicest on my mail route."

"Danny. Some of my grandmother's mail is missing. She thinks you stole it. Is that why you're not working today? Have you been fired?"

"I'm working today."

"Where's your uniform? Why are you dressed up in a suit?"

"Maybe I have a hot date. Maybe I'm trying to get kissed again."

Tears fell from Jane's eyes. "Danny, I know you're going through difficult times. But you've got to get help. Please, Danny. Don't cause trouble. If you stole some of the mail, you better give it back. You wouldn't survive a day in prison."

I drove away from dulcinea and out of the city, hoping the gravel roads would lead to that feeling of life beginning again. But after ten miles or so of random driving, I found myself approaching some gnarled and dying oak trees huddled around an abandoned farmhouse. The oaks had been planted a hundred years ago in a happy circle to block the wind and provide some shade. Now the breeze was moving through the tree limbs as if passing through bones.

I stopped the truck in the middle of the road and climbed out. This farm was in the vicinity of ours. I scanned the horizon, but I must have been in a slight hollow. There was nothing in the distance but corn and sky. And memory.

When I was ten, I peeked through a window into the living room. Grandmother was sitting upright in the love-seat, her face beaming, her callused hands nimbly opening a garment box that lay across her lap. My mother and my little sister stood at opposite sides of the loveseat, leaning in. Grandmother solemnly lifted a wedding dress out of the box. It was her wedding dress, and my mother's wedding dress, and someday it would be Holly's.

Holly was only seven and already she was a dreamer for marriage. She had been begging my mother constantly for permission to try on the heirloom.

I inched closer to the window. My breath on the cold glass formed rings and halos around the women and girl. All three were talking excitedly, but I couldn't understand their words.

Grandmother handed the wedding dress up to my mother, who then held it for my sister. Holly danced, clapping her hands. Then she became perfectly still, her arms upraised. My strong mother, her face weakening, helped Holly slip into the dress.

And my little sister was suddenly gone, as if swallowed up by a great shimmering ghost.

Years later, on a rainy day in late October, my mother opened the garment box and showed the wedding dress to my new girlfriend. Rachel Golding had recently moved to Iowa City from New York. She had wild curly hair and wore outrageous bohemian skirts. She was smart and funny. And our love was crazy; already we were talking about marriage and children and normal happy things.

Mother had been drinking too much wine since the double funeral for Grammy and Holly, and she was smothering Rachel. "You have no idea what a blessing you've been! Rachel, sweetie, as soon as you finish your degree, you marry my little boy!"

Rachel smiled politely and reached for the dress.

Mother said to me, "Get! Outside and find your brother."

"But I wanna see Rachel—"

"No. You're not seeing anything until your wedding. Understand? Now go find your brother."

Rachel nodded for me to go, so I slouched outside and followed the trail of smoke that led to Jonathan. He was sitting on the porch, watching the rain.

"You look cold," I said.

Jon took a deep drag on his cigarette.

"You look cold," I repeated.

"I'm used to it."

I sat on a rocking chair beside him. "Rachel's gonna try on the dress. We're getting pretty serious."

Jon flicked ashes on the porch floor. "Yeah, I heard something about a Christmas wedding."

I paused and let the subject drop, aware that my older brother should be the first one to have a serious girlfriend. It saddened me that he never seemed to find love among his many admirers.

"Danny," he said, his face dark with smoke. "Let's you and I sing."

"Really?"

"Yeah. Let's sing your song."

"My song?"

"You know. 'This Old Time Religion.' "

"Yeah, sure. In harmony, or call and response?"

Jon tossed his cigarette out into the mud. He cleared his throat, smiled, and put his arm on my shoulder. "Harmony."

"*Oh, this old time religion. This old time religion. This old time religion. It's good enough for me. . . .*"

Perhaps, I thought, gazing sadly through the gnarled oaks, I should get in my truck and drive over to our family's farm and see if the buildings are still standing. Perhaps I should go over there and say a prayer. It's been years.

Suddenly a gray Volvo came speeding down the gravel and almost crashed into me. I stood frozen, holding up my arms. The Volvo swerved and spun in a circle, and sputtered and stalled. A bald-headed man, wearing a green shirt and brown khakis, climbed out into the dust. We exchanged awkward pleasantries. One of us used profanity, and one of us didn't.

I said, "Do you realize your words float in the air forever?"

He said, "Listen. I work at the Fermi Lab in Illinois. I know what is in the air."

I asked, "Are you a meteorologist?"

He said proudly, "I am a physicist. I work with atoms."

Atoms. The word struck me like Scripture, and I remembered how my science teacher in fifth grade, Mr. Stratford, had made me dizzy by proclaiming that his wood desk was not actually solid, despite all appearances, but was more like "a spinning series of invisible events in the guise of a desk, with enough potency in its tiny movements to energize the whole world. Or destroy it."

Meeting a physicist on a gravel road in Iowa is a never-in-a-lifetime experience for most people, so I wanted to make the most of the situation. I wanted to ask him a really good question, but instead I blurted out, "You smash atoms just to see what will happen."

He stared quizzically. "That is sort of what we do."

I looked into his eyes. "Aren't you afraid?"

"Why should I be afraid?"

"What if," I asked, "you smash the wrong atom? Aren't you afraid of all Hell breaking loose?"

The physicist rubbed his bald head, making his bushy eyebrows lift and lower. He looked surprised, and then angry, surprised, and then angry.

"You know," the Atom Smasher said, "I knew a man like you in Chicago. When he got on the proper medications, he got better. Maybe you could get better, too."

"Why should I get better when I'm already charged?"

"Charged?"

"Yeah, full of heavenly fire. Watch this."

I stepped back and then sprinted forward and jumped on the hood of his car, and up to the roof. "I'm lighter than air, light as an angel! See? I can't be as dense as you think."

The Atom Smasher picked up a large rock. "Get down from my Volvo."

"On one condition," I said.

He let out a sigh. "What is your condition?"

Actually, I didn't have a condition. And I really liked

this guy. But I felt the need to scold him for some reason. I said, "Mister, from now on, you leave the atoms alone."

Thunder rumbled in the distance. Lightning flashed. The physicist dropped his rock. "My colleagues warned me about coming to Iowa."

"Oh, you'll grow to love it here," I said, jumping to the ground. "Maybe you'll even find your soul mate here. Iowa's very romantic, a good place for a guy like you."

"Romantic? I've been divorced three times."

The wind was singing and wailing from the west, with a large black thunderhead following.

I wasn't sure what to say to the physicist at this point. The possibilities were infinite. So I asked him, "Do you think fireflies are miraculous?"

"Hmm," he said. "No. Absolutely not."

That made me laugh. And that made him laugh. I think we both thought the other one was the crazy one.

I climbed into my pickup and turned the key. With a spark and a backfire, the truck inched forward, slowly built up speed and eventually began flying over the gravel. I drove toward the oncoming storm, eager to lose myself in the deluge; but when I came to a crossroads, I felt a tug to the north—as if magnetically pulled by some old prayer—and lit out for the clear skies of Minnesota.

Driving away from my home state, with a rainstorm in the rearview mirror, I remembered splashing the sky with colors, making a rainbow while watering Grammy's rosebushes. The garden hose sprayed a fine mist into the speeding spectrum of light that just a few minutes earlier had waved away from the sun.

While I journeyed northward, every glow and flicker

caught my attention. The delicate flash of a goldfinch in a shrub. The glimmer of a red squirrel swimming through the branches of a lone oak. The momentary halo around a floating leaf.

Further up and farther into the north, the ocean of corn became smaller, and the islands of trees became larger. At dusk, crossing the border into Minnesota, the first thing I saw was a lake. The sight of it was so powerful that I had to pull over. The blue reminded me of a canoeing trip I'd taken with my father to the Boundary Waters when I was eleven.

The wind had shifted that first day of October, changing the weather from warm to cool to freezing. My father, in green fatigues, paddled furiously across the lake as if pursuing or escaping something. We had no idea that this was where my sister would someday drown, but the colorful leaves around the lake were bursting with death.

"This is far enough," my father said.

Finally, he had stopped striking the lake with his paddle. His voice became as soft as a child's. "Look at those beautiful birch trees. I wonder how long it took God to think them up. Or maybe 'think' is the wrong word. Maybe everything was sung into being. Isn't that how it happens in one of your books, Danny? A great lion sings the universe into existence?"

A flock of geese flew over, huge Canadian honkers, piercing the sky with their cries and triumphant V.

"Look," I said, pointing up. But my father hung his head, staring down at the water.

"Well, we've seen enough," he said, blowing steam.

"We better get back to the farm. There's a lot of work to do before harvest. And the band needs to practice."

"What? We just got here! Aren't we going to make camp? Aren't we going to see the aurora borealis?"

"Maybe next time," he said, paddling furiously, turning us around. "If there is a next time."

An hour later, while securing the canoe to the pickup, I noticed that my father was crying. I refused to look at him or show concern in any way. How could he be so cruel when the miracles of the North were just beginning to show themselves? I caught a glimpse of a black bear trudging through the leaves, probably seeking her winter den. Father didn't notice the bear, even though she must have been a sign. I gnashed my teeth at the thought of spending the night in the truck, passing over mile after mile of boring cropland.

In the middle of the night, somewhere in Minnesota or Iowa, my father poked me in the ribs, waking me from a nightmare.

"Danny, look," he said, pointing at the rearview mirror. "There's your aurora borealis."

"Where? I don't see her. Oh, now I do!"

Blue, red, and green streamers were flowing down. The aurora seemed to be following our pickup from a playful distance. My heart pounded and ached. "She's so beautiful."

My father drove to the side of the road. "Let's get out and have a better look. I wish we had a camera."

"We don't need a camera," I said. "We'll just remember everything."

He laughed. "You'll have to remember for the both of us. My brain is on the fritz."

We scrambled out of the truck. The streamers grew brighter and closer. My father whispered, "The sky's really taking shape."

I smiled and reached up.

The light faded and disappeared.

Sitting in my pickup near a small body of water, not sure if I should go deeper into Minnesota, I wondered if the Atom Smasher was right. Maybe I just needed some medications.

As the day deadened, the lake turned from sky blue to campfire red. A gathering of cumulus clouds formed a fiery crown around the setting sun.

What a failure, I thought. First I lost the farm, and my family, and my fiancée. Now I'm going to lose my job at the post office. And possibly my mind. I can't seem to keep anything.

The sun, crown and all, sank into the earth, leaving me wondering in the twilight: how do other people manage to find love, keep jobs, have children, and live normal happy lives? Couldn't I be normal and happy, as well?

"I awoke to a woman yesterday morning," I whispered, "and she kissed me."

It was only a dream.

"She was the most beautiful woman in the world."

In your dreams.

"She wants to marry me."

Dream on.

Hands cold and trembling, I put the truck into drive and turned around. I abandoned my search and drove back to Iowa City, taking the well-paved roads all the way.

chapter two

GRAMMY SANG, *"How sweet the sound!"* and flung a handful of flour at the dough.

The kitchen table was my favorite place to ask her questions. When I was ten, I snuggled beside her and asked, "Why are Baptists louder than Catholics?"

Grammy grinned. It was the morning after our first Gospel Family concert, and I was referring to the fact that her backup vocals had almost drowned out my father.

"Hmmm," she hummed, rolling out the dough. "Baptists can get a little wild. But what do you expect from a group whose namesake fed on locusts and wild honey?"

I smiled and pointed at the bread-to-be. "Anything wild in there?"

Grammy laughed and ran a floury hand through my hair. "Oops, I made you sparkle."

"Do I look silly?"

"No. Very smart."

I stood quietly for a time, watching her work while she sang again, *"How sweet the sound!"*

"Grammy," I asked, "do you think John the Baptist was a good gospel singer?"

She pounded the dough and thought for a while. Finally, she said, "He probably chirped."

"Chirped?"

"Yes, like wilderness at sunrise."

"I don't understand."

My grandmother gave me a knowing look. "Danny, you're kind of a chirper yourself."

Two days after the kiss, I shaved and got dressed for work, hoping to salvage whatever normalcy remained in my life. But visions of delivering the mail for the next thirty years overwhelmed me with depression, and I collapsed on the couch, holding my head in my hands. I tried to pray my way out of the depression, but the pain continued to increase, rising to a level that seemed untenable, until I fell, mercifully, into the most wonderful dream—harvest sunshine, followed by a snowfall, and then the exchange of vows in a cathedral lit by the northern lights, and the kiss, and the bride so perfectly lovely.

And then my cat, Doggie, must have swatted or bitten the remote for the TV, and up flashed CNN, awakening me with the news: two mailmen had died of anthrax poisoning.

I rubbed my aching chest and prayed, "God have mercy."

Doggie pounced on the remote again. Up flashed the local news with a story about an Alzheimer's patient who had wandered away from a nursing home. A photograph of the man filled the screen, showing a wrinkled, weather-kissed face with a long white beard.

It was Jack Williams, an old friend of my family.

My father and Jack had shared farm equipment for many years, enabling them to avoid serious debt. They had named their sharing "neighborism" and took turns planting and harvesting. Sometimes whoever harvested second would end up losing some money, but nothing compared to the price of owing everything to the banks. Neighborism was the perfect system. However, the relationship between my father and his friend went sour when Jack began to lose his memory. Several years in a row, Jack harvested first. My father didn't confront him—not until the third time it happened. That year, Christian words became curses. Helping hands became fists.

After the confrontation, my father rushed out and bought expensive new equipment, all on credit, even though a bad fall was predicted.

"It was wise," he said to our family at the dinner table. "Wise and prudent. God helps those who help themselves."

Grammy Dorrie, on the far end of the table, didn't say a word. That was unusual because most nights she and my father debated all sorts of issues. Freedom of speech and religion were preached in my family because of my father's service in Vietnam. At the age of twenty-two, he'd enlisted in the fight against atheistic communism, even though he himself had no faith. My father had sent many Vietnamese souls to the next life and was almost spirited away himself. However, he survived his wounds and returned to Iowa a Catholic, pious and devout. And he vowed that his family would be allowed to believe anything their hearts desired. The only condition was that everyone must attend Mass together, "to preserve the Union."

"Dad," I asked, hoping that my questions would not be taken as attacks, "what if we have a bad harvest this year? What if we have a bad harvest next year?"

My father was dressed in his singing clothes, all black, his elbows on the table, a large bamboo crucifix hanging low.

"Dad? What if the crops aren't blessed?"

Father said nothing, and the crucifix loomed.

Silence seldom visited our dinner table. That night, it hovered over us with a heaviness that seemed all-powerful. Finally, the lull was lifted by Holly slurp-slurping a glass of milk. Jon and I laughed, thankful for the comic relief, but Father scowled. "Holly. Haven't we taught you proper manners? What's wrong with you?"

Holly flinched. "Sorry. I was just trying to—"

"Shush," my mother said softly.

My father's face reddened. Beads of sweat appeared above his furrowed brow. He scratched his head furiously as if trying to claw into his skull. "Danny," he said, "we will not have a bad fall. Not this year. Not next year. Everything is under control."

"Okay, Dad."

Jon grabbed a knife and sliced open a biscuit and began slathering on the strawberry jam. He raised the delicious mess to his mouth. "If we lose the farm, we lose it. We don't have that many acres. It won't be the end of the world."

Grammy slapped the table. "Put down that biscuit! And bow your head. We forgot to say Grace."

We all bowed and gave thanks. Like so many other families, we spoke to God with tense voices.

A few weeks later, unable to sleep, I heard my parents talking in bed. They were arguing about Jack Williams. My mother said, "You have to forgive him."

"No. Not until he admits that he lied and cheated, and asks for my forgiveness."

"Peter, if everyone waited for someone else to make the first move spiritually, then we'd all be doomed."

"I'm not forgiving him until he acknowledges the truth."

Mother sighed. "Perhaps he knows not what he does."

"Don't twist the Scriptures," my father said. "Don't twist them around my neck!"

I knew that Holly down the hall and Jon in the room beside me were lying awake, eyes wide open.

The tolling grandfather clock, downstairs where Grammy slept, struck its way to midnight.

When the tolling stopped, I was afraid the arguing would begin again, so I cleared my throat and began to sing, "*It's me, it's me, it's me, oh Lord, standing in the need of prayer. It's me, it's me, it's me, oh Lord, standing in the need of prayer.*"

Jon chimed in. "*Not my brother or my sister, but it's me, oh Lord, standing in the need of prayer. Not my brother or my sister, but it's me, oh Lord, standing in the need of prayer.*"

We paused, allowing someone else to pick up the song.

Holly yawned loudly and then sang dreamily, "*It's me,*

it's me, it's me, oh Lord, lying here in my bed. I'd like to sleep, I'd like to sleep, I'd like to sleep in peace, lying here in my bed. I want my brothers to shut up and my dad to be good, and everyone be nice to Mom—"

Father shouted, "Holly!"

Our golden-haired girl went silent. The whole house seemed to hold its breath, waiting for the next harsh word. Before it could be spoken, Holly chirped, "Dad? Can I help you?"

He cleared his throat. It sounded like the beginning of a scold. "Holly! That song you were singing . . . it was very interesting."

"Yup. I think it was."

"Hmm. Perhaps we could perform that song at our next gig. Do you have the new lyrics all memorized?"

Holly giggled. *"It's you, it's you, it's you, oh Dad, making friends again with Jack. It's you, it's you, it's you, oh Dad, making friends again with Jack."*

In the morning, after a pancake and sausage breakfast, Father pushed his chair away from the table. "Well, if nobody needs me here today, I'm thinking about driving over to the Williams place—maybe have some coffee or something. Maybe fix up a few things over there."

My mother said, "That sounds good."

My grandmother said, "Take a plate of pancakes."

Unfortunately, the meeting between Jack and my father didn't go perfectly well. There was a reconciliation of sorts, but not a partnership, and my father decided to keep all of his new equipment. So although our family was on good terms with our neighbor again, we still had enormous debts.

Years later, Jack was moonlighting as a custodian in the university's Newman Center, sweeping dust down in the Catacombs, where I was reading a Valentine's poem to my fiancée.

Rachel was wearing what she called her Manhattan Delight, an all-white blouse, skirt, and knit hat, with long dangling earrings, a Star of David brooch, and a gold necklace cross. Rachel was so moved by the Valentine's poem that she wrapped her arms around me and wept. I felt like the greatest poet ever. And then my beautiful fiancée, very slowly but with complete determination, returned the poem to my hands.

"Everything you write is about life on a farm."

"Well, more like a garden."

"Danny, we've talked and talked about this. You don't have a farm anymore. Or a garden. You live in the trailer park. You work at the post office."

There was a long, familiar, awkward pause.

"Danny. I'm transferring to NYU."

I laughed. "Is that in Des Moines?"

Rachel wept. "Danny. This isn't working. I love you. But I can't stay in Iowa. There's nothing here for us."

"But the farm, our garden. The heirloom wedding dress—"

"It doesn't exist. It's all gone, Danny. You have to stop dreaming."

"I can't."

"You have to."

"I can't."

Rachel stood and walked out of the study room and began climbing the stairs. I let the poem fall to the floor.

When it came to rest, Jack Williams appeared with a broom and swept it up.

"Thanks," I said. "Please throw it away."

Jack hovered near the trash can, his whiskery mouth mumbling the words of love. "This is beautiful," he said. "Are you sure you don't want this poem?"

"I'm sure. It's over."

Jack ripped the paper into little shreds and dropped them like confetti into the trash. Then he tapped his temple with a callused finger. "I'm keeping that poem right here. You just find me when you want it back. I'm easy to find."

Now Jack was loose from the nursing home, wandering, shivering, and afraid, maybe in a back alley or out among the cornfields. My old neighbor was lost, but I was going to find him.

Wearing my mailman uniform, I left the trailer and climbed into my pickup and drove over to the nursing home, hoping I could sense which direction Jack had gone. Looking at the rows of unlit windows, I felt guilty for not having visited him during the past year.

"Which way, Lord? Which way?"

The evening was growing dark, dangerous for the vulnerable.

"Lord, there are four directions. Which one should I take?"

There was no answer, but the city lights grew brighter. And that made me think: if Jack is in town, he'll be found very soon. But if he's out among the corn, he could stay out of sight until the harvest, until he's dead.

"Lord, an old lamb is lost. Please tell me where to find him."

A minute passed. And another. The truck hummed and rattled. More minutes passed in the darkness. "Which way? I just want to help."

All I needed was a direction. One of four. It would be so easy. "Lord, you know where Jack Williams is. I'm here. I'm willing. Show me the way."

Silence.

"Please. Show me the way."

Silence.

I sat at the wheel for an hour, waiting, listening, watching.

Eventually, the door of the nursing home opened and two young nurses walked out. One of them lit a cigarette and exhaled a great cloud. My first thought was: nurses shouldn't smoke. And then I noticed that the cloud was taking a strange shape in the air, drifting under the streetlight, riding the wind dead south.

Dead south. That was my direction.

"Thank you, God."

I gave the Chevy a good dose of gas and sped through town. I drove out into the cornfields, hoping for the best. Several times per mile, I stopped and stuck my head out the window and shouted for my old friend. "Jack!"

And I waited for a response.

There was no response.

After midnight, when my tank was nearing empty and my throat was scratched with grief, I gave up the search and drove the pickup back to the trailer park. It made no sense to me that God was allowing Jack Williams to suffer, especially because I was willing to do anything for his rescue. I went to bed angry, pulled the pillow over my face, and then tossed and turned for the next several hours, forced to endure another night of war exploding from the neighbors' TV.

Shortly after falling asleep, I was awakened by the moon. There are nights, especially in autumn when the weather is turning, that the moon is not so much a reflection of the sun but a burning white flame. I rubbed my eyes and thought about the ancient hermits in the woods, monks in the cliffs, and warriors of prayer in the desert. Sometimes they must have been so overcome by the fire in the night sky that they couldn't help but wander away from their dreams.

I arose from the bed, put on jeans, a T-shirt, and sneakers, and went outside. The moon led me down a glowing path. Dead leaves crackled and crunched with every step. An owl somewhere on a branch in the air wanted to know who, who, who I was while I crept toward the river. Although the river was brown during the day, the water was a glittering blue in the middle of the night. It may have been an optical illusion, but what a lovely one.

"Goodness gracious," my father exclaimed on our way to the Boundary Waters. "Look at that lake! Just look at it."

Lake Superior. The coldest, deadliest body of fresh water in the world.

Father drove slowly down the hill, allowing us to have a good long view of the harbor and what seemed to be an ocean beyond.

"It's not possible," my father said. "It's just not possible for anything to be that blue and that deep."

But it was possible, because my father was that blue and that deep.

After passing through the great harbor town of Duluth, we turned away from Lake Superior and journeyed into the Iron Range, a strange land of deep scars and blood-red mounds of ore. We stopped for lunch in a small town called Tower, filled our bellies with fresh fish, and then we drove into the deep woods, venturing further into the wilderness until my father found a small meadow. "Let's stretch our legs," he said.

"Okay. But let's not stretch too long. I wanna get on the water."

We jumped out of the truck and waded through the long grass that turned into a brown carpet of needles under a stand of evergreens. The smell of balsam fir made me think about Christmas and my sister. At the age of six, Holly had chosen Christmas for her personal religion. She celebrated the birth of Jesus every day and we began to call her a Christmasist. Holly kept a plastic tree in her room, decorated with lights and colorful ornaments. Every morning at breakfast she handed out presents—small things like pheasant feathers she'd found in the cornfields.

Father and I lingered for a long while among the whispering evergreens.

"This is the place to live," my father finally said. "Up here in God's country."

"What about Iowa?"

My father plucked a pine needle and snapped it in half. He breathed deeply and said, "I feel more alive in this forest than on our farm."

"Then let's grow some trees," I said. "Let's turn our farm into a forest."

Father rubbed his chin and smiled. "A forest in the corn? That's not a bad idea."

We walked over to a grove of sugar maples. Their sweet leaves were buzzing with bees and hummingbirds.

"How strange," my father said. "They think the autumn colors are spring flowers. The bees and hummingbirds have gone crazy."

"They've gone beautiful," I said.

Father laughed and put his arm around me. "C'mon. Let's get on the water."

With that memory of my father, I braved the dark edge of the Iowa River, singing, "*Oh, we are pilgrims here below. Down by the river. Oh, soon to glory we will go. Down by the riverside.*"

I took a step forward. The reflected stars scattered as if swimming away. I took another step, trying to walk on the water. Other people had done this. I wouldn't be the first. Or the last. Who knows, I thought. Maybe some day it will be normal for people to walk on lakes and rivers.

And down I sank, off the deep end of the sandbar, way down into the murk. The river rolled into my lungs, and I rolled downstream. While drowning, my mind wandered from psalms to fireflies to flickering images of grandchildren playing on the farm. And then a white-bearded face appeared. Jack Williams. His gentle eyes made me panic. How can I find him, I thought, if I'm dead?

I kicked and thrashed and reached out of the water and caught the branches of a weeping willow hunched over the river. I pulled myself ashore and coughed and spluttered and lay in the grass for several minutes, shivering. Eventually, the wind whispered me to my feet. And the moon lit a path away from the water.

Sloshing out into the countryside, I should have felt happy to be alive, but everything itched. My T-shirt was stuck to my skin, my jeans clung heavily to my legs, and my feet were in agony. Every so often, a massive blister would burst inside of my shoes.

It was a miserable march, but I just kept limping along, searching for signs of Jack Williams. The wind and moon guided me for several miles, and then disappeared when I came to a mysterious farm. The place was surrounded by an electric fence, and that was strange because there were no livestock. The farm was silent, unblessed by the breath of dreaming animals or the snorting of those awake. And there were no eyes around the yard, peeking out from behind corners or between woodpiles. The farm seemed dead. So why was it surrounded by an electric fence?

Touch it.

What?

Touch it.

Excuse me?

Reach out and touch the fence.

On purpose? Are you crazy?

Nothing will happen if you touch it. You won't die. You won't even get hurt.

"Listen," I said, "all I want is a normal happy life. All I want is a wife and a family and a farm. I never asked for a spiritual charge. I never asked for—"

I reached out and touched the electric fence. My first

thought was: this doesn't hurt very much. My second thought was: I've become all fire.

And I was sent flying over the fence.

The fall when Holly was thirteen, she had a bad feeling about visiting the Boundary Waters alone with our father. He'd been depressed and suffering violent nightmares and flashbacks to Vietnam. Holly feared that our father might try to drown himself or lose himself in the woods. My little sister had pleaded with me. "I know it's my turn to make the trip, Danny, but maybe we could break with tradition this year. Maybe two of us kids could go. Will you go with me? Please?"

I was sick in bed. "What about Jon? Did you ask him?"

She shook her head. "Jon is gone. After his chores, he drove the motorcycle into town. He's with those potheads in the trailer park. Oh, Danny, I need you to be healed. I need you to help me watch Dad up there in the woods. Please be healed. Please help me."

I was nauseated and not myself. And in my sickness, I said, "Not every day is Christmas. Tough it out, sis."

Holly put on a brave face and walked out of my room. An hour later, she waved from the Chevy while it slowly pulled out of the yard.

Waving back too late, I shivered at the sight of the upside-down canoe, fastened to the truck's roof, gliding away into the morning sky.

Three days later, after the canoe had killed her, my father packed Holly in the bed of the pickup, covered her with a blue tarp, and drove her down from the Boundary Waters back to the farm.

I was upstairs sweating and shivering under the covers when I heard my mother and Grammy making a commotion on the porch. I rolled over to look out the window, and there between the ripened cornfields was the red truck crawling up the driveway.

I heard my mother say, "Where's the canoe? Where's Holly?"

Grammy prayed, "Lord Jesus, please be with us."

Mother ran to the truck and nearly threw herself into the open window, asking my father what had happened; and then she turned and reached down into the payload and pulled back the blue tarp. "Holly, what are you doing? Sweetie, wake up." She gave my sister a shake. "You're home now, Holly. C'mon, sweetie, wake up."

Father spoke in a faltering voice. "She's not sleeping. She flew away."

There was a thud on the porch. I heard it in my chest. Grammy had fallen, her heart pumping more than she could bear.

Several weeks later, on Thanksgiving morning, I crept into the kitchen and asked my mother, "Is it okay to invite them back?"

Mother stood facing the stove. There was nothing cooking. No turkey. No pumpkin pie. She was barefoot, trembling in her bathrobe. An empty bottle of wine glowed between the burners.

I stepped closer. "Remember how Lazarus got called out of the tomb?"

No answer. She just trembled.

"Mom, I've been praying for Holly and Grammy to be raised from the dead."

Mother whirled around, her face pale and anguished. "Danny. Please don't pray that way. Holly and Grammy are much better off where they are."

I came to consciousness on my knees, my body still tingling with electricity. Floodlights filled my eyes, making them water. A silhouette stood between me and the farmhouse. The silhouette exuded mystery and strength and a sense that something spiritual was afoot on this farm.

The silhouette stepped closer, and snarled, "You're trespassing. You flew onto my side of the fence."

I mumbled, "I'm sorry. I was just searching for somebody."

The silhouette pulled out a shiny pistol and aimed it at my chest. "Trespassing is a sin. Trespassers can be put to death, especially in these days."

"I wasn't trying to trespass," I said, struggling to stand. "Is there a gate to get out?"

The silhouette groaned, "Get on your belly, trespasser, and crawl out the way you came in."

Without a word, I got down on my belly and crawled, very carefully, under the pulsating fence.

"Trespasser, trespasser," the silhouette sang in a mocking voice, "searching for nothing but trouble."

Continuing onward, I walked deep into the night, and I prayed for the silhouette, and I prayed to find Jack Williams, and I prayed for Rachel and everyone in New York, and I prayed with all of my heart for the whole groaning universe, and I prayed for another kiss. And a few miles up the road, a huge dog bounded out of nowhere, put his heavy paws on my shoulders, and licked my face as if he'd been searching for me.

"Okay," I said, pushing the Saint Bernard down. "That's enough. Now find Jack Williams. He needs our help."

Woof!

Away we went. I limped down the middle of the road, holding the scruff of Bernard's neck, hoping this was the will of God and not just craziness. Suddenly, a soulful meowing arose in the distance. The melancholy music called out to us, with each note suggesting a moment of greater urgency. Bernard did his best to guide me toward the kitten, but I was afraid we were too late. The meowing stopped.

Bernard and I stood silent. For several minutes we did not move, waiting for the kitten to regain its strength and send us another signal. Eventually, Bernard began to whine.

A man with a spiritual charge should always be full of faith and hope, but I began to feel a twinge of panic. Having failed so far to locate Jack Williams or the woman who'd kissed me, what if I couldn't even find a little lost kitten? What if I couldn't find anything?

Now the night became full of wings as a prowling owl pounded the darkness, scattering the air in all directions. The wings, serving the terrible claws, dove into the grassy ditch, rose again, and then beat a path back into the sky.

There was no meowing. No melancholy music. Nothing. I fell to my knees and crawled into the ditch, just in case the owl had missed its mark. I searched in small circles, eventually reaching the edge of the cornfield. There my face touched the whiskers of a silver tabby in a basket. Poor thing. She was lifeless.

I whispered, "Why should I even try anymore? I am so sick of death."

The kitten reached her little paw out of the basket and swatted me hard on the face, as if to say: where ya been?

Bernard walked over and snuffled the kitten. The great dog acted like a mother cat, giving the tabby a bath with his tongue. And then it was time to get on with the mission. And so we went, Bernard and I and a kitten in a basket. We searched and shouted, barked and meowed, but nothing stirred in the corn.

"Jack! Jack! Where are you?"

About an hour before sunrise, Bernard began sniffing hard at the gravel road as if he'd found a hopeful scent.

Woof-choo!

I wondered: what kind of a bark is that?

Woof-choo!

It wasn't a scent in Bernard's nose. It was an allergy. Bernard couldn't smell a thing, and the sneezy drooler was leading us like a blind seeing-eye dog.

"We're getting nowhere," I said. "My feet are killing me. C'mon, Bernard, let's call it a night. You go to your home, and I'll carry this kitten to the trailer park."

The dog kept plodding forward, dragging me along for at least another mile. He sneezed and drooled, sneezed and drooled, while the kitten meowed and meowed and reached out of her basket and swatted me. And then a small light appeared, hovering in the distance. And the light eventually became a lampstand in front of a familiar farmhouse.

Woof-choo!

The dog announced our presence and then bounded away into the corn. A few seconds later, the door of the farmhouse opened and Melissa appeared. She stood tall and strong in her fuzzy white bathrobe.

"Danny? Was that you barking?"

I explained the whole situation. She listened patiently and then invited me inside to the kitchen. She gave food and water to the kitten. Then she said, "I'll butcher some eggs for us."

"That sounds, um, good."

Melissa fired up the stove. "Danny, that's sweet of you to search for Jack Williams. I saw the story on the news. Very sad, no family in the area. No wife, no kids. Now, put the kitten back in the basket and wash your hands."

I washed while Melissa began cooking. She said, "When I saw the old man's picture on the TV, I felt like searching for him, too, but I didn't quite have the energy."

"You had a good thought," I said, "and that's like a prayer."

Melissa made omelets oozing with cheese and stuffed with sweet onions and green peppers, and she toasted home-made bread and stirred a pan full of hot chocolate. The chocolate was all creamy and frothy with little marshmallows floating on top. I offered to help cook, and she offered to hit me with the spatula. When the feast was ready, we sat at the kitchen table and talked.

"You know, Danny. After you left the other day, I felt inspired to do some writing. It wasn't my best work, but it was something I can build upon. Thank you for that."

I took a bite of buttery toast. "You're welcome."

"I sell farm goods and antiques for the cash," Melissa said, "but my real passion is writing."

I gulped some hot chocolate and gulped some more. "What do you write about?"

She sighed. "Relationships. Love. Breakups. Death. You know, life."

I swallowed hard. "Yeah, I know."

"Danny. I'm really glad you appeared the other day. I hadn't been getting much writing done. Not since September. All I've been doing is watching TV and getting depressed. I don't remember ever crying so much."

My heart pounded and ached. Why hadn't Rachel called? Didn't she know I'd be worried? Didn't she care?

"Goodness," Melissa said, looking at the playful kitten. She reached down and scooped her up. "Are you giving her away? Last month I lost my cat, Musie. I really need another Musie. Look at this little tiger's face. Oh goodness, she's so alive. Are you giving her away? Please, Danny. May I keep her?"

"Sure, I'll trade the kitten for a phone call."

Sitting somewhat tall and especially wide in the cab of his tow truck, Grease glowed in the first rays of sunlight. His unwashed T-shirt was a Rorschach of oil stains and tobacco juice.

"Listen," he said as I climbed into the truck, "I'm not a taxi driver."

"You're a good man, Grease."

He spit a juicy wad of tobacco out the window. "I'm a lady's man. That's the only reason I drove out here. When you called from Melissa's house, early in the morning, I put one and one together and figured you were hanky-pankying all night and would need my advice."

"I wasn't hanky-pankying."

Grease wiped his mouth. "Did you kiss her?"

"We were talking. That's all."

"Yeah, right."

He put the truck into gear and accelerated away from Melissa's house, while she stood shimmering on the porch with her new Musie.

Grease rubbed his dirty face with a grimy hand, pinched his pink nose, and said, "Danny, man alive, you smell like sewer."

"I fell in the river."

"You smell like sewer mixed with dog."

"Yeah, I should probably take a shower, just in case someone wants to kiss me again."

"Melissa?"

"No. She's wonderful but she's not the one. I'm talking about the real her. Understand? HER."

We rode in silence the rest of the way into town. Near the trailer park, Grease pulled into a parking lot. A few cars and trucks were scattered about as if embarrassed to be seen with each other. A neon orb glowed sickly above the strip club.

FULL-MOON—DANCING. 24 HOURS. FULL-MOON—DANCING.

"What do you say, Danny? Wanna see some mooning?"

"Grease, you know that's not good for your soul."

"Yeah, I know," he said, "but my flesh is weak. Very, very weak."

"You could try prayer and fasting instead of TV and pork chops."

"Yeah, I know," Grease said, staring longingly at the strip club. "I'm just lonely. And I have some bad news."

I wasn't sure if I could bear any more. "Bad news?"

Grease turned to face me. His eyes were bloodshot and watery. "I was listening to the scanner a few hours ago. The police were searching the reservoir for Jack."

"The reservoir? That's way north of town. How could Jack have walked that far?"

Grease rubbed the tears into his face, making a dirty mess. "The cadaver dogs picked up a scent, Danny. They think the body's in the lake."

I took a long, hot shower, and then put on my blue suit and sat in a chair beside the bed. Outside my window, a congregation of black-capped chickadees twittered and chirped, welcoming the new day and begging me for their daily seeds.

Twitter, twitter. Chirp, chirp. Twitter, twitter. Chirp, chirp.

"Okay, birds," I said. "I hear you. But I'm waiting for someone."

Twitter, twitter. Chirp, chirp. Twitter, twitter. Chirp, chirp.

"Birds, don't you care about my love life?"

Twitter, twitter, twitter!

I arose from the chair and went into the kitchen, where I kept a sack of sunflower seeds under the counter. I plunged a plastic scoop into the bag, lifted a mound of seeds, and shuffled outside.

"Here, little birdies. Get your yum-yums for your tum-tums."

Instead of rushing to the feast, the chickadees flung their plump bodies away from the house and flapped out of my yard. They flew above the neighboring rooftops and then paused at the edge of the trailer park. The flock of birds hovered in the blue as if inviting me to follow.

I didn't want to be superstitious or deceived in any way, but I also didn't want to consider myself above and beyond the wisdom of the One who chose to speak through the donkey-brained ass of Balaam. Perhaps the chickadees were speaking to me with their chirps and twitters and wings.

I filled the feeder with seeds, dropped the scoop in the grass, and then jumped in my truck and followed the birds.

Why not? It was a warm-cool day with a crisp wind that made me shiver with hope. Leaves of orange turned in the wind as the October sun baked everything gold. Why not follow birds on a day like that?

We didn't get far out of the city before we came to a farm that was so abandoned it had only one remaining building. It was like a black-and-white photograph that seems lifeless but makes you imagine more life. The birds hovered for a few moments and then hurried back toward the trailer park, hungry for the seeds. I climbed out of the truck and walked up to the cracked and rotting building. Once upon a better time for farming, it might have been a small barn. Or a large chicken coop. Now it was leaning ever closer to the earth.

And it was padlocked.

"A brand-new lock," I whispered. "This is very mysterious."

At the sound of my voice, the ruin came alive with rustling noises.

I squinted into a crack in the door and called out, "Hello? Is somebody in there? Do you need help?"

The rustling noises got louder.

"Don't be afraid. I'll get you out of there."

I yanked on the padlock but it would not give. So I focused on the rusty hinges. I worked my fingers into the gaps, ignoring the slivers that needled under my nails, and I was able to rip the hinges from the rotted wood and fling the door open.

"Come on out," I said, "you're free!"

The rustling became a stampede, and I had to leap away from the door. A great cloud of dust and a herd of swine billowed into the sunlight. The pigs pounded the earth, snorting and squealing into the corn.

Maybe I should chase them into the field, I thought.

No, just let those pigs fly.

Caw! Caw-aww! A musical crow appeared from behind the ruin and floated with the wind like a beckoning prayer; and I got into the truck and followed. Why not? If God wanted to use a musical crow to serve His purposes, then who was I to argue? I followed the bird for several miles, even though she didn't fly as a crow is supposed to fly—straight—but kept going this way and that way, and I began to worry about that creature's ability to serve its Creator.

A few minutes later, the crow led me to a brick building rising out of the corn. It was the Rural Mental Health Clinic.

The bird whirled in midair and landed on top of the flagpole. Caw-aww! she sang over the stars and stripes. Caw-aww! Caw-aww!

The clinic looked more like a veterinarian hospital. Something told me that I'd been there before. Something told me not to go inside. But I slowly climbed out of the truck and walked toward the one-way glass entrance.

"Come in," a man said, opening the door. He was short and round and his jowls wiggled when he spoke.

I felt uneasy and thought about running away.

"Come in, Daniel," Dr. Parsons said. "I haven't seen you for a while. But I knew you'd want to talk with me today."

It was the anniversary of my mother's death.

chapter three

THERE IS A moment in late autumn in Iowa when it seems the sun so adores the earth that the cornstalk leaves go all a-swirl and leap like love-struck flames. When I was a teenager in love, I was caught up in one of those moments when everything that could be seen was nothing but fiery, golden grace; and then my mother's voice fluttered out of the sky. *"This little light . . . this little light . . . my little light . . ."*

The words were a sing-song mess of grief that drew me out of the shadow where I was leaning against the barn. I stepped into the sunshine and had the squinting thought: what is she doing atop the silo?

She was singing, slurring, *"Holly little light . . . Grammy little light . . . my little lights . . ."*

My mind, slipping into a panic, was unable to move my body beyond slow motion, while Mother swayed in the sky in the near distance—so far away in a white dress—her arms uplifted, her wind-blown hair parting like wings.

After hitting the ground, she survived in the hospital for six days. On the last day, after several clergymen had visited and done all they could do, Jon and I were asked to leave the room so our father could say good-bye to her alone. We lingered at the door while the words "I love you" were whispered into an ear that was already hearing the same thing from God.

Just a year after the funeral for Holly and Grammy, we had to face another burial.

Jon and I shuffled down the hall. In the waiting room, I slouched in a cold plastic chair, picked up an issue of *Clean Country Living* from the magazine table, and began reading an article about the miraculous life of insects. At the bottom of the page was a large photograph of a female mosquito, her belly swollen with scarlet. The caption read: "Our blood makes her babies."

I lifted the magazine to my brother's troubled face. "Look at that mosquito," I whispered. "She's beautiful."

Jon's eyes narrowed. "I don't know why God made mosquitoes." He sighed heavily. "I don't know why God made anything."

Now, I can't speak for all mosquitoes. But the one that appeared in my pickup after my meeting with Dr. Parsons was a very helpful guide. At first I ignored her while she flew around the cab. But after a while, I noticed that she was extremely gifted. The mosquito seemed to know whenever we came to a crossroads. She buzzed and zipped to a side window as if telling me to turn. Or sometimes she sat still on the dashboard, pointing her stinger straight ahead.

Considering the fact that I had just visited a clinic for my mental health, I politely declined to have any communication with the mosquito. I just let her do her thing while

I minded my own business, randomly driving around on the gravel roads. After a while, however, the sound of her wings became impossible to ignore, resounding like the high strings of a violin. It was beautiful. And every move the mosquito made seemed to make sense. When she wanted me to drive straight, she squatted directly in the center of the dashboard. And when she wanted me to turn, she flew to a side window.

And so we went, crisscrossing the Iowa countryside, all day long. I thought my guide might leave me when I stopped to get gas in Amana. I even opened the window to set her free, but when I returned from paying the cashier, the mosquito was perched patiently on the dashboard.

In the reddish light of sunset, I followed the directions of the talented mosquito, until eventually I was led to Saint Isidore's Church and around to the cemetery. In a frantic flash of buzzing wings, the mosquito flew to the rear window. Apparently my guide wanted me to hit the brakes. So I did, and when the dust settled, I could see half of a man among the gravestones.

It was my brother, Jonathan, kneeling in the middle of our family's graves, his lips moving. After a few minutes, he stood and brushed himself off. He wiped his eyes and looked at the truck. He smiled painfully, took a deep breath, and walked slowly down a row of the dead. The rays of the setting sun gave a glow to the rust-colored scar on Jon's cheek. He was as skinny as a skeleton and wore a pinstriped suit. His dark hair was still as thick as trouble, and his eyes were a mix of sorrow and joy.

I wondered: what does Jon have to be joyful about?

He climbed into the truck. "Hello, Danny. Are you visiting the family?"

I stared at the gravestones and the growing shadows. Grandparents, parents, and Holly, all buried before their time, or before a time that I could understand. "I can't deal with this, Jon."

"Okay, Danny. Let's go for a drive."

I gave the truck a foot-load of gas and sped away from the cemetery. I looked around the cab to see where the mosquito was. I wanted to introduce her to my brother, the great lawyer, but she was gone.

Jon said, "Watch out!"

I swerved to avoid hitting a large hog, and made a quick left turn at the crossroads. The pig followed in pursuit, galloping in a waddling sort of way, before finally disappearing from view.

"That was very strange," I said. "Jon, have you noticed strange things happening lately?"

My brother didn't answer. He stared out the window while the final glint of sunset left the face of the sky. And he began to sing, "*Walk you in the light. Walk you in the light. Walk you in the light of God.*"

It was a song our family had always performed at our barn dances.

Our great red barn, which hadn't housed livestock in ages, was filled with Christmas lights on my sixteenth birthday. Holly had wanted to decorate a tree for me, as well, but I said the lights were good enough. On September 11, 1992, the party included my friends (Grease, Jane Jones, Mud Eye, and Slopper) and neighbors (Jack Williams and the

Lancaster, McCuskey, and Manifest families) and various people from Saint Isidore's and Grove Baptist, and about a hundred strangers that Jon had invited. He'd blurted out at a concert, "You're all invited to my little brother's birthday party! Come to the farm next Saturday night."

Even without receiving proper directions, people showed up for the celebration. My father, the decorated military man, spent most of the evening directing traffic and giving out parking warnings. "Hey, don't hit the septic tank!"

For many of our guests, this was their first barn dance. Grammy was our caller and Holly was our fiddler, and they had everyone clapping and holding hands, locking arms and going allemande left and right. They had the dancers forming circles and squares, crossing and casting and making the grand chain. Grammy called out the commands as loudly as an evangelist, and Holly fiddled to beat the band, and they had everyone promenading and do-si-doing under the summer Christmas lights.

Outside, with a good moon rising, there were mountains of food dishes on a long line of tables. Fried chicken, baked ham, mashed potatoes, potato salad, egg salad, fruit salad, sweet peas, green beans, baked beans, corn bread, corn on the cob, chocolate cake, chocolate-chip cookies, and pies: apple, strawberry, lemon meringue, and blueberry. With sweet iced tea and lemonade and thick black coffee. Some people danced while others feasted, and I went with the flow, spending most of the night with Plain Jane until her parents drove her home.

After receiving a year's worth of handshakes, hugs, and "Happy birthdays," I snuck away from the remaining revelers and went behind the barn. In the moonlight, I strolled in the grass beside the cornfield. Fireflies hovered and blinked, and I paused to consider them. Heaven loves light so much, I thought, even insects get a share.

I held out my hand to a firefly, and it disappeared.

Swish, swish, swish, a half-lit girl came walking toward me, taking the shape of a woman as she got closer. She swished right up to me in her red skirt and purple sash. I'd never seen a gypsy before, or a Spanish dancer, or whatever this wild-haired woman was. She was almost my height in her bare feet. And with no awkwardness, hesitation, or formal introduction, she planted a kiss on my cheek. "For Danny, the birthday boy."

I stuttered, "Th-thanks."

The woman laughed and lifted her face to the moonlight, as if expecting a kiss in return. Clumsily, I pecked her glowing cheek.

"Sweet," she said. "I'm Rachel Golding. And tonight is my birthday, too."

"That's weird. I mean cool. Happy Birthday! Are you sixteen?"

She laughed. "Eighteen. I'm a freshman at the university."

Impressed, even enthralled, by Rachel's bohemian attire, I asked, "Are you from Des Moines?"

"New York," she said.

"New York? Really?"

Her eyes grew mournful and her voice tense. "Can I tell you something, Danny?"

I felt like I'd known her forever. "Of course. Tell me."

She took my hand and we sat in the grass among the

reappearing fireflies. Rachel told me about growing up in Manhattan, where her mother and father, a Catholic and a Jew, had owned a nice little wine shop. Life had been strange and good, they had all kinds of interesting friends, and Rachel was considering working in that wine shop and attending NYU, and just enjoying the city for the rest of her life, until some dangerous people wanted more than wine.

Something horrible happened to her parents. Rachel didn't say what it was. She choked back sobs and whispered, "I was sent here to Iowa . . . to be safe."

As I drove further away from the cemetery, Jon kept singing, "*Walk you in the light. Walk you in the light. Walk you in the light of God.*"

Fog rose like smoke out of the corn. Jon stared out the window and eventually fell silent. I drove us deep into the Iowa gloom. My brother and I met up like this every year on the anniversary of our mother's death, and the night always ended the same, with a bitter argument and a return to the cemetery, where we hurried our good-byes and went home in opposite directions.

But on this particular night, before the bitter argument, we happened upon a roadside oasis called Kate's Home Cookin'. And I slowed the truck.

"Are you hungry, Jon?"

"Starving."

"Me too."

My brother put his hand on my shoulder. "Danny, let's try to have a good meal together. Like the old days. Remember the good meals? Remember the good conversations?"

Of course I did.

When we were young, the dinner table had been a feast of both food and theology. Almost every evening, my father and grandmother debated the deepest mysteries of the faith, but never with their mouths full. They had developed a system of giving short speeches, followed by taking a huge bite of food and chewing it slowly while the other person spoke. They would debate the history of the Church, the role of Rome, the sacraments, the saints, the interpretation of Scripture, and the varieties of worship. My father and grandmother disagreed about many of the Mysteries, and sometimes the discussions got heated.

I listened with equal-sized ears to everyone in my family. I knew that each of their souls had some of God's secrets. And I considered myself a collector of any wisdom that anyone had to offer.

Mother knew the Bible so well that she never argued about religion. She was a warrior of prayer in the closet, and she knew from her childhood how quickly a shared table could explode into chaos. Her father, she once told me, "Preached Hell and proved it with his hands. But please don't tell Grammy that I told you that. She never stopped loving that man, even when he was violent."

Like everyone else in my family, I was an extreme. Of all the spiritual possibilities, I had chosen to be a slave. Why? Because of the songs. I believed the slave spirituals were as inspired as King David's psalms, and if the Bible were ever updated, many spirituals would bless the new pages. When I chose to be a slave at the age of ten, I often went without eating, and did extra chores, and a few times whipped myself with a belt. But I was never able to write a song like "Swing Low, Sweet Chariot" or "This Little Light of Mine" or "Didn't My Lord Deliver Daniel."

Holly, who believed it was Christmas every day, gave us the gift of asking innocent questions. Often it was her curiosity about the nature of reality that inspired my father and grandmother to spar and grapple for the truth.

Jon, our resident agnostic, loved to stir up trouble, but because of his charm, he rarely got into trouble. He could get away with saying things that would have gotten me punished. Sometimes I tried to get punished, for example, the time I painted LET MY PEOPLE GO in large black letters on the side of the barn. I wanted to get whipped, but my parents knew what I was up to.

"Danny," my mother said gently, "you don't have to be a slave to write a song."

"But I want to write a spiritual."

"Don't wish for suffering, Danny. It's not fair to those who've really suffered."

Jon and I went inside Kate's Home Cookin' and were greeted by the glorious stench of Iowa soul food. Hog fat boiled in oil.

A farmer at the counter was eating pork chops and mashed potatoes. The harvest was fast approaching, and the old man was gorging as if it were his final meal. Another farmer stood at the cash register. He wore, like many Iowans, both a belt and suspenders. He was a man who would never get caught with his pants down.

"Good ribs tonight," he grunted.

"Say it with a bigger tip," the cashier replied.

My brother led me to a corner booth. On the walls were black-and-white photographs of pioneers. Dirty, sweating, unsmiling men and women and children.

I sat and stared at the photographs, searching for signs of hope in the eyes of the pioneers.

Jon picked up a greasy menu. "Well? Do you want to hear my good news?"

"Good news?"

Jon stared at the specials on the back of the menu. "I'm engaged."

I bit my tongue.

He smiled. "She's a lawyer."

"Hmm." I searched the menu for anything healthful. The special was tenderloin. "Surprise, surprise."

"She's a good lawyer, Danny."

"A good lawyer? Isn't that a contradiction in terms?"

"You'll like Marta. She fights for the rights of migrant workers. You know there are thousands and thousands of migrant workers in Iowa."

"Yes. I know. They get abused by the corporate farms."

"Marta helps the workers receive a living wage, sanitary housing, basic health care, and education. She was recruited by Cesar Chavez, the great human rights activist, while in college."

"Berkeley," I guessed.

"Stanford. And then Harvard Law School. Marta is perfect, I'm telling you."

Part of me wanted to congratulate my brother. Part of

me wanted to smack him. And all I could offer was a dead pause.

"Hmm," Jon said, disappointed by my silence. "I wonder if the applesauce in this place is homemade."

"I'm sorry, Jon."

"The applesauce is from a can?"

"I don't care about the applesauce. I think you know what I care about. I was engaged once. And you sold the farm, and burned the heirloom wedding dress, and ruined everything."

Jon took a deep breath. "I had to make some difficult decisions. I did the best I could with the wisdom that I had."

"You were stoned half the time."

"I plead guilty. I'm sorry, Danny. You and I are the only Gospels left. And I want you to be my best man. It's going to be a Christmas Eve wedding in Des Moines."

The best man in my soul wanted to say yes, and the worst man still wanted to smack him. So I changed the subject. Or rather, I kept the subject but changed the focus. "Remember when Holly got engaged?"

Jon nodded, slow and sad.

When Holly's fifth-grade classroom got wired for email, young Miss Drake was so excited about corresponding with other cultures around the world that she allowed Holly to use the computer during lunchtime, unsupervised. During the spring semester, my little sister built a relationship with a sixteen-year-old boy who claimed to be José from South America. Some of the emails were shown to Miss Drake. Other emails, the romantic ones, were printed out, put into

Holly's backpack, and erased from the computer. And she carried her secrets home.

Having never heard of Internet prowlers, Holly had offered up her heart to the illusory Web. And she had divulged her greatest desire: to give birth to a baby named Jesus.

José told Holly that he had an uncle named Jesus and he would gladly name his own children after the Savior. "Jesus will be our first boy," he wrote, "and Christina our first girl."

Holly emailed back: "Dearest José. I can't wait to meet you. Love, the Christmas Girl."

Jon had discovered some of the printed emails down in the root cellar among some old gunnysacks where he kept a stash of marijuana. He led me down to the cellar one night and showed me the correspondence.

"We have to find this guy," Jon said, "before he and Holly have a chance to meet."

Under the speckled light of a dusty bulb, my brother's face seemed old and hard.

"Holly's a smart girl," I said. "She won't do anything stupid. She's just playing a game. It's puppy love. She'll never really meet this guy."

Jon lit up a joint and took in a deep drag. He exhaled into a corner full of cobwebs. "I'm not being paranoid," he said. "I really have a bad feeling about this."

The next day after school, I met Jon in his room. He was slouched on his bed with his boots on, smoking a cigarette beneath a poster of Bob Dylan. I sat at Jon's desk. It was strewn with twelve months of Christmas presents.

"She can't fly to Brazil," I said, picking up a pheasant feather. "Are you really afraid she might meet this boy?"

Jon exhaled loudly. "What if he lives in Iowa? What if he isn't a boy?"

"What?"

"It could be a filthy old man. Some murderous old pervert in the trailer park. This world is a hellhole. I've fallen into it the last couple of years, and I know what I'm talking about, Danny. I've seen things. I've heard things. I know the truth. The world is mostly evil."

"No," I said. "The world is mostly good. Evil is just a small part of the story."

"You wish."

I pointed the feather at him. "You're not the only one who has seen and heard things. That hell-raiser who scarred your face is now in seminary, serving the Lord. I'm telling you, the world is full of love."

"Read the newspaper, Danny. Watch the TV. Love is not in the news."

I wanted to be hopeful, ever hopeful, but the image of Holly being hurt scared me to death. Maybe we should search her room, I thought.

Jon could see that I was reconsidering. He said, "Listen. Holly's out in the fields with Dad. Let's go into her room and look for a card or letter. She must have something more than the emails that she keeps in the cellar. We need to find a street address for José, or whoever he is. We need to track him down. And if he's a devil, we need to exorcise him."

Jon spit into his hand and snuffed out his cigarette. He

dropped the butt into a soda can beside the bed and jumped to his feet. "C'mon, Danny. If something horrible happens to Holly, you'll never forgive yourself."

I turned and peered out the window. Many acres away, out among the spring-green shoots of corn, my father and little sister were standing in the muddy field. We'd had two bad years in a row. Father and Holly were praying, hands raised.

"Okay," I said. "You keep an eye on Mom and Grandma. And I'll search Holly's room."

"I want to look with you, Danny."

"No. You won't be careful enough. She has nativity sets all over the place. You'll step on a baby Jesus, and that'll be the end of you."

Jon was surprised. "You've been in her room before? I didn't think she let anyone in there except for Mom and Grandma."

"Yeah, I've been in there. Holly and I have discussed whether or not to search your room."

Jon laughed and then slipped out into the hallway and down the stairs to spy on the ladies in the kitchen.

I snuck into Holly's room and searched her dresser and closet and under the bed. I peeked inside of shoe boxes and crayon boxes. I searched in the manger of the large nativity set and in her backpack. And I found nothing. It appeared that José hadn't sent anything through the mail. I breathed a sigh of relief and sat on her bed and thanked God, and then I stood and impulsively reached under the mattress. There was a stack of about ten cards and letters, tied with a red Christmas bow.

I untied the bow and examined the first envelope. It was

expensive, ivory, scented with cologne. There was no return address, but the postmark was from Slow Creek, a small town about sixty miles away. My hands trembled when I opened the envelope and pulled out the card.

It was a Mother's Day card, with a scratchy handwritten note. "Soon, you'll be a mother. And we'll name the child Jesus. Love, your Secret Boy."

A few minutes later, when I showed the card to Jon, his face went ashen and he was quiet for a long while. Finally, he said, "We're driving over to Slow Creek in the morning. Bring your knife."

We ate breakfast with the family at first light. Jon and I nibbled dry toast and sipped some orange juice in silence. We let Grammy and Father do all of the talking as they debated the Resurrection of the just and whether or not those who rise from the graves will still have some of their earthly wounds, just as Jesus kept his.

Grammy adjusted her glasses. "The disciples needed to see those wounds, and touch them, in order to fully believe. But when Jesus ascended to Paradise, his wounds were healed."

Father shook his head. "In Heaven, we'll all be showing our wounds—to remind us of where we've been. Scars in Heaven will be beauty marks."

Jon and I excused ourselves from the table. We kissed Mother on the cheek, smiled at Holly, and waved good-bye to Grammy and Father, who were oblivious in their talk of new flesh.

We put on our sunglasses and went out to the utility shed and fired up Jon's motorcycle, a junkyard special that was part Honda and part Harley and really an accident waiting to happen. We rumbled down the gravel driveway and paused at the mailbox. However, instead of turning toward the rising sun and going to school, we went west, speeding toward our conjoined shadow. Jon wore his leather jacket and I was dressed in denim. He was seventeen and I was fourteen.

I never put my arms around my brother when we rode the bike, but that morning was different. I could feel the knife in the pocket over his heart, and I knew he meant business. The knife was a Rambo, cinematically deified in *First Blood*. With its long wide blade and secret compartment in the handle, the knife could do anything—give you true north, catch a fish, cut down a tree, start a fire, and scare the hell out of José.

My own knife, a Bowie, continued to rust in the shed. While praying through the night, I had sensed God telling me the weapon would not be needed.

We sped down the country avenue, and I wondered if Jon had prayed about this situation. And I wondered if he'd gotten a message.

"Let's sing," he said, his words rushing past my ears.

"Good idea!"

Jon cocked his head slightly. Even though I couldn't see his face, I could tell he was smiling, thrilled to be on a mission, speeding down a road of wild flowers and greening fields.

"Go Down Moses!" he shouted.

And we sang: "*Go down Moses, way down to the land of Egypt. Tell old Pharaoh to let my people go. Go down Moses, way down to the land of Egypt. Tell old Pharaoh to let my people go.*"

We sang spirituals, hymns, and Dylan songs until we reached the city limits of Slow Creek. The town was small and yet stretched, as if reaching to be put on a map; and the moment we zoomed past the welcome sign, a mongrel dog began chasing us.

"Good boy!" I said.

The dog suddenly turned toward the morning freight train as if the cars were full of bones or other treats.

Slow Creek seemed desolate as a ghost town. Not a soul in sight, until we saw a mulleted mailman ambling down the sidewalk.

"He's a sign from God," I said.

"Maybe," Jon said, slowing down.

He steered the motorcycle over the curb. The bike bounced and rattled as if breaking apart, and I was nearly thrown to the ground. Jon drove into the grass between the road and the sidewalk, put down his leg for support, and reached into his leather jacket.

The mailman's eyes were wide. "Don't rob me. It's just a Tuesday. I don't have many paychecks."

Jon said, "We're not here to rob you. We need your help."

The lanky mailman stared quizzically. After a few moments, he seemed to believe that we weren't bandits. "I think I've seen you before," he said. "At the state fair."

Jon pulled out the ivory envelope. "Do you recognize the handwriting? Do you know who wrote this?"

The mailman squinted. "Hmm. Maybe."

"Who is it?" I asked. "Is it a boy named José? Is he really sixteen? Is he nice?"

The mailman shook his head. "Can't tell you. It's against the law."

"Tell us who this creep is," Jon threatened, "or else—"

I covered Jon's mouth and said, "We respect your rule of secrecy, but our little sister, Holly, is involved in something that could be dangerous. We're just trying to make sure that she's safe. You might have a young sister, or a daughter, so maybe you can understand how we feel. We're afraid she could be involved with a stalker, or even a rapist. Please understand, this is urgent. Will you tell us who addressed the envelope? Is it really a boy named José?"

The mailman held his breath for a moment. He sighed and shook his head. "Can't tell you. I could lose my job. I have three children at home."

My hand still covered Jon's mouth. He bit into a finger and freed his lips. "One of your children," he said to the mailman, "could become a victim of the creep. We're doing you a favor by confronting him."

The mailman ran a hand through his mullet. "I'm really sorry, but I can't tell you whose writing is on the envelope. But I can tell you that we have a hog processing plant. It employs many immigrants, legal and illegal. You could probably find someone named José among the butchers."

"You're a good man," Jon said, "and a good father. Now, which way is the processing plant?"

The mailman pointed. "Go six blocks to the last street in town, and turn left. Then just follow the smell."

"Thank you," I said.

Jon revved the motorcycle, and we sped away.

The hog plant was a hulking cement building that squatted over an oversized parking lot recently paved with new
tar. Despite the noise of the motorcycle, we could hear
shrieking pigs when we pulled up beside a large truck. Pink
snouts were poking through the breathing holes.

We jumped off the bike. Jon muttered, "Poor
things."

"Maybe we should set the pigs free," I said. "They could
help us by causing a diversion."

"We don't need a diversion. Listen, Danny. Things could
get ugly inside. Stay behind me, okay? Follow my lead with
everything."

Inside the plant, we were immediately confronted by
a short man in a white smock. His nametag said "Mark
Taylor, V.P." He looked us over and demanded to know,
"What is your business here?"

Jon gave him the ivory envelope. Mr. Taylor slowly
opened it, and smirked.

Jon said, "The man who signed the card is trying to
have relations with my little sister."

There was another smirk.

Jon spoke with a threatening voice, "Mr. Taylor, if one
of your employees is doing anything illegal, or is perhaps
in the country illegally, you could get some bad press. Or
big fines. Maybe even get shut down."

Mr. Taylor's smirk got angry. "You son of a sow," he
said.

Jon, who was over six feet tall, glared down at the V.P.
"What did you say?"

"Son of a sow," Taylor repeated, putting the card back into the envelope. He shouted, "Olsen!"

Through the sounds of breaking bones and ripping flesh, a voice replied, "Yeah, Boss?"

Taylor pointed at the source of the voice and said, "There's your man. You can ask him your questions, as long as you do it after work."

"Okay," Jon said. "But can we just talk to him now?"

"Well, all right. I'll give you two minutes. That's it. We have pork chops that need chopping."

Olsen, a fat forty-year-old with boils on his nose, frowned when we strode over to his cutting table. "Get away from me," he said. "I have work to do, and you boys are breaking federal regulations."

Jon was seething, too angry to speak. So I asked the butcher, "Have you been sending cards and letters to someone named Holly?"

Olsen scratched his nose, inflaming the boils, then spit on the floor.

"Speaking of federal regulations," I said.

Jon pulled out the envelope. "Did you send this to my little sister?"

Olsen took the envelope in his red hands and glanced at the handwriting. He removed the card, read it very slowly, and smiled. "No," he said. "I don't think I wrote this. My *L*s are much more elegant."

He shoved the bloody card back into the envelope and handed it to me. "You boys go home now."

Jon went berserk. He lurched toward the cutting table

and pounded his fists into the hunks of pork. "You messed with the wrong family!"

Olsen laughed and grabbed a knife.

I tried to pull Jon back to safety, but he wouldn't budge.

Olsen spit on his blade as if for luck. Some of the spit hit Jon in the face and, in an angry flash, the Rambo knife appeared.

I yanked Jon back a few feet—it took all of my strength— and whispered into his ear, "Cut me."

"What?"

"Cut me. It'll scare him. Just do it."

Many times before, I had asked my brother to hurt me, believing that suffering would inspire me to write a spiritual. But Jon had always refused, telling me I was crazy.

Olsen, his face crimson and sneering, said, "Bring it on, hero. The winner gets to kiss your sister."

Jon turned and slashed down on my chest with the Rambo knife, and I didn't flinch.

Olsen trembled.

Jon shouted at him, "Admit that you sent the card!"

"It wasn't me," his purple lips lied.

Now a crowd of meatcutters had formed. Knives of all shapes and sizes surrounded us. The cutters could have ended the situation, but they allowed the scene to play out.

My brother leaned over Olsen's table. "You claimed to be a teenager named José! You were going to rape her!"

Jon's eyes were animal-wild. In the next moment Olsen would be dead.

We've taken too much into our own hands, I thought. We never should have come here. Now I'm bleeding and somebody is about to die.

Jon tried to stab Olsen's heart, but I pulled him back just in time. We wrestled until my body was between Jon's and the cutting table. I could feel Olsen's furious panting convulsing out of his nose and mouth; and I could see the murderous glint in Jon's eyes. His knife was already familiar with my skin, and I wondered if he would cut me again, this time deeper.

He gritted his teeth. "Danny, what are you doing?"

"Saving you."

My brother put his knife to my throat. "Saving me? Or saving him?"

My head was swimming. The strain of the fight and my bleeding and the stench of carcasses caused me to sway and nearly faint. Just then two meatcutters grabbed my brother and Olsen, and several others helped to wrest the weapons away. There were shouts for 9-1-1 and bandages.

Suddenly I was down on the floor, passed out and dreaming, and someone brought me back to my senses by pouring cold water on my face and chest.

Mr. Taylor appeared with disinfectant and a towel. He helped me get my T-shirt off and dabbed at my chest. "Sorry if this stings, but it doesn't look like you'll need stitches. I don't know what your brother was trying to prove, but at least the cut is superficial."

Jon, being restrained by several butchers, kept saying, "I'm sorry, Danny. I'm sorry. I'm sorry."

Eventually, the sheriff's deputy arrived. He questioned everyone and then made a few phone calls and took Olsen into custody.

"I didn't do anything!" he shouted. "That girl wrote to me!"

The next day, the deputy visited our farm and asked Holly to turn over the correspondence she'd had with the fictional José. After that, for the entire summer, she moped around the farm, suffering her first and only broken heart. Yet she still kept handing out Christmas presents every morning.

Jon leaned back in the booth and sniffed the air wafting through Kate's Home Cookin'. "Pork still smells good," he said, "even after that day in the hog plant."

I nodded, although I disagreed. And then I changed the subject. "If Holly were alive today, what would she be?"

Jon smiled. "A musician and an artist, and everything she already was."

"I think Holly would have gotten into some kind of church work, maybe youth camps and things like that. She would've inspired a lot of kids."

Jon and I both teared up, and I was beginning to feel very close to him again.

A muscular woman strode out of the kitchen and overshadowed our table. Her blue sleeves were rolled up. "What's with the weepy eyes?" she said. "Did I cut too many onions?"

"We were just reminiscing," my brother said, "and wondering how things might have been different."

Kate looked puzzled for a moment. She ran a hand over her hairnet, found a few loose ends, and yanked them out. She winced. "Hey, I know you. Jon and Danny. How are you?"

Before we could answer, Kate leaned over the table, reached out with her strong arms and forced a group hug. Everyone in the café stared, including Dot, the waitress. She shuffled over, saying, "Hey, aren't you guys part of the Gospel Family?"

"We used to be," I said.

Dot beamed. "I saw your family play in Iowa City one summer on the Fourth of July. It was better than the fireworks."

Kate nodded and said, "I have a great idea! Why don't the Gospel Brothers give us a little concert—something inspiring on this gloomy night?"

Jon shrugged, deferring to me.

"We don't have our musical instruments," I said coldly. "Jon sold them at the auction."

Dot grinned, oblivious to the tension. "In the middle of your concert, everyone left the circle of torches except for you two. Remember? You stood arm-in-arm and sang, *"I've got a song, you've got a song. All of God's children got a song."*

Dot paused, waiting for us to join in. We didn't, so she continued. *"When I get to heaven, I'm gonna sing a new song. I'm gonna sing all over God's heaven."*

Jon applauded politely, but I sat motionless.

"C'mon," Kate said, "sing one song for us. And I'll cook for you, free of charge. I'll even pay for my own tip."

Dot, who was not a small waitress, began jumping up and down. "Please, please! Sing! I love those old songs, like 'That Old Time Religion.' They don't make songs like that anymore. Please sing for us. Please?"

The look on my brother's face suggested he'd be willing to perform, but I was hesitant. For years now, I felt like it was all over—the singing, the shouting, everything.

After Holly and Grammy were buried, the Gospel Family mourned, and then regrouped and started performing again. That's when the audiences began to sing along. We had lost two voices and gained thousands. But when Mother died, I thought the band was finished because her harp had been the heart of our music. At Mother's burial, my father could barely stand, slumping near to the grave. My body was tense and electric, and my ears were ringing with expectation after the final amen of the service. Dad was going to say something, or perhaps pray something more, or maybe softly sing to his wife's memory. Raising himself to his full height, shoulders straight, he tilted his head heavenward. Half smiling, his eyes narrowed into the blue-gray sky, and he whispered, "If you kill us all, who's gonna sing for you?"

The customers in Kate's café were waiting, not eating their food, not drinking their coffee. Eventually, Jon stood and said, "Thank you for remembering us. But my brother and I don't sing anymore, at least not together. We haven't seen each other since last year. And we're just going to have some dinner now, if everyone would kindly respect our privacy."

Dot was not giving up. "But you're the Gospel Boys. That's your gift. You sing for people."

"Sorry," I said. "We are not the 'Gospel Boys.' Once upon a time, we were part of the Gospel Family. But those days are over. Understand?"

Dot did not understand. "God gave you a gift, and you're supposed to share it. Just like the song says: 'Hide it under a bushel, no! I'm gonna let it shine!'"

Jon's eyes darkened. He glared. "Find someone else to soothe your soul. We're not in that business anymore."

Dot burst into tears and retreated into the kitchen.

Kate shook her head at us. "This is why people don't believe in Christianity. Because people like you pretend to be followers of Jesus, but deep down you're just selfish and mean."

Jon stood and grabbed my arm and pulled me from the table. "I'm sorry, Kate," he said. "Danny and I are trying to work out some issues. But that's no excuse to be selfish and mean. I apologize."

He pulled out a fifty-dollar bill and placed it on the menu. "C'mon, Danny, we need to leave these people alone."

Kate followed us, fretting. "You both look so skinny. Why don't you stay and eat?"

Jon shook his head. "Not tonight. Maybe next time, when things are more normal."

Just then something told me to turn and run into the kitchen; so I rushed through the swinging doors and nearly fell on the greasy floor. Dot was standing beside the cutting board table, dabbing her eyes with her apron. I rushed up and wrapped my arms around her.

She sniffled, and sniffled again, and finally spoke. "Danny, I became a new person at your family's concert.

I was so inspired by the music, with no preaching and no collection plates, and I could feel the presence of God. And I let Him into my heart."

I squeezed Dot tight and whispered into her ear, "*Sing together, children. Don't you get weary. Sing together, children. Don't you get weary. Oh, shout together children. Don't you get weary. There's a great camp meeting in the Promised Land.*"

Dot kissed me on the cheek, a warm wet kiss of tears. "Danny, you have to sing with your brother."

I touched her gently on the face. "I know. It's killing me."

The cook shouted, "Order up!"

Dot gathered the heaping plate of barbecued pork. And I returned to my brother. We got in the truck and I drove us to the cemetery, without a word spoken. Every moment felt like hell.

"Well, here we are," I said, stopping the truck at the gate.

"Here we are," Jon said.

We waited for the other to start saying the things that needed to be said. It seemed like the gravestones were leaning toward the pickup, listening.

Finally I broke down and asked, "Jon, do you think Mother committed suicide?"

He stared out the window. "No, Danny. She fell."

"But why was she up on the silo?"

"She wanted to fly away."

"She jumped?"

"No, Danny. She fell."

"It wasn't suicide?"

Jon looked at me with sorrow, his eyes full of kindness. "Mother didn't mean to do what she did. She loved us, Danny. You know that."

"But I had to watch it happen. She was wearing her good white dress."

Jon put his hand on my shoulder. "I know."

"She seemed to think she had wings."

Jon turned away and looked at the graves. "She was drunk. She didn't know what she was doing."

"Jon, I tried to catch her."

"I know, Danny."

"I almost caught her. I was just a few steps away, praying real hard."

"It's a good thing you didn't get there in time. The weight would have killed you."

"No. She was floating. She didn't hit the ground very hard. I think I could have caught her."

Jon turned to face me again, with sorrow, with kindness.

"Danny. About the farm . . . After all of the funerals, I wasn't thinking clearly."

Unforgiving words overpowered my tongue. "Yes, you made lots of mistakes. And I ended up with nothing."

"You got the truck."

"That's it."

"Danny, listen. I'm not going to talk about this now. I thought maybe we could make some progress tonight. I thought we could meet somewhere in the middle."

"In the middle of what, Jon? The cemetery?"

A tear trickled down the side of my brother's scarred

face. "Danny, I heard you're having problems at the post office, and financial troubles."

"Who did you talk to? Grease? Plain Jane? They don't know the whole story. What I do with my money is none of your business. Maybe I gave it all away, or maybe I put a down payment on some farm equipment. What if I told you I'm going to start farming again?"

Jon pondered the idea. "Where would you farm? Do you have a property in mind?"

"I'm not starting over unless I start from the beginning. The family farm. The Garden of Eden. If I'm going to start over, I'm starting from there."

"Danny, you have my phone number. You have my address in Des Moines. Call or visit any time. Okay? Don't be a stranger. And Danny?"

"Yeah?"

"Did you want to pray over the graves with me? We've done it every year on this date."

"No thanks."

"Are you sure? You always find comfort in it."

"No thanks. Not this year. They never rise, anyway."

"Your prayers? Of course they rise."

"No, I mean the dead. I've prayed a thousand times for them to rise. And I've really believed it was possible. But my faith doesn't bring anyone back."

Jon whispered, "I'm back."

I shook my head.

"It's true. I'm actually a pretty good lawyer now. And I want to be a good husband and father. Danny, I hope you'll be the best man at my wedding. You don't even have to attend the rehearsal or anything. Just stand up for me."

"I don't know. Maybe."

Jon nodded, satisfied with that answer. He climbed out of the truck without saying good-bye and walked, very slowly, toward the cemetery gate.

I put the Chevy into gear and sped down the road. And I remembered the day after Mother's funeral. Jon and I had walked away from the mourners at our farm. Mile after mile, we'd walked in silence, ending up at the gravel pit. I paused at the edge, while Jon slowly descended the steep, muddy path. His head hung low, my brother searched the path for signs. There were some tracks, heart-shaped, fresh from the morning, when a doe and her fawn had climbed out of the pit to eat the grass above the ridge. Jon fell to his knees and traced a finger in one of the hearts. He seemed to feel haunted by the coolness of the clay, his whole body shivering. Something told me to rush down there and kneel beside him. But I stayed above, watching.

My brother stood, as if answering a call, and walked deeper into the pit.

"You're suffering, Daniel."

I looked out the window of the Rural Mental Health Clinic. I thought I could see the tops of the twin silos above our farm, but they were only clouds.

"It's called post-traumatic stress," Dr. Parsons said. "Everyone in the history of the world has suffered from this disorder, but you've got it bad. You're worse off than the soldiers I've treated."

I turned away from the window. "So, I'm mentally ill?"

"Yes, Daniel."

I tried to smile. "Being mentally ill is illegal in Iowa, right? Isn't everyone in Iowa required to live a normal happy life?"

Dr. Parsons folded his arms over his chest and leaned back in his chair. "I'm suffering, too."

"You are?"

"Of course."

"Really? How?"

He sighed. "It's a very long story, Daniel. But let that be. We each have our sorrows for not being angels."

chapter four

WHEN MY FRIEND Grease was a child, he was bullied at school. The kids called him Retard and Tardo and Hog Pile. But his mother and father treated him like a child of God and encouraged him to dismantle and rebuild lawn mowers and other small engines and spark them back to life. He eventually mastered the mechanics of cars, trucks, and tractors. By the time Grease was eighteen, he could fix anything. And after his parents lost the farm and filled their pickup with carbon monoxide, Grease got a job at a gas station in town. A few years later, he bought the station and increased its revenue by restoring and selling antique automobiles.

Grease has his faults, like everyone else, but when he realized that I'd lost some weight, he arrived at my trailer loaded with so many barbecued ribs that I wondered if any pigs were left in the world.

Fasting, I let Grease eat most of the food. He stuffed himself and spilled various sauces and condiments all over his shirt and my couch, while I politely nibbled a bit and soaked my aching feet in a bucket. I'd gone back to the mail route that morning, and the work seemed harder now, and I came home limping and exhausted. It didn't help that some people at the post office were gossiping about a bag of stolen mail.

While Grease ate and ate, he sometimes paused to share his conspiracy theories. "Danny," he said, his eyes wide and bloodshot, "listen to this. I was plowing the Internet—"

"Surfing," I said. "You surf the Internet."

"Not me. I plow it. And today I found out why so many cell phones are ringing in church, making it harder to worship God."

"Is it because people are forgetful?"

Grease whispered, "No. It's the terrorists."

"What?"

"The terrorists are disrupting church services. They know how people lose their minds and forget about Jesus whenever a phone rings."

"You're a lunatic, Grease."

But he was my best friend, and occasionally wise. So I asked his advice about my love life. "Do you think Jane is the kind of girl who would sneak into my trailer at sunrise and kiss me?"

"Plain Jane Jones?"

"Yeah."

"Your old girlfriend from ages ago?"

"Yeah."

"The one who works at dulcinea?"

"Yeah."

Grease mulled it over. "Hmm . . . I don't think Jane would enter your bedroom unannounced. She'd politely knock first. She wouldn't just appear and start stripping for you. She'd call ahead. Plain Jane plays by the rules. Or maybe she has a wild side like Princess Diana. Yeah, it's possible Jane could be a secret stripper, now that I think about it."

"It was an innocent kiss, whoever it was. Don't ruin it. That kiss is all I have right now."

Grease trudged into my kitchen and filled half a thermos with coffee. As usual, he added a cup of sugar and a cup of chocolate sauce. He returned to the couch, took a big gulp of the potion, and began to have visions. "Danny," he whispered, "I'm working on something that will change the world. I'll tell you about it if you swear to secrecy."

"Swear? No, I won't swear. But I'll keep your secret."

"Shhh," he said, looking suspiciously around the room. "Now don't tell a soul—not even your stripper. Listen, Danny. I'm developing a toothpaste that also cleans the sink. And the toilet. And the floor. You just spit, and it whitens everything! It's called Spitzoclean. And I'm gonna be a billionaire."

Grease chugged the rest of his syrup-coffee, and his eyes grew so wide that you could almost see into his brain. It was scary.

I turned on the TV and found the local news. It was a follow-up story about Jack Williams. A bubbly blond reporter stood at the edge of the reservoir and proclaimed, "Tomorrow a dive team will arrive and begin searching the depths. And we will keep you updated about this tragedy."

After the news, I told Grease to make himself at home, which he did by taking off his shoes and socks and showing me his craggy yellow toenails.

"Hey, Danny, do you feel like clipping these things?"

I pulled my feet out of the bucket and went slip-sliding toward the door. "Jack Williams is not in the lake."

"Where is he?"

"I don't know. But he's alive."

"Can you find him, Danny?"

"I'm gonna try."

"Want me to help?"

"No, Grease. Stay here until the coffee wears off."

"Okay, Danny. Can I read some of your books?"

"Sure, buddy. Help yourself."

Grease went over to the bookcase and grabbed *The Wisdom of the Desert*. "Hmm . . . Does this have pictures?"

Not bothering to put on my shoes, I hurried out to the pickup and sped away, searching. The gravel roads that night seemed to go toward everywhere, toward nowhere, and I tried to imagine where a man might wander if he had no memory of wandering. Here and there as I drove, I saw harvesters crawling through the fields with their bug-eyes and ferocious mouths chewing up the last of the corn. I hated those machines and their heavy debts that had brought down so many family farms. But then again, the harvesters were helping with my mission, clearing away the hiding places.

I stopped the truck and shouted out the open window. "Jack! Jack! Where are you?"

Electricity crackled the air. Perhaps a storm was brewing. No, the sky was clear. The electricity was not outside. My fingers were warm and slightly glowing. That hint of holy fire should have fueled my faith, but my mind immediately fell into doubt. Maybe my spiritual charge was nothing but nitric oxide, the gas of the firefly.

The glowing dissipated, and I left the truck and went

for a walk. Breathing the crisp air, my head became clearer, and I wandered aimlessly up the road. It was cold and hard and my bare feet had to step lightly. The gravel gleamed as if the Milky Way had spilled a million frozen stars. Directly in front of me, a deer crossed over with a constellation on its head. And then a fox with a comet's tail. The road was busy with brilliant animals moving from one field to another, avoiding the harvesters. All night long, I limped up and down the road, with all of creation crossing my path and slipping away.

When the stars faded over the horizon that morning of Halloween, I knew it was time to go home. Not to the trailer park, but really home. Even if the Gospel Family's farm had been bought by a corporation and ruined in a dozen ways, I still had to face my hauntings. I limped to the truck, climbed inside, and turned the key. Nothing. Not even a click. I said a little prayer and turned the key again. Nothing. The truck was dead.

I went outside and laid my hands upon the frost-covered hood. "Please, God," I said, "if you wanted to, you could fix this thing."

There was no flash of heat. Nothing. I raised my numb hands above the hood in a kind of blessing. "Good-bye, old truck."

Into the field of golden stubble I stumbled, blowing steam and shivering. For some reason, there was a lone tree standing near the road. The tree stood dark and leafless, as if death were written all over it, and I felt somewhat afraid to approach because it seemed to portend something painful beyond. My heart sank at the thought of continuing, and sank further at the thought of turning back, and then the sky did its heavenly thing, opening up and finding a way to turn the desolate, unwelcoming tree into a greater picture of gold. Everything became glorious in the sunrise, the whole landscape backlit with a hint of God's own brightness. And I continued onward, searching for home.

After an hour of walking, I figured the family farm was just a few more miles away, east and into the light. I squinted and searched the horizon. But I couldn't see the house, the barn, or the twin silos.

The second silo was our final debt, the death of us. During a fit of cancerous madness, Father believed he could double our production, forcing miracles from our humble acreage. And he acted like it was all for my benefit.

"You'll be the King of Iowa."

In our faded overalls, we leaned against the side of the original silo.

"I'm building another tower," he said, wiping his brow with a red handkerchief. He paused, his breath labored. "I want it to be a monument to my mother, your mother, and Holly. And that fancy girl of yours—"

"Rachel."

"Yes. Rachel will be more likely to marry you and live on the farm if we add cows and honeybees."

"What?"

"Milk and honey, Danny. We'll fill up two silos."

"Dad, are you feeling okay?"

My dying father stared at a large empty space in the sky. "Believe me, Danny. I'm building another tower."

Where he was looking, the blue sky just kept going and going, high above and beyond our farm, to where Iowa wasn't even a place anymore.

Wandering through the corn stubble, searching for home, I stepped into many memories, most of them fleeting, while others, like the morning of my thirteenth birthday, lingered. After doing my chores, I was about to shower when I looked out the bathroom window. The September corn was ripening in the sunrise, and I believed the best year of my life had moved from the horizon to the house. In my vision, our cornfield and the neighbors' fields that had rolled away to the sky were all returning in a tidal wave of perfect calm, not too high above the earth, delivering into my eyes a perfect floating garden with a happy family and a divine hint, among the blue and green and golden blessings, of more light to come.

Just then, my father ended the vision. He stomped into the room with a straightedged razor in one hand and a cup of foam with a brush in the other hand. He grinned and said, "Happy birthday, old man."

I grinned back and rubbed my sparse chin. I hadn't thought about needing a shave, and even if I had, an old-fashioned straightedge was not something I wanted to hold at my throat.

Jonathan appeared in the doorway. "Danny, look at that field of whiskers on your face. Maybe I should go start up the harvester. We might be able to get that field clean by sundown. I think we could get forty bushels off that face."

Father laughed and reached out with the straightedge. "We can get fifty, maybe sixty bushels."

I pushed my father away and threatened to snap him with a towel. "You guys get out of here. I'm not shaving today."

"Danny," Jon said, "the girls all want a smooth gospel singer, not a rough one. Smoochy, smoochy!"

I snapped the towel. The sting missed my brother's face by an inch. "Get out," I said. "Let me sing in the shower in peace."

My father set the shaving gear on the sink and backed away. He and Jon stifled their laughter and ran stumbling down the stairs. I wrapped myself in the towel and leaned over the sink and stared at my aging face in the mirror. There was a light in my eyes that seemed to be shining from a place that was beyond me. I stared more intently. Was that the soul looking back? Or just the natural light passed on through generations?

My grandmother had a forbidding apple face that seldom smiled, yet people knew that she loved them. Whenever we played a concert, she opened the show by softly strumming a few chords and then saying, "They call us the Gospel Family. On both sides of the family tree, we're farmers all the way back to the furrows of Adam and Eve. The Gospel Family has known joy, weeds, insects, war, and all kinds of suffering. We've had our share of death. And we know about resurrection. Just like your family, we've experienced what the world has to offer, good and bad. This first song is called 'This Little Light of Mine.'"

Limping through the harvested field, headlong into the blinding sunshine, not sure if I was on the right path, I thought about my wonderful grandmother, and I sang into the fiery sky. "*This little light of mine. I'm gonna let it shine. This little light of mine. I'm gonna let it shine, let it shine, let it shine . . .*"

Midday, the sky filled with clouds. At first they were a

welcome relief from the relentless glare, but as the day wore on, the clouds grew thicker and darker, threatening a cold rain. Already I felt half dead. By late afternoon, the wind seemed wicked and I was hardly moving, my blistered feet plodding. I was starving, parched, and trembling. My mind began to wander. I daydreamed that I was back in high school, senior year. It was English class and everyone was yawning and nodding off to sleep, bored to death with Edgar Allan Poe, until our gray and wrinkled teacher grabbed the apple on her desk and rolled it into the center of the room. There it swelled into a giant pumpkin. Carved like a Halloween castle.

"Okay, students," Mrs. Older said. "One at a time. Go see what's inside."

A line formed, and I found myself last. The clock ticked and tolled. The students entered the castle, stayed inside for a while, and then came out glowing like fire. Even Grease and the Samsonov brothers—Mud Eye and Slopper—came out as clean as the sun.

With one minute remaining before the end of school, it was finally my turn. I entered the castle, praising Mrs. Older's name and trembling with excitement. I thought: this is the best assignment any teacher has ever given; this is what literature is all about.

In the flickering light, in a corridor that led to a throne room, stood Plain Jane Jones. She was wearing a wedding dress. "Danny," she said, smiling, "fancy meeting you here."

While I stumbled deeper into the corn stubble, the night crept up behind me and passed through the field and filled it with darkness. Good, I thought. That should reveal a light of some kind. Even if our farm was not nearby, there must be something. A gravel road. A truck driver. Anything.

There was nothing. Limping onward, I began to imagine the aurora borealis swaying above the clouds, dancing colorfully like nobody was watching, and I tripped and fell facedown in the dirt. Suffocation covers the mind so quickly, especially if part of you wants to leave the world, but I rolled onto my back, coughing, and I thought: how could this happen? How could I end up lost in a cornfield? If my body is found, will the people of Iowa laugh or cry when they hear that Danny Gospel died of exposure in his own backyard?

I wondered if my family members in Paradise were allowed to watch this.

"Rise and shine," I imagined them saying.

And down from the sky came a cloud of bright blessings. I jumped to my feet. "The first snowfall!"

The frozen blossoms fluttered to earth, the crystal flowers so extravagantly fragile that even the dumbest tongue, like mine, could melt a heavenly masterpiece in one open-mouthed instant.

For several minutes, I feasted upon the snowflakes. I felt childlike and wondrously alive, and I did a little dance.

The wind blew harder and the swirling snow thickened and the scent of Minnesota pine trees began to fill my head. Balsam fir, Christmas trees on Halloween. I wondered: how could I have walked hundreds of miles north, and how could I have crossed the border without anyone seeing me? The farm should be right here. Iowa should be right here.

Limping deliriously deeper into where I was, I became convinced that the blizzard was probably a dream and I would soon wake up at the post office, going about the world's business as if nothing strange had ever happened. And then I heard a rumbling. Was it a freight train? Had I wandered onto the tracks? Or was I hearing thunder in the blizzard?

Neither a train nor thunder, the rumbling became hoof-beats, heavy but quick and coming right at me.

Don't fall, I told myself. Don't fall. You might never get up again. And I struggled to stand firm while the pigs descended upon me. The herd seemed to be coming from all directions, or maybe running in a circle, snorting and squealing, turning me around and around, until they finally disappeared, beyond the swirling curtain of snow.

I took a shaky step forward into a wind that smelled like manure and Christmas trees, and then another step forward, and I was able to limp without falling. My feet could feel nothing, and I had no sense of direction; but at least I was moving. That was my best chance of staying alive.

After a while, the moon peeked out from behind the clouds, and the blizzard became a few harmless flakes. Without the wind, the air felt warmer, and it seemed as if the danger had passed. I sat heavily and massaged my feet for a long while, bringing them back to life. I cried out at the burning, again and again, sentences that only made sense because of the pain.

And then I looked up and saw a shadow, or a person, standing in the field.

I shouted, "Hey! My name is Danny Gospel and I need some help."

The shadow, without speaking, slunk away through the snow. I painstakingly stood and followed, trying to keep up, but soon I was far behind. The shadow paused and waited for me to stagger closer; and the forced march began again. I stumbled and was horrified by the thought that my feet might be frostbitten and have to be amputated. I plopped to the ground and rubbed my left foot; rubbed and cried out until the pain blessed me with the assurance that I could keep it. And then I rubbed the right foot; rubbed until the agony became all fire. "Th-th-thank God," I chattered, while the shadow just stood and breathed, steam rising toward the moon, and then suddenly walked away.

I stood and stumbled forward, and an image immediately came to mind of the next day's news, the TV showing cadaver dogs sniffing the snowdrifts. This was not the way I had planned to spend my last day on earth. I had planned on having my children and grandchildren around my bed, singing.

South of the moon, a light appeared. I stared and thought it could be a planet. Perhaps Venus. And then another light appeared. Maybe Mars. And then another. And I wondered: how many planets can be seen with the cold naked eye?

A fourth light appeared, and now they all grew brighter. The shadow changed directions slightly, moving toward the cluster of lights.

A farm, I thought. A farm!

The shadow quickened his pace, and I tried to keep up, but my numb legs could barely wobble and my head was pounding. My mouth and throat were so dry that every breath choked me. I paused to eat some snow and began to lag far behind while the shadow hurried toward the farm. Soon he reached the house and stomped up the stairs to the porch. The shadow paused for a moment, as if remembering something, and then laughed and opened the door.

A golden glow poured out, and there was a shout of joy, followed by another shout of joy. I wanted to enter that house and its warmth, but instead I slumped to the ground at the edge of the field, unable to move forward. And then I curled painfully into the snow and went to sleep, and dreamed. Dreamed of Genesis . . . farm . . . festival . . . music . . . ocean . . . wedding . . . funeral . . .

I awoke facing a fire. Someone had wrapped a red blanket around me and I was pleasantly hot, sitting in a rocking chair. At my feet, which were covered with wool slippers, sat an empty water glass and a dinner plate that had remnants of mashed potatoes and gravy. My stomach was full and I felt perfectly comfortable. My toes were alive and wiggling.

On the mantel above the fireplace was a framed photograph of two brothers with their arms around each other. One of them had a smooth face and fancy clothes and the other had a beard and wore overalls. The bearded one was Jack Williams.

A voice whispered, "Are you awake?"

I looked up, hoping to see Jack, and there was Shelby Williams, appearing beside the fireplace. He wore a dark shirt and a red tie and was holding a bottle of beer. His deep-set eyes blinked and flickered.

"Son," he said, with a hint of a drawl, "you wanna beer?"

"No thanks."

"Hot brandy?"

"No thanks."

Shelby nodded. His face was like hardened clay, ruddy and square, strong but capable of kindness. "You feeling better?"

"I feel fine."

"How are your feet? I washed them and bandaged the blisters."

"My feet feel good. Thanks."

"You enjoyed the baked ham and mashed potatoes and corn?"

"Yeah. I must have."

Shelby grinned. "After flying into Cedar Rapids, I drove the rental car straight to the nearest grocery store and picked up several deli lunches. Five pounds for six dollars. Gotta love Iowa."

"You flew in to search for your brother?"

"No," he said, and then paused, and swallowed hard. "I'm here to identify the body."

Shelby Williams, whom I barely remembered but had often heard stories about, had left Iowa long ago to seek fame and fortune and apparently some trouble in New Orleans. He had kept the broad shoulders he'd earned as a boy on the farm, and now he'd added a broad belly after years of booze and gumbo. However, his most prominent feature was his hair, a thick black mass combed upward and curved back in the style of an old-time Hollywood actor or TV preacher.

Shelby took a long drink of beer and said, "I almost fainted when my brother came bursting into the house in his pajamas and slippers."

"Your brother? Jack? He's alive?"

Shelby nodded. "Yes. The first thing he said to me was, 'Gospel brought me home.'"

I should have known. "Jack was the shadow I'd been following. Did he say anything else?"

"Something about some pigs and a big dog. It didn't make any sense."

"It makes sense to me," I said, looking around the room. "Where is Jack now?"

Shelby gulped his beer. "I took him to the hospital."

"Oh, good," I said, and wondered: why aren't you with him?

Shelby smiled warmly. "So. You're a Gospel."

"I'm Danny."

"My brother wrote letters telling me about your family, how you formed a band and stirred up quite a following, had a harp and everything. You know, Danny, it's been twenty years since I've seen you. You were just a little kid, racing around your farm with your brother."

"Jonathan."

"Yes, I remember he had a blue bicycle and you had a red tricycle. And bless your heart, you covered more ground. You were quite the traveler. In fact, one day you rode all the way down to our farm. I don't know how you escaped from that grandmother of yours. But somehow you showed up at our house, and I remember how you tugged on Jack's beard and asked, 'Are you real? Are you Santa in summertime?'"

I rocked slowly in the chair, smiling, my heart aching, remembering.

Shelby peeled the label from his beer bottle. "Not long after your visit, I flew to New Orleans and left my brother alone on the farm. He was seven years older, set in his ways, satisfied with going to his grave in familiar ground. And I was so restless. I would have killed to have gotten out of here."

Not wanting to address any rumors, I asked innocently, "What did you end up doing down south?"

"Oh, a little bit of everything. Maybe too much of some things."

"But you like it down there?"

Shelby became solemn. "New Orleans is an angel. It's an angel that rebelled against God but didn't give up its faith. I've traveled the world, and the Big Easy is the most tangibly evil and good place on earth. You can feel Hell and Heaven on every street corner."

He paused, his eyes glinting. "Hey, Danny, wanna hear about the ladies?"

"Only if they're dressed in white."

"Well, most of mine wear black. Silk lingerie and—"

"So," I said, changing the subject, "Jack was doing okay at the hospital?"

"A doctor checked him over and said he was healthy as a horse. And then a nurse's aide, a cutie pie named Abigail, helped him wash and doted on him."

Shelby winked. "She was dressed in white, Danny, if that makes you feel better."

"I feel good," I said, rocking at a quicker pace.

"Dixie" began playing on Shelby's cell phone. He stood and took the call. "Yes, it's about time. Hold on." He patted me on the shoulder. "Excuse me, Danny." And he walked into the kitchen.

I tried not to listen, but some of Shelby's words were too

loud. "Future considerations . . . outright lies . . . unwilling to compromise . . . vendetta . . . unusual cash flow . . . devil to pay . . . history of bad business . . . necessary precautions . . . don't wait and see . . . someone has to suffer . . . that's life . . . I understand . . . be careful."

Shelby returned from the kitchen with another beer for himself and a glass of water for me.

"Drink," he said, sitting next to me. "You're still dehydrated."

"I feel fine."

He thrust the glass into my hand. "Drink. Or else I'll have to drive you to the hospital. I'm sorry about offering alcohol to you. That was unwise. Now help me make amends. Drink the water."

"Okay," I said, and raised the glass.

Shelby raised his bottle. "Cheers." He took a long swig. "Son, I'm still shaky from seeing you at the edge of the cornfield. I thought you were dead."

"Yeah. I seemed dead to me, too."

"When I drove back from the hospital and caught a glimpse of your body in the headlights, I was sure you were a corpse. I was sure you were gone. But when I got out of the car and investigated, I saw that the snow was melted in a circle around you. And you were just sleeping peacefully, covered with blotches of hair."

"The hair must have been from a sneezy drooler. Bernard."

"A dog?"

"Yup. And a Saint. He must have kept me warm."

Shelby seemed confused. He swigged his beer and still

seemed confused. "Well, anyway, Danny, I want to thank you for finding my brother and bringing him home."

I laughed. "I didn't find Jack. He found me. I was the one who was lost."

More beer flowed down Shelby's throat, and his eyes narrowed as he tried to think. He wiped his mouth and sighed. "So, anyway." He stood and stretched. "We'll figure this out in the morning."

"Aren't you going back to the hospital tonight? To make sure Jack's okay?"

"No. They told me to stay here so I wouldn't distract him. They said I could return in the morning."

"I want to go to the hospital with you."

Shelby nodded, grateful. "Yes, Danny. We'll go bright and early."

"Be sure to wake me."

He yawned. "Good night, Danny. Feel free to use the spare bedroom. It's just up the stairs and to the right. And the bathroom is across the hall. Make yourself at home."

"Thanks. I'll probably just stay where I am. I like this chair."

"You want some pajamas?"

"No, I'm comfortable."

"All right then," Shelby said with a fatherly voice. "Let me know if you need anything."

"I'll be fine."

He turned toward the mantel and stared at the photograph. "You know, Danny, I'm something of a legend in New Orleans, but in reality, my brother is all that I have. I can't imagine going on without hearing his voice again."

"At the hospital, we can ask him to recite a poem."

"A poem?"

"Six years ago, when I was nineteen, Jack memorized a Valentine's poem that I wrote for my fiancée."

"Well," Shelby said, turning to face me, "I wouldn't count on him remembering it now."

"I'm not counting on it. But I'm hoping."

"Good night, Danny."

Late in the morning, I wandered into the kitchen and found a ham and cheese sandwich and a tall glass of water waiting for me on the table. On the chair was a pair of socks, a flannel shirt, underwear, overalls, and boots. "These are my brother's," a note said. "They're nice and clean and I think they'll fit you. I'll be at the hospital all day. Help yourself to anything in the house. We'll talk tonight."

I was upset that Shelby had failed to awaken me, but it was good that he wanted to spend time alone with his brother.

I gathered up Jack's clothes and went upstairs and took a bath, scrubbing with a good soapy brush. Then I put on Jack's clothes, went downstairs, and ate the sandwich, drank the water, felt my strength increasing, and called Grease to see if he could drive out with his wrecker and help me find my pickup.

"Find it yourself," Grease said. "I spent the whole night searching for you. I'm always hauling you out of trouble, and you always get into more. Now I'm hauling myself to church."

Click.

"Yeah, go to church," I said to the dial tone. "Go to church and leave me stranded."

I hung up and walked over to the window and glared at the frost-covered pane. I scratched angrily at the frost, making blue-gray lines that crossed and little circles that joined until a viewing hole appeared.

In the melting driveway, shining as bright as rust can shine, was the old red truck.

"How on earth . . ."

In a flash, I was behind the wheel and turning the key. The Chevy fired up like it was hot off the assembly line.

"Grease," I said in amazement, "you're the greatest!"

chapter five

DRIVING AWAY FROM the Williams farm, I was tempted to peek over at our old farm. There was a strange blurriness in the fields, but I didn't take a good look because I knew the blur would distract me from my mission.

I drove through the slush into town, over to the university hospital, and circled up into the ramp. It seemed completely full, but the Chevy eventually found a parking place up on the roof. I limped down the stairs, praying out loud, "God, please heal Jack Williams. Please take away the Alzheimer's and let him be himself again."

I passed through the glass doors into the hospital lobby. A barrel-chested man at the welcome desk smiled warmly. "Hello, son. How can we help you?"

A large cross hung from the man's neck. I stared, and the gentleman repeated, "Son, how can we help you? Are you okay? You look like you've seen a ghost."

"I'm fine," I said. "It's just that . . . you reminded me of someone."

The desire to be crucified had obsessed my father in the

months after losing his wife. He began to wear a dozen crosses, day and night and even in the shower—rosaries, crucifixes, and crosses made of various plastics, woods, and metals. At our final concert, in the spring of 1994, when Father and Jon and I performed as The Gospel Trio, Dad stood wild-eyed in a circle of fire near the Iowa River and ranted about Vietnam.

"My neighbors in the jungle, in the rice paddies, in the villages and monasteries, everywhere, they carried their crosses. They carried their crosses through burning bushes, scorched trees, and under smoldering earth. Grandparents, mothers and fathers, aunts and uncles, sisters and brothers, they all marched, limped, and crawled with their crosses. And I carried mine. My government said I could love God and neighbor by killing my neighbor. I don't know how much of that is true or false, and I wasn't even a believer, but I carried my cross. I carried a lot of crosses for you."

"Dad," I whispered, "please don't do this."

Sweating and trembling, he shouted, "We killed whole families! Grandparents, mothers and fathers, aunts and uncles, sisters and brothers. We piled up the bodies as if Heaven would smile down on the slaughter. We were told that it was possible to love both God and country, and we ended up doing everything that was the opposite of love. Now look at my neck, strangled with all these Christs! Look at what I'm carrying for you."

Someone shouted from the audience, "Shut up and sing!"

"Dad," Jon said, putting his arm around him. "C'mon, let's sing some gospel."

The ex-marine stood tall, on the verge of fainting, and

proclaimed to the crowd, "There's no gospel without the cross, no matter how good the music is."

When Father collapsed at the end of the concert, he refused an ambulance. Members of the audience helped carry him to the back of the pickup, and Jon held him for dear life while I drove through the park and up the hill to the hospital.

That night, with the cancer consuming everything in his skull, Father shook in bed so violently that the staff had to strap him down and remove his crosses. In the morning, when he regained a semblance of consciousness and saw that he was alone with his boys, he said, "I can carry more. I'm giving you a direct order. Make a big cross. And put me on it."

"Shush," Jon said, adjusting the blanket. "Get some rest now."

"Boys," Father whispered. "Crucify me. That's an order."

Jon nodded yes but obviously meant no.

I said, "Yes, Father. We'll do it. I promise."

Dad smiled, fell asleep, and began doing battle with someone in his dream. The bed straps strained to keep him in place.

Jon glared at me. "We are not going to crucify him. That's crazy. Do you understand? He needs a higher dose of morphine. He needs to pass on peacefully."

"But I made a promise."

My brother reached out and grabbed me by the throat. "We are not hurting him, Danny! I'm calling a nurse, and I'm getting more morphine."

He loosened his grip. I could smell alcohol and pot on

his breath. "Fine," I said, straining to speak. "You make the decision. You're the elder brother."

"That's right," he said. "You won't be making any of the important decisions."

"Fine, ruin everything," I said, abandoning the room.

When I returned a few hours later, Jon was asleep in a chair, his face shadowed with stubble and his eyes darting fitfully under bulging lids.

I'd been to the home-improvement store and party store for supplies. I'd tied the strings of a dozen large balloons around a two-by-four as tall as I was. Multicolored, the balloons were a mix of smiley faces and exclamation points at the end of wishful clichés:

GET WELL SOON!

BETTER DAYS AHEAD!

DON'T WORRY, BE HAPPY!

At my father's bedside, I removed the balloons from the wood and sent them floating to the ceiling. Jon lurched awake in his chair to see me maneuvering the two-by-four under Father's bony shoulders.

"Danny, what are you doing?"

"Help me," I said.

Father's eyelids fluttered open. He focused slowly on my face. "Is it time?"

"Yes. It's time."

Behind my back, I showed Jon that I had a hammer but no nails. And I hoped he could see the plan.

We would pretend to crucify him.

Without a word, Jon helped me untie the restraints. We placed Father's limp arms on the lumber and then retied his wrists.

"Yes, yes," Father said, closing his eyes. "I deserve this."

Tap, tap, tap, I hit the makeshift cross with the hammer, careful to avoid Father's fingers.

He grit his teeth. "Harder! Pound the stake through my palm!"

While I tapped slightly harder, Jon came over to my side of the bed and stuck his finger into Father's hand and pushed down forcefully.

"Good boys," Father said. "I can feel it now. I can feel it. I can feel . . ."

Jon and I exchanged nervous glances. The plan seemed to be working.

"Okay," I whispered, "go poke your finger into his other hand. Make him believe that we're really crucifying him."

Jon obeyed, circling around the bed. However, when he touched the left palm, Father opened his eyes and shouted, "Where's my blood? Am I all out?"

The question caught us off guard. We didn't have any fake blood. Jon said, "Oh, umm, wait a second. Okay, Dad, here comes the blood. Just close your eyes. Please. Close your eyes."

He took out a pocketknife and opened the blade.

I said without saying: don't you dare cut him.

The knife glowed sickly pale while Jon thrust the blade into his own palm. He held the dripping wound over Father's hand and gestured for me to pound the hammer.

"Good, good boys," Father said. "Now it's flowing. And there he is . . . there he is . . . here they are! Here they are!"

Jon leaned over him and whispered, "Shhh. You need to rest easy now."

Father opened his eyes, grimacing, the morphine wearing thin. "It's time for last rites."

Jon touched Dad's face, very gently, and kissed him on the cheek. It was the most beautiful thing I'd ever seen my brother do.

Father blinked tears. "Jon and Danny. You're the only ones left in the family. Please, always be friends. Always sing together. Be the Gospel Brothers."

In the next moment, Jon and I would have hugged our father, together, and told him that we loved him, but a nurse's aide walked into the room. She saw the blood and the crucifixion board, and she screamed. A mad chaos of nurses, doctors, and security officers appeared. They took Jon and me into the hallway to answer questions while our father was cut loose from the board, cut loose from the world, once and for all.

Father went to be with his loved ones.

And the Gospel Brothers went to jail.

With my one phone call, I dialed Rachel's number. She was living in the dorm and I wondered which roommate might answer. After six rings, I was afraid the answering machine would pick up and leave me speechless, but my fiancée finally answered.

"Hello?"

"Hi. I'm in jail."

"Danny! What did you do?"

"Me and Jon—"

"Did you get into a fight? Are you hurt?"

"Rachel. Listen. My father died today."

"What?"

"He died. And the police think Jon and I killed him. At the hospital, we pretended . . ."

"I don't understand. I thought you had a concert last night. I thought your father was feeling stronger."

I explained everything about his death, and broke down several times. Rachel listened and cried with me. After a long while on the phone, the jailer motioned for me to hurry up.

I said to Rachel, "Tell me something good. Please. After everything else that's happened, I can't take another death. I can't take it."

Rachel was silent. It felt like the end of the world. And then she spoke very quietly. "Your father, like everyone else in your family, will always be with you. The memories will give you strength, Danny. Listen. Today I remembered a morning when I was three, somewhere in New York City, near a shimmering fountain. My smiling father, drenched in a cologne that smelled of sky, smiled and lifted me from the ground that was covered by a flock of gray pigeons; and I was soaring above the birds, soaring into the blue. My father showed me the heavens, Danny. That's my favorite memory. And that's what I cling to."

"What about me? What can I cling to?"

The jailer took the phone out of my hand, but I still heard Rachel say into the air, "Everything. Cling to everything, Danny."

The man wearing the cross made me sign the hospital guest book, and then I took the elevator up to the fifth floor and limped out into Intensive Care. I started to look around for Jack Williams' room and was immediately accosted by Mrs. Flynn, the head nurse. Every step she took was a great stride, and when she approached, you became small and obedient. Her eyes said: don't cross me. Her mouth said: don't sass me. And her bosom said: I will defeat you.

"Stop," she said. "Only family members are allowed to visit."

I nodded. "I have a relative up here, Jack Williams."

Mrs. Flynn frowned. "You're not a relative. You're my mailman. So tell me, Danny, what's the problem at the post office? Since the anthrax scare, I've barely received any mail."

"The system is a mess," I said, stepping forward. "I'll try to get it sorted out later."

Mrs. Flynn blocked the hallway. "Danny, stop! You can't go any farther."

I stared down the corridor. "Please. Let me go."

"No. I'm sorry. Family members only."

"But Jack has something I need, buried in his brain, or down in his heart."

"It'll have to stay there. We have rules."

Because a rule is different from a law, I scurried around Mrs. Flynn, saying, "You have to let me visit Jack. If he can miraculously remember a poem, then maybe I can get married to the woman who kissed me. And we can have children and live on the farm. And that's how the world begins again, with one normal happy family."

"I can't help you," she said, pursuing. "Danny, you have to stop."

I kept on walking.

"Listen," she said, grabbing the back of my overalls.

"You're not allowed in this hospital. You're going to be arrested. Again."

A man stepped out of a room. It was Shelby Williams, dressed in a black suit fit for a funeral. His hand seemed to be strangling his cell phone. He hissed, "Considerations . . . cash flow . . . city administrators . . ."

"Hello, Shelby," I said, trying to squirm out of the nurse's grip.

Ignoring us and finishing his conversation, Shelby said, "Get it done, you worthless—" And then he was all smiles and manners. "Good morning, Mrs. Flynn." He bowed and kissed her free hand. "Thank you ever so much for escorting Danny. He's the one who found my brother last night. He's the one, bless his soul, who saved Jack's life."

Mrs. Flynn was charmed by Shelby's style. "Good morning, Mr. Williams," she said, blushing. And she released me into his care.

"Myrtle, you're a doll," Shelby said, winking. And when she turned away, he whispered into my ear, "A voodoo doll."

"No, she's a good nurse," I said.

Shelby nodded, and I noticed his eyes were full of fear. He gestured for me to enter the room. And there on the bed was poor Jack Williams, motionless.

"He hasn't spoken for several hours," Shelby said. "The doctors say he's slipping away. He seemed fine last night. Maybe we should have kept him at the farm. He was so energized to be home. We should have kept him there."

Shelby sniffed angrily, the way strong men do when they are about to cry. "Excuse me," he said, "I need to use the rest room."

He stomped into the rest room, and I stepped closer to the bed and remembered how much I'd always loved my next-farm neighbor. He was truly salt of the earth, a preserver of plain old goodness.

Heal him.

What?

Heal him.

I want to. But I'm not sure how.

You know how.

I do?

Heal him.

As if I'd done this sort of thing a thousand times, I leaned over the bed, placed my hands over Jack's forehead, and whispered, "Our Father, who art in Heaven, hallowed be thy name. Thy kingdom come. Thy will be done, on earth as it is in Heaven. Give us this day—"

A doctor walked into the room, looking puzzled. "What are you doing?"

"I'm trying to heal him."

"Who are you?"

"Danny Gospel."

"Security!" the doctor shouted, pushing the emergency button. "Security!"

Shelby burst out of the bathroom. "What's going on?"

"I'm trying to heal your brother."

"How dare you," the doctor said. "How dare you touch a patient! The contagions on your hands could kill him."

"God can heal him," I said, "no matter how dirty my hands are."

The doctor ignored me and asked Shelby, "Did you invite Danny into the room, against hospital policy?"

Shelby's eyes narrowed as if trying to figure out possible lawsuits, counter suits, and insurance claims; and then he shrugged. "No. I didn't invite Danny Gospel, nor do I know why he assaulted my brother."

Jack's eyes opened slightly, full of light. His lips moved, trying to form a word; and a security guard ran into the room. The guard grabbed my arms, twisting them behind my back, and yanked me away from the bed.

My muscles were ready to spring with whatever force was needed to break free. Jack had responded to my prayer of healing, and now I wanted to finish God's work.

Shelby helped the security guard wrestle me into the hallway.

I shouted, "Don't you want your brother to be healed?"

Shelby's face was red and contorted. "The doctors will heal Jack, or else he'll die, and that's it."

"No! That's not it! Why not let God be involved?"

Shelby gave me a final shove. "Leave us be. I'm not explaining nothing to you. Just go away."

Not sure if I should fight harder for Jack's healing, I allowed the security guard to drag me down the corridor. It felt like my heart was not merely pumping blood but actually bleeding. At the nurses' station, Mrs. Flynn showed no mercy. "Danny, don't ever come back here, not even if you're dying."

When I returned to my trailer, there were several messages on the answering machine. One from Plain Jane. One from Grease. And one from my supervisor at the post office.

"Danny," she said, "you've been let go. But I wouldn't

go anywhere. You're under investigation for mail tampering."

Not sure how much I was guilty and how much I was innocent, I went into my closet to pray. I lit a candle, brightening the eyes of the icons of my loved ones. For the rest of the afternoon and into the early evening, I prayed and sang while the candle melted down to a little flicker and eventually went out. And I continued to pray and sing in the dark.

Doggie scratched at the door and yowled, and then my neighbors turned up the volume on their TV. The McCuskeys were watching *Saving Private Ryan*, bullets ricocheting over screams. I filled the chapel-closet with my best attempt at a baritone, like my father's voice: "*Swing low, sweet chariot! Coming for to carry me home . . .*" when suddenly a soldier cried out for his mother, cried out and died inside of the McCuskeys' TV. And that made Doggie get the crazies. I could hear the cat flying around the bedroom, banking off the walls and leaping from my dresser to the lamp to the table, and then he knocked over my bedside radio.

Music began to play with angelic voices ascending into and beyond the mural of the Garden of Eden on the ceiling. I don't know what radio station Doggie had found with his crazies, but it sounded heavenly.

And then static cracked and crackled out of the radio, drowning the angelic voices. I stumbled out of the closet, turned on the light, and tried to fine-tune the station, but nothing came in for several minutes. Finally, a deep and troubled voice tried to make itself clear. "We apologize for the interruption in the music. We are experiencing problems due to the solar flares that have been so active lately."

Solar flares? Was that the strangeness in the air? Was that why so many weird things had been happening?

Someone knocked on my front door. I turned off the radio and went to the living room to answer.

McCuskey burst into my trailer in all of his glory, wearing a pea-green shirt and red polyester pants. In his hand was a twenty-two pistol that he often used to kill gophers, crows, squirrels, and other creatures that called the trailer park home.

Back when he farmed, McCuskey never killed anything. He didn't even butcher for meat. He was known to be a friend of animals, and his farm was famous throughout the county for being a good home for abandoned cats. After the foreclosure, the bank listed "good pets" as an item to be auctioned, but McCuskey drowned all but one of the cats in his bathtub the night before the sale.

Doggie hissed, and I stared into the murderous man's eyes. McCuskey cursed and pointed the gun at my chest. Emotions that I thought were under control suddenly welled up into adrenaline, the combustible that so easily sparks into violence. I, a Gospel, felt like stealing his weapon and shooting him. The law might not even consider that a crime, much less a sin, considering the circumstances. But I imagined the headline: "Gospel Kills Neighbor." And I began to laugh. I laughed and pointed. "Hey, McCuskey. Look behind you."

"What are you pointing at, you freak?"

"There's a herd of swine on your property."

"Ha-ha. Nice try." McCuskey pulled back the hammer on his gun.

I kept pointing. "Look behind you. I'm serious."

"You're seriously disturbed, you—"

Snort! Snort!

Squeal! Squeal!

There really was a herd of swine rooting around his house. McCuskey turned, incredulous at the sight, and I reached out and took his gun. He ran into his yard, yelling and cursing, causing the hogs to stampede. One of the pigs pounded up the steps of his trailer and crashed through the door. Mrs. McCuskey shouted, "No! Not on my good rug!"

I shoved the pistol into my jeans, scooped up Doggie, and carried him to the truck. Then I sped away to the Newman Center.

There is an underground parking area beneath the church, with a large door that can be activated by pressing a button on the wall of the entrance; and with that knowledge I descended into the Catacombs. That's what Rachel always called the subterranean enclave of study rooms. Down there was a scattered congregation of artists, homeless people, couples making out, and graduate students studying, sleeping, or muttering to themselves.

I entered the hallway and began walking through the dim light. Doggie yowled, scaring a young couple that was making out in a study room. The girl said, "Did you hear that?"

"Shh. It's all right, baby. Nothing can hurt you. Not here in church."

"We're not exactly in church, Frank. We're under it. And we're not exactly praying down here."

I padded through the hall and down another flight of stairs, and then turned left into dimmer light. Doggie dug his claws deeply into my chest. My pace quickened while Doggie hissed and yowled.

A door opened, and Brother Paul appeared. A tall Franciscan with a ponytail, he looked at me with a mix of friendliness, concern, and bewilderment. "Danny, are you okay? What's that blood on your clothes? What are you doing with that cat?"

Knowing that Franciscans traditionally get along with animals, I yanked the cat out of my flesh and said, "Doggie needs sanctuary."

Brother Paul took the animal into his arms. "Good kitty. Good kitty. Ouch. Don't scratch." He hurried up the hall and into his library, held the door for me to enter, and slammed the door shut. A library may not be the best place to pacify a yowling cat, but Doggie immediately sprang through the air, hit the ground gracefully, and began sniffing at the books as if his nose were hungry for theology.

Brother Paul sat at his desk, whispered something to God, and then asked me quite bluntly, "Are you taking any medications?"

I turned away to browse a wall of books. There must have been a thousand volumes. I said, "What would medication do? Make me numb? Why would I want to be numb?"

"Well, are you still feeling depressed?"

One of the books on the wall was called *The Problem of Pain* by C. S. Lewis. I'd read that book three times. After each reading, I'd felt better for a while. And then the pain returned. And that's the problem.

"Yeah, I sometimes feel depressed. Who doesn't?"

Brother Paul had seen me in pain before. He was quiet

124 — David Athey

for a while and then asked, "Did you want to talk about Rachel?"

"No. Not tonight. Maybe tomorrow."

Brother Paul searched my eyes. "Danny, what's going on? I can't help you unless you tell me everything."

"It's a complicated story. Anyway, my trailer is no longer safe. Would you please take care of Doggie for a while?"

"Sure, Danny."

I reached for the gun and placed it on his desk. "Can you turn this into a plowshare?"

The Franciscan's eyes grew wide, and then he nodded gravely. "I'll turn the pistol over to the police."

That sounded like a good plan, because the last time I saw Brother Paul with a gun, he seemed intent on killing someone. And he wore animal horns.

When I was fifteen, my father gave me permission to go into town for Halloween, "As long as you remember that Good and Evil are at war and not at play." My mother had mixed feelings about my going. "Danny, be careful. It's a dangerous night. And please get me some chocolate." My grandmother was strongly against Halloween. Fist on hip, frown on face, she said what she'd been saying for years. "It's paganism, pure and stupid."

"But I'm not a pagan."

She nodded. "Right. You're a Gospel."

"Grandma, I won't do anything creepy. I'll just be myself. I won't even wear a costume."

Her fist was so buried into her hip that she could have been the angel that had injured Jacob. And yet there was a slight twinkle in her eye. "Oh, you'll wear a costume all right."

"I will? What costume?"

Her whole face brightened with a mischievous grin. "You'll wear the costume that I made for you."

I gave her a hug. "Do I get to be King Arthur?"

"Better."

"Francis of Assisi?"

"Better."

"Billy Graham?"

"Better."

My costume, as it turned out, was Scripture itself.

Grandmother had taken an old choir robe and sewn Bible verses onto it. Not only was I wearing my faith on my sleeve, I was wearing it from head to toe, with large words sewn in red. On the front of the robe was the Twenty-third Psalm. THE LORD IS MY SHEPHERD . . . And on the back was John 3:16. FOR GOD SO LOVED THE WORLD . . .

My brother came down the stairs and strode into the living room, laughing. "Danny, you look like an idiot."

Holly came down the stairs and showed me a little Christmas card. She said, "It's not quite finished, but it will be in a few hours. I'm making one for Jon, too. I'll leave them on your pillows tonight."

The card was decorated with a magic-marker image of a manger beneath an autumn tree. Inside were the words: "Christ is born this day! October 31st, 1991. Love, Holly."

"Thanks for showing me that," I said, and gave her a hug.

She held on tightly and whispered into my ear, "Jon's in trouble. Help him, Danny."

I whispered into her ear, "I'll do what I can."

Jon grabbed my robe and tugged me toward the door. "Let's go, bro. It's your big night."

He drove us into Iowa City, nervously smoking a cigarette and muttering to himself about money. Then he dropped me off at Brown Street, near a large Victorian home, where I was scheduled to meet some friends. I climbed out of the truck, closed the door, and spoke into the open window. "Why don't you join us, Jon? You could sing with me."

"Sorry, Danny. I have work to do."

"What kind of work?"

He revved the Chevy. "I'll pick you up in three hours. Right here."

"Jon, why won't you sing with me?"

My brother shrugged. "I don't have a robe."

"You can wear this one. I'm fine with a T-shirt."

He laughed. "See ya later, Danny."

The truck rattled over the old-fashioned brick pavement. I waved good-bye half-heartedly, knowing Jon wasn't looking back. And when the Chevy disappeared down the road, I found myself looking to the sky. It was a perfect twilight, and there was something about the wind and the geese near the clouds that made everything seem more alive than ever. While I thought about All Hallows' Eve and what it really meant, in church and out of church, the darkness descended or arose or appeared as if out of nowhere. Standing on the street corner in my Scripture robe, while ghosts and witches and little clusters of pop-culture creatures began swarming the porches, I kept glancing at the sky, the gloaming drawing my mind away from the fun-filled pretenders, reminding me, like Grandmother, that real powers and principalities, in all of their manifestations, were just one fell swoop away.

Grease suddenly appeared, waddling down the sidewalk, dressed as a pig.

"Oinky Halloween, Danny!"

"Yeah, oinky to you, too."

The Samsonov brothers were with him. Slopper was dressed as a vampire. He didn't have fangs, but he had big yellow dentures jutting out of his mouth. Mud Eye shuffled stiffly about, all wound up with toilet paper, a cheap mummy. The brothers carried candy bags that were already half full.

I asked, "What time did you start trick-or-treating?"

The mummy smirked through his toilet paper as if keeping a secret.

The vampire drooled through his dentures. "We're carrying rotten eggs. We've been saving them since August."

Grease leaned down for a sniff. "Yech. These things are killers."

I leaned down for a sniff. "Yech. Oh, please, don't throw those eggs within a mile of anything with a nose."

The mummy and the vampire laughed, mad laughter that went on and on, while Grease and I waited patiently for the fit to pass.

Finally, the streetlights flicked on, buzzing like firebugs.

The mummy said, "Now is the official start of Halloween. Let's egg the next car that comes down the road."

The vampire agreed, and the brothers reached into their rotten bags and grabbed a handful of stink bombs.

The next car to enter the neighborhood was a truck, a garbage truck that wasn't stopping to pick up any garbage. The Samsonovs waited until the monstrous vehicle was almost upon us, and then hurled their horrid grenades.

Splat! Splat!

Sploosh! Sploosh!

Ooze like gangrene slimed down the windshield, and with the hissing of air brakes, the truck came to a sudden stop beneath the streetlight. Despite the ooze, we all saw the driver clearly enough, and that sight must have terrified the brothers, because they'd just egged the biggest hell-raiser in Iowa City. Paul Renkendorf, the twenty-year-old son of a garbage man, was a known drug dealer with a habit of bizarre violence. He rolled down the window and stuck his head out. It was horned. Paul had somehow fastened antlers to his head. Real antlers. He looked both silly and murderous.

"I'm gonna kill whoever threw those eggs," he said.

The mummy and the vampire dropped their bags and went flying up the sidewalk. Paul yanked his antlers back into the truck and drove off in pursuit, leaving me and Grease behind in a cloud of dusty stench.

Grease said, "It's gonna be a great night."

"Are you sure?"

He nodded. "You're gonna sing and I'm gonna eat."

Grease grabbed the collar of my Scripture robe and dragged me into the yard of a fine home with a jack-o'-lantern grinning in the window.

And for the next few hours, while my friend rang

doorbells and begged for treats, I stood beside him and sang hymns and spirituals and Christmas songs. Some people stared at me like I was from another planet. Others laughed, and a few hurled insults. But many appreciative people recognized me from the Gospel Family concerts. One nice old lady said, "Danny, I think you understand this night better than anyone else. Here, have a pie."

Grease and I sat on her steps and ate a whole apple pie (he had five of the six slices), and then we continued our journey through the sacred night. I sang my heart out and shared the Scriptures while Grease filled his bag and himself with sugars to the point of bursting. We stayed out later than most of the other trick-or-treaters, visiting all sorts of neighborhoods throughout Iowa City, and by the time we circled back to the Victorian homes of Brown Street, it had begun to rain. Shimmering water kissed the trees, and the last of the leaves swirled in the air.

It was one of those strange late-autumn storms without thunder but strobed with lightning. In the flashes we saw the last of the Halloween creatures scurrying away for shelter.

"Well," Grease said, yawning, "I'm supposed to meet my mom over at the Cottage Deli. I better hurry over there before she eats too much potato salad."

"Your mom didn't have to come into town. Jon could've given you a ride."

"No, she won't let me ride with Jon. She says he's a party animal. Anyway, see you tomorrow, Danny."

"See you tomorrow."

Grease waddled away, hefting his candy bag. And now the rain and the lightning, which had been wildly inspiring, began to bother me while I shivered beneath a tree and waited for Jon's arrival. It must have been half an hour, or maybe a whole hour later, when the headlights of the old Chevy appeared, peeking through the raindrops as if searching for me. The truck squealed to a stop near the sheltering tree.

Jon opened the window a crack. "Hurry, get in!"

Before I moved, a garbage truck came roaring up the road behind us. It hissed its brakes and proclaimed its stink. Paul Renkendorf jumped out into the storm, his antlers flashing white in the lightning.

While Jon scrambled out of the pickup, Paul pulled out a gun and aimed it at the Twenty-third Psalm and my heart. "Aren't you one of the kids who egged me tonight?"

"No. I've just been singing."

Jon rushed toward Paul, who then pointed the gun at my brother.

"Back off, Gospel."

Jon stopped dead in his tracks. "Okay, okay." And he whispered, "Danny. Let me handle this."

I almost said, "Will you handle it like you did at the hog plant?" But I bit my tongue.

Paul said, "I don't take kindly to people getting into my territory."

Jon forced a smile and tried to act cool. "Paul, you and I aren't really competing. I know it's all yours. And I'm only temporary. Just passing through town until the farm is good again."

Paul laughed, his antlers shaking. "You're pretty slick, Gospel. If it weren't for your family's music, I'd hire you to work for me. But I'm not a hypocrite, understand?"

Jon nodded. I noticed how the raindrops fell darkly on his pallid face. He looked ancient and miserable.

Paul re-aimed the gun at me. "Don't look so stupid, you idiot. The banjo player has been stealing my hard-earned business. Do you understand?"

I nodded.

My brother had been selling marijuana to make money to save the farm. Back in the summer, he'd suggested that our family sell an album of the songs we performed. Father, who was anguishing over a failing corn crop, listened carefully and then slapped his elder son. "We will not profit from the gospel!"

"So be it," Jon had replied, his lip bleeding. "There are other ways to save ourselves."

Paul stepped closer and aimed the gun at my mouth. "Danny, I've heard you sing. And I don't like you."

Jon whispered, "Danny. Step back, very slowly. I'm going to make my move now."

"No."

"Danny. Step back. Let me handle this."

"No."

"Danny—"

I whirled around, offering Paul the words on the back of my robe. There was just enough streetlight and lightning for Paul to see FOR GOD SO LOVED THE WORLD . . .

The son of a garbage man was silent for a few moments, and then he burst out laughing, as if God's love were the funniest thing on earth. I turned around and said, as gently as possible, "God is not mocked."

Jon made his move and threw a punch at Paul's face. He missed, and the horns came down quick and gashed

Jon's cheek to the bone. He fell to his knees, dazed, while the blood poured. I rushed over to apply my robe to the wound. Paul leaned toward me, swinging his antlers, and one of the horns cut viciously across my chest. I fell to my knees beside my brother.

Paul immediately put the gun to Jon's head and squeezed the trigger. I tried to punch the gun away, but I wasn't fast enough. In a flash of lightning there was a click. My brother flinched and I shuddered and Paul laughed. The pistol wasn't loaded.

Paul laughed again. "God might not be mocked. But you are."

Then he jumped into his garbage truck and revved the engine and roared down the street, and it seemed like the lightning was giving chase.

Jon and I knelt in the rain for a while, and I could hear him praying under his breath, and cursing, and making promises, and mostly just breaking down; and finally he stood and pulled me up. "That's enough of that. Let's go home." And we got into our pickup and drove out of the city.

"Danny," Jon said, grabbing my robe and holding it to his face, "I was only trying to save the farm. And I was only selling to people who were already smokers. Please don't think I'm a bad person."

"I don't think you're bad."

"Thanks. That means a lot to me."

I looked into his sorrowful eyes. "I think you're lost."

We drove in silence into the fields while the rain turned to open sky and burning stars.

When we reached the farm, my big brother wandered

off toward the root cellar while I sloshed into the house. Everyone was in bed except for our mother, who was re-clining on the sofa, reading a Bible. Her hair was laid out beside her like two silky blankets.

"Danny," she said sleepily, "it rained. I hope you didn't catch a cold."

I leaned down and kissed her cheek. "I forgot to bring you a chocolate bar."

Mother smiled. "I don't need it. I'm full of good words."

"Like my costume."

She noticed the torn bloody robe and jumped to her feet. "Danny! What happened?"

"I'm fine. It's just a surface wound. It doesn't even hurt."

She dropped her Bible on the sofa. "Let's get you cleaned up."

"Okay, but first listen to what happened tonight."

"You're bleeding."

"No, it's stopped. I'm okay, really."

"Where's Jon? Is he down in the cellar, smoking? Was he involved with you getting hurt?"

"Please, Mom, sit and listen. Something very important happened. I think Jon is starting to believe in our songs."

"Are you sure?" Mother sat nervously. "Tell me what happened."

I related most of the night to her, and she smiled at the beginning, especially at the part about the pie, and cried at the end. "Oh, Danny. What are we going to do? What's going to become of our family?"

"We're gonna keep singing."

She wiped away tears with her hair, and then hurried into the bathroom to get some rubbing alcohol, a washcloth, and bandages. She hurried back. "Danny, take off your robe and shirt. And stand very still."

Her voice was weak, but I obeyed.

Farm wives see a lot of blood in their lives, and this wound shouldn't have bothered her much, but my mother's hand trembled while she rubbed my chest. "At least the scar will be in the same place as the other one," she said.

I grinned. "Makes it easier to find my heart."

She covered the cross with large bandages, and suddenly got angry. "I'm calling Paul's mother. Doris needs to know what's going on. A gun? And animal horns? I'm calling her right now."

"No, Mom. You have enough to worry about. I'm a big boy. You don't have to watch over me."

She stood on her toes and kissed my forehead. "I'll always watch over you, Danny."

chapter six

I SAID GOOD-BYE to Brother Paul and Doggie and left them in the Catacombs. I wound my way up the stairs and out the door. Through the brisk November air I walked over to Dave's Foxhead Tavern. The place is famous for being the hub of the Iowa Writers' Workshop. On any given night, you can exchange words and shoot pool with poets, novelists, and playwrights. The Foxhead is a small wood-frame rectangle that resembles an old train car. When I entered the tavern, it was half empty but filled with a sense of momentum.

The bartender, wearing a blue racing shirt with yellow stripes, said, "How can I help you?"

"Water," I said, bellying up to the bar.

The bartender threw a wet towel over his shoulder and walked away.

Knowing it was his job to return, I waited patiently and contemplated the three shelves of antique clocks on the wall behind the bar, clocks of many shapes and sizes, including a stately grandfather and a funny cuckoo. All of the clocks had their hands mixed up. And I tried to imagine a scene for every hour and minute.

5:34 p.m. A young boy in Beijing glances up from his rice bowl and grins at the girl outside the window.

8:24 p.m. A husband with his eyes closed reaches for his wife's hand during a scary movie in Madrid.

3:58 a.m. An old weathered man in the Arctic Circle smiles warmly at his old weathered wife.

10:01 a.m. A young man in Iowa says, "I love you." And a young woman in New York is silent.

The bartender reappeared. "Tap water or spring?"

Transfixed by the clocks, I said, "How are we inside of time, and how are we outside?"

"Tap water or spring?" the bartender repeated. "What do you want?"

The clocks swirled in my mind.

The bartender waved his hand in front of my face. "Are you still with us? I don't have time for this. Listen, I really don't have—"

A woman's voice sang out, "I have time!"

The voice sounded familiar, yet strange.

I turned to see a woman with wild red hair, fiery blouse, hot pink skirt, and torrid orange stilettos. A cigarette dangled from her scarlet lips.

"Plain Jane? Look at you."

She curled her fingers and stared at the reflections in her ruby fingernails. "I have been looking at me," she said, nodding her approval. She stared at the dry blood on my flannel shirt and pointed at me with her cigarette. "Look what the cat dragged in."

Another woman's voice rang out. "Is that Danny Gospel? Hey, Danny!"

I craned my neck to see Melissa. I only knew her in

white—the peasant dress and the bathrobe—but now she wore a black cocktail dress, so tight that the designer must have used a single strand of night sky to weave his magic around her curves.

I wondered: what's with all the flesh tonight? Don't the women know that the weather turned cold? They could catch their deaths.

The bartender asked, "How can I help you?"

Jane flicked cigarette ashes at the floor. "Two bottles of Harp for the girls. And spring water for Danny. Put everything on my tab, Bubba."

"Okay," Bubba said, "but my name is Frederick. Did you see the latest issue of *The Atlantic*? My poem—"

Jane laughed. "Whatever, you'll get your tip. Now, Danny, we were just talking about you. Some new rumors are floating around. Come sit with us."

Before I could decide if that was a good idea, Jane dragged me around the pool table and over to the corner booth.

"Hey," I said, "take it easy. What's gotten into you?"

"Don't be shy, Danny," she said, shoving me across from the scantily clad Melissa, whose eyes widened at the sight of blood on my shirt.

I shrugged. "Cat."

She nodded, fully understanding. "My new Musie has already swiped me. See the scratches on my wrists?"

Jane started humming the chorus of "Cat Scratch Fever" while the bartender, apparently the only person working that night, appeared with our drinks. "For the ladies, here are your Harps. And for the gentleman, cool clear water."

Jane winked. "Thanks, Bubba."

"I'm Frederick Madison," he said, "and I'm featured

in *The Atlantic*." He frowned proudly and scurried off to serve other customers.

Melissa swigged her beer and then pulled out a Swiss army knife. She opened the blade, sliced through the air, and stabbed down hard on the table. For years, poets and other customers in the Foxhead have wielded blades of all shapes and sizes, carving temporary immortalities into the tables. Most of the graffiti is typical: various initials heart other initials; a few people rule; and on our table, there was a crude but lovely scraping of Van Gogh's *Starry Night*.

"One last star in the swirls," she said. "There. Now it's finished."

"It's wonderful," I said.

Melissa beamed, her black dress and gold skin shining across the table. She pointed the knife at me. "Danny, you never told me the story about your scar."

I looked down. "Can we talk about it some other time?"

Melissa hesitantly agreed, and gently placed the knife on the table, the blade pointing at herself.

Jane sighed and tossed her cigarette to the floor, right where a group of revelers stood with their drinks. Jane extended her plain leg and snuffed out the cigarette with one stomp of the orange stiletto.

A tall blonde swayed dramatically and said, "Ex-cuuuse me, Miss B!"

"Only God could excuse someone like you," Jane said.

The blonde's boyfriend, all muscle inside of a white cashmere sweater, glared at the cigarette butt and then at me, and said in a challenging voice, "Are we cool?"

"Sorry about that," I said, not wanting any trouble.

The muscle man smirked. "So, we're cool?"

"Yeah," I said, analyzing his weak spots and noticing the overripe Adam's apple, "we're cool."

The blonde hissed in my direction, "Sooo not cool. Flannel shirt and overalls. Beyond retro. Loser!"

"At least his chest is real," Jane said.

The muscle man's face grew pensive, as if considering the validity of the comment, and then his brow unfurrowed and he laughed heartily. "A real chest! That's funny."

Everyone in their group agreed, laughing, except of course for the blonde. "That's sooo not funny," she said. And she dug her nails into the cashmere sweater and dragged the muscle man toward the bar. "You better make it up to me, Kendal. I want an Irish car bomb."

I whispered into Jane's ear, "You've never caused trouble in your whole life. What's happened to you?"

She lit another cigarette. "I met Melissa."

"So? I've met her, too. And I didn't start acting crazy in public."

Jane raised an eyebrow. Melissa raised an eyebrow.

"Okay, okay," I acknowledged. "But you girls have gone off the deep end. Last week, you were fine. And now you're . . . you're . . . this."

"It's called a makeover," Melissa said. "I just walked into dulcinea on a whim and started talking to Jane about clothes and men and terrorism and the end of the world, and we decided to change our lives."

"Make over our lives," Jane said. "You understand that, Danny."

I nodded sympathetically. "Yeah, I understand."

Melissa sipped her beer and started bobbing to a blue

tune that was jazzing from the jukebox. "I just love Miles Davis."

"Me too," Jane said, bobbing along. "Man, they have the best jukebox in here."

Heads were bobbing throughout the bar, which was now almost full, and I joined in, enjoying the call of the muted trumpet.

When the blue tune was over, the next song was "I Go Walking After Midnight" by Patsy Cline, and I felt as if the whole crowd in the Foxhead was in the moonlight with me, searching, searching for—

"Danny," Melissa said, "have you written any songs?"

"Huh? What?"

"Religious songs," Jane said. She blew on her Harp bottle as if it were a musical jug. "You've always said you were going to write hymns."

"Spirituals," I said. "I've always wanted to write something as good as the spirituals. But I haven't suffered enough."

"Danny," Jane said, taking my hand, "you've suffered—"

The bartender and his racing stripes appeared with another tray of drinks. "On the house," he said. "Say, that Patsy Cline song reminds me of the poem I published in this month's *Atlantic*."

Jane and Melissa looked away, hoping he'd take the hint. I gulped some more spring water and said, "Tell me about your poem, Frederick."

The bartender glanced around the busy bar and convinced himself that nobody needed him. He squeezed into the booth beside Melissa. "My poem was inspired by my cousin's wedding in Greece. The ceremony took place in a domed church on a mountain overlooking the Mediterranean. I don't have a religious bone in my body, but I loved the artfulness of the ritual. The entire service was sung. I didn't know a wedding could be sung! And the bride and groom were crowned with flowers. Imagine that, my pregnant cousin Lorraine and her swarthy plumber—the king and queen of the world!"

Several customers waved for Frederick from the bar. "Excuse me," he said, scooting back out of the booth. "I better get back to serving."

"Bubba," Jane said, flirting, "you're my third-favorite author."

"Bubba," Melissa said, teasing, "you're my second-favorite author."

Frederick replied, in all seriousness, "I will be signing copies of *The Atlantic* at the Prairie Lights Bookstore next Saturday. I'll see you all there."

Despite Frederick's problem, it was good to be in a place where literature is considered sacred. And I asked the ladies, "Who is your favorite author—for real?"

With her red blouse glowing in the smoky room, Jane expressed her newfound admiration for Dostoevsky. "I just started reading *The Brothers Karamazov* and it seems to be about everything," she said. "Love, hate, faith, doubt, kindness, cruelty, men and women, and everything with a passion."

Melissa swigged her beer. "Hmm. I cast my vote for Emily Dickinson. She wasn't as extreme as Dostoevsky or as fancy as Shakespeare, but sometimes I think about her when I'm alone on the farm, notebook in hand, staring out into the sky. Emily reminds me of the largeness and loneliness of the soul."

Jane said, "You should call Ethan."

Melissa sighed. "Oh, Ethan . . . with his mismatched arms and asymmetrical head . . . Hmm. Maybe." She reached out and spun her knife. The blade whirled with light in the middle of the table, eventually slowed and stopped, and ended up pointing at me.

Melissa asked, "Who is your favorite author?"

I sipped more spring water and thought about people like Dante, Chesterton, Flannery O'Connor, and a host of others who loved words and the Word.

Jane tapped her ruby fingernails on the table. Tap, tap, tap. "Tell us," she said. Tap, tap—

"My grandmother," I said. "She wrote wonderful little stories. Every person she created was heroic and foolish and struggling to do God's will. Her characters were heavenly, and stuck in the Iowa soil, just trying to be normal and happy."

Jane and Melissa enjoyed their Harps and I gulped my water, and we sat quietly for a while, listening to the conversations rising and falling. The jukebox, awaiting the next round of quarters, flashed and blinked in silence.

Melissa said, "Danny, do you still have your grandmother's stories? You should try to publish them."

I shook my head. "Everything is gone. When my brother sold the farm, the people in charge of the auction burned several boxes they thought were full of junk, including Grammy's notebooks and an heirloom wedding dress."

"Those auctioneers are criminals, stealing from their neighbors," Melissa said, fingering her knife.

Jane rubbed my shoulder. "Danny, you really have suffered."

"Look, turn around," Melissa said, pointing at the TV

above the bar. "They're showing a picture of that poor old man, the Alzheimer's patient who wandered off."

My eyes filled with tears. "Jack Williams," I whispered.

"They found him," Jane said. "Turns out he wasn't in the reservoir, after all. Thank God, he's alive!"

"Yes, he's alive," I said, wiping my cheek. "But I don't think the doctors can keep him alive."

"You know him, Danny, right?" Jane asked. "Didn't Jack Williams live near your farm?"

"Yes, he was a good neighbor."

In the next booth, someone whispered loudly, "Do you remember that music group made up of farmers, the Good News Family or something? Danny was in that, but everyone died and he went crazy. Or I should say, crazier. Then his fiancée left him and moved to New York. Since 9/11, Danny has been terrorizing half of Iowa, driving through farms and stalking people."

"Maybe," I said to Jane and Melissa, "we should go somewhere else. Maybe we could find some good live music."

One of the guys at the pool table shouted, "Will! It's your game! C'mon, shoot 'em up!"

My stomach felt sick.

"Will! Where are you?"

From the far side of the bar, a stocky guy in jeans and cowboy boots came strutting. The guy had pale blue eyes, a clean strong jaw, grinning teeth, and a self-inflicted buzz cut.

Jane and Melissa rolled their eyes, amused.

I was not amused. Because this strutting grinner was Will Bentley, the guy who had messed with my girl.

It's interesting how a horrible memory often begins with

144 — David Athey

a scene of bliss. On a summer day, Rachel and I were sitting under a tree near the reservoir.

"Why did the Lord create the leviathan?" Rachel asked, her toes wriggling in the spillway creek.

I smiled. "Just for fun."

Rachel nodded, her wild hair sparkling. "And why the brontosaurus?"

"God loves to move mountains. So He gave the mountains some feet."

Rachel laughed and reached for my hand. "And why did the Lord create a man?"

I pulled her close. "Man was made to walk in the Garden."

"Is that all?"

"And to farm the Garden."

"Sounds boring."

I leaned in for a good kiss.

"Now you're talking," Rachel said.

It was one of the few good days that I had after my father's death. My fiancée did her best to get me through the summer, helping with the farm and everything. But when the season changed to fall, and the crop was failing, Rachel no longer wanted to talk about marriage. And then came the auction and my move into the trailer park, and a cold winter, with Rachel hardly ever talking about anything except New York. And then on Valentine's Day, she wept over my beautiful poem and dumped me.

I didn't speak to her again until the second week in March, when the snow was melting. I called her on the phone and kept the conversation light, telling her strange stories about working at the post office. She actually laughed. And something inside of me blossomed and I couldn't help myself. I began talking about the farm and having a normal happy life.

Rachel responded, "I want to be happy, as well. You know how much I love you, Danny. But I can't stay in Iowa."

"And I can't leave."

There was a horrible hush.

"Danny. I'm returning to New York at the end of the semester."

"I know."

"And I'm going to stay there."

"I know."

Yet something way down in my heart kept telling me that Rachel and I had a future.

Perhaps I shouldn't have followed my ex-fiancée the morning of her last day in Iowa, when she visited the reservoir. In my wishful-thinking mind, I thought Rachel was driving out there as a sort of pilgrimage to recall how we'd played with the big questions and answered them with a kiss.

I followed her red Jetta from a distance and then parked my pickup beside her car after she'd walked up the trail toward the spillway. Silently, I climbed out of the truck and searched through the trees where Rachel had disappeared; and when I was almost to the clearing, I saw the shimmer of her white blouse. I took a step closer and saw her kissing another man.

Will Bentley. On the lips? Or just on the cheek? What did it matter? The damage was done.

Rachel saw me out of the corner of her eye and didn't say a word. She didn't even wave or acknowledge my existence.

I thought she might at least phone me later and try to

explain. But she just delivered her leased Jetta back to the dealer and flew to New York.

After that, it was wretched enough living in the same town with Will Bentley. But he made everything worse by moving into a house on my mail route. Sometimes he'd appear at the window with puckered lips. He'd kiss the glass, and wink, and laugh.

Certain men would have killed him. But I wasn't certain men, so I just dropped most of his mail into the black metal box and walked away.

"Jane and Melissa," I said, sliding out of the booth, "please excuse me."

"Where are you going?"

I climbed on the pool table, my head in the cloud of smoke near the ceiling.

Will Bentley glared. Jane and Melissa smiled nervously. Other people, including the blonde and her muscular boyfriend, pointed and murmured.

"I'd like to recite a poem," I said, swaying. "I just made it up, with help from King Solomon. The poem is called 'Song for the Woman of My Dreams.'"

A hush fell upon the tavern.

"*Behold,*" I said, "*You are beautiful.*

"*Your eyes are new-born stars. Your hair is the swishing of Pegasus' tail.*

"*Your teeth are pearls of good prices.*

"*Your lips are red roses with no thorns.*

"*Your cheeks are halves of a pomegranate, like the good kind you get at the Farmers' Market.*

"*And your neck is a leaning tower in Babylon, making everyone babble about its beauty.*

"*And your breasts, if I may say so, are two happy fawns, dappled with freckles because of your sunbathing.*

"*As the day breathes heavily, I will travel the roads of myrrh and frankincense and gravel.*

"*Come down from Heaven, my love, with wings or just the way you were.*

"*Let us kiss one another and become the lovers that enter the Garden again.*"

Jane and Melissa whistled and clapped their hands.

The blonde said, "That was really cool. And really hot."

Will Bentley scoffed.

"Encore!" Melissa shouted. "Encore!"

"Okay," I said, swaying. "Here's one called 'Song for the Woman of My Dreams, Part Two.'"

Several amazing words were dancing on the tip of my tongue when Will Bentley jumped up and joined me on the pool table.

"You're the mailman for Brown Street," he said. "You're the stupid mailman, right?"

"Yes, Will. I sometimes deliver some mail on Brown Street."

"Well, I'm missing several bills, Danny Boy. What did you do, throw my mail in the garbage?"

"Don't worry about your bills. When my angel marries me and turns the world into Eden again, everything will be free. No more debts."

Will slid closer to me and assumed a grappling position, reaching out with thick arms. "Tell me what you did to my mail, or else I'm gonna throw you against the floor. And when the bill collectors start calling me, I'm gonna direct them to your hospital room."

"I did you a favor."

Will shifted his weight slightly away and then smirked the same smirk I'd seen at the reservoir after he'd kissed Rachel. "Listen, Danny Boy. I'll make you a deal. You and me sign up for the marines tomorrow, and I won't kick your butt tonight."

I laughed. "Me? A marine?"

"Join up with me. C'mon, Gospel Boy. Let's go to the Middle East and make them pay for what they've done."

"I'm not gonna fight," I said. "Not with you or anybody else."

Will exploded. "What kind of a freaking coward are you?"

I shook my head. "It's not about fear."

He inched toward me, seething with rage.

Melissa stood and shouted, "Catch!"

She tossed her Swiss army knife, and I managed to catch the handle.

"Butcher him," she said.

In a flash I brought the knife to Will's throat. The temptation was exhilarating, and everyone in the Foxhead reacted in wildly different ways—gasping, cheering, cursing, clapping, threatening, and I heard animal noises from human mouths, or noises that were not even animal—and I dropped Melissa's knife to the floor.

Will didn't hesitate. He lowered his center of gravity and grabbed my waist and hoisted me up, knocking my head into the ceiling, and then he shoved off from the table. We flew for a moment, my back vulnerable to the ground with Will's entire weight upon me. He grabbed my chin and arched my neck to make my head hit the floor, but something turned us around in the air. Will hit hard, and the sound of his skull breaking was horrific. Blood poured from him.

There were cries for an ambulance, and the blonde told everyone to stand back because she was a nurse and the entire bar broke into chaos and I stood near the growing pool of blood, and one of Will's friends called me a murderer and tried to punch me in the face but accidentally hit the blonde's muscular boyfriend, and then everyone began fighting, and I was shoved into the jukebox and it shattered and some coins tumbled out and Jane and Melissa were helping the blonde save Will's life, wrapping his head with somebody's scarf, and suddenly my attention was drawn to a figure in the doorway, shimmering. Shimmering like an angel.

Could it be? Was it her? The one who had kissed me?

No. It was Grease. With his filthy hands, he plucked me out of the crowd and threw me over his shoulder. And the two of us disappeared out the door.

chapter seven

GREASE DROVE MY truck across the university bridge. "You're in a heap of trouble, Danny. The police will be looking for you."

"Well, if they catch me, it's probably for the best."

Grease ran a red light. "For the best? Are you crazy? They'll throw you in a clinic and ask you personal questions. They'll peek into your head and push drugs up your—"

I sat up suddenly, feeling clear-minded and strong. "Let me get this straight. They're gonna throw me in a loony bin, while guys like you run free."

Grease ran another red light. "Yep."

He drove us over to Coralville, a small but growing town named in memory of the ocean that once ruled Iowa, the thought of which always set my mind to swimming. In the genesis of Genesis, the world was one shimmering circular sea. Bright leviathans schooled and lolled for the playful Lord. The liquid flames in the center of the earth leapt and gurgled at the chance to help build mountains, deserts, fields, forests, and cities. . . .

We descended into the heart of the warehouse district, a place that was relatively unknown to me.

Grease said, "This is where I work on my top-secret projects."

His workshop was tucked between a self-storage building and a strip club. Grease drove down a dark alley that opened into a vacant lot behind a large anonymous garage. He rolled down the window, stuck out his arms, and clapped loudly. The huge door slowly opened. Grease grinned. "My invention is called the Applauder. It's like the Clapper, only for stronger hands. I'm gonna make a billion dollars from this one, Danny. And I'll retire to Palm Beach and live with Donald Trump. We'll swap business wisdom, and I'll probably marry some of his ex-wives."

"What?"

Grease drove my pickup into the garage and stuck his hands out the window and gave himself another round of applause. Lights erupted in all directions, revealing junk and a dozen cars in various stages of repair. Grease climbed out of the Chevy, came around to my door, and tugged my arm. "Danny, we need to get you out of Iowa. I'm afraid you started a war tonight."

"All I did was make up a poem."

Grease led me to the far side of the garage, where a large white sheet covered a hulking vehicle.

"What's under the sheet? An army tank?"

"No, just you wait and see."

Like a magician, Grease ceremoniously yanked the cloth. "Behold! The car of my dreams!"

"A pink Cadillac," I said. "Hmm."

"From Key West, Florida. I've been restoring her for a couple of years now. Is she a vision or what?"

I circled the Cadillac, bewildered by its classy trashiness. Grease had converted the convertible into a high-rider. With oversized wheels and flamingo mud flaps. "This car," I said, taking a step back, "does not belong on this planet."

He grinned and then bent down and hugged a headlight. "I love her. And she loves me."

"Grease, this is a pink monstrosity."

He stood and opened the door and shoved me inside. "Fly away, Danny! Here are the keys. Just go."

"What?"

"Don't even tell me where you're going. And don't call. I'm sure my phone is bugged."

I shook my head. "Listen, Grease. I can't simply drive away from my problems."

"Danny. If they catch you and put you in a psycho ward, you'll never get out. Will Bentley's family owns half of the city, and a third of Johnson County, and a sixth of the state."

I gripped the steering wheel. "I didn't bust Will's skull on purpose. I have witnesses."

"Witnesses can be bought."

"I have good witnesses."

"Good witnesses can be bought."

"I can't run away from Iowa. This is home. This is where all the stories make sense. Even if they lock me up, this is where I'll still be Danny Gospel."

"Turn the key, Danny, and go."

"The post office said I can't go anywhere. I'm under investigation."

Grease grunted and plodded across the stained cement floor over to a refrigerator covered with fleshy calendars. He flung the door open and started grabbing food and drinks and tossing them into a plastic cooler. He returned to the Cadillac and placed the cooler in the back seat. "You can't return for a long time, Danny. The cops, the post office, and the Bentley family are all after you. Everyone is after you."

"I'm in deep, that's for sure."

Grease closed the back door and began searching through piles of boxes and junk until he found a case of motor oil. He told me to grab the lever that opened the trunk, and he placed the case inside. "Don't worry, Danny. I'll figure out how to contact your brother without the Feds finding out."

"Jon won't get involved with this."

"Of course he will, Danny. You're his best man."

Grease slammed shut the trunk and returned to my window. He looked at me funny. "This reminds me of a good movie I once saw. The hero got away, nursing just a few gunshot wounds. And his sidekick got hung and eaten by buzzards."

I smiled at my friend. "I don't want you to get into trouble, Grease. By helping me, you're breaking the law."

"Oh, I'll risk anything to help you. The sheriff can throw me into a hog lagoon, but I won't complain. I'll just call Johnnie Cochran, and he'll say, 'If the Grease is slick, you must acquit.'"

I laughed. I didn't want to. But I did.

Grease reached into his grimy overalls and pulled out a money clip. "Here," he said, stuffing the clip into my overalls. "Business has been good lately. I've been really blessed. And it's not just money. At church yesterday, I heard the voice of God."

"Is that a fact?"

"Yep. The voice was loud and clear, with a Canadian accent."

I shook my head. "And what did the voice of God tell you?"

"STAY OUT OF STRIP CLUBS, EH?"

"Oh boy," I said, turning the key. "Maybe I should get out of here."

"Danny."

"Yeah?"

"The voice also said, "TELL DANNY TO STOP WORRYING ABOUT RACHEL. SHE'S FINE."

I gave the pink high-rider some gas and it roared to life, squealing out into the empty lot. I cranked the wheel and the car spun in a half circle and headed toward the alley. I saw Grease in the corner of my eye, applauding, while the garage door closed down.

The pink Cadillac took me to I-80 and accelerated east toward Chicago. Okay, I thought, perhaps the City of Big Shoulders can carry my burdens for a while.

However, before I'd gone fifty miles, something told me that I should take the next exit and return to Iowa City and face my accusers. Something told me that I should trust the legal system and allow the courts to judge the proper punishment for my crimes, even if I hadn't committed any in the spiritual world. Something told me: if you flee, you'll never see your brother, the farm, or the woman who kissed you, ever again.

I prayed through the windshield, beyond the midnight stars, "God, even if I'm going the wrong way, please bless this journey."

After praying some more, I switched on the AM radio and dialed around for a soothing melody. Considering all the great songs in the world, finding one shouldn't have been difficult, but the only sounds up and down the dial were monologues and diatribes. Finally, I settled for a talk show that was exploring the mysteries of outer space. An astronomer from Oxford was talking about his search for intelligent life in the universe. I was struck by the words "intelligent life," and I wondered: if the Oxford astronomer reached the outer limits of the universe and found just one measly life-form, a man dressed in bloody overalls, praying like an imbecile, would that count as intelligent life?

Crossing the bridge and the border into Illinois, I had to decide if I should continue toward Chicago or take the loop going south. It occurred to me that the pink Cadillac might draw too much attention in the Midwest, and I would be better off driving to a destination that was full of wild and colorful cars. Miami came to mind, and then a better idea: Key West, the absolute end of the line.

"That's where I'll go. I'll take the high-rider to visit its home."

In the early light of morning, I was still in Illinois, which was just like Iowa except for a few more trees. There was an atlas on the passenger seat, and I grabbed it and propped it against the steering wheel and scanned the United States and was amazed by how far Florida was from the rest of us. Out in the Atlantic Ocean among exotic islands, Florida seemed to be more mythological than real, a geological dream, with all of the roads on my atlas seemingly drawn to that kingdom like magic.

My stomach rumbled hungrily, and I reached back into the cooler and pulled out a Greasy surprise, a barbecued pork sandwich. It was awful and quite good, and after the first bite I remembered to say grace. Or rather, I remembered to sing it. "*Oh, the Lord is good to me. And so I thank the Lord, for giving me the things I need, the sun and the rain and the apple seed. The Lord is good to me.*"

That was Holly's favorite grace. And she would have sung it in the Boundary Waters, sung it so faithfully, if she had just survived a few more minutes.

While Father fried a sizzling walleye over the campfire, Holly paddled the canoe over the calm lake, just a hundred feet from shore. This was her third trip to the Boundary Waters, and because she had proven her abilities, Dad was letting her paddle alone. He knew how important it was for her to experience God in the wild. Every few seconds, he looked up from the fire to see that his thirteen-year-old daughter was okay.

Holly glided across the blue water, singing. "*Why should I feel discouraged, why should the shadows come, why should my heart be lonely, and long for Heaven and home, when Jesus is my portion, my constant friend is He? His eye is on the sparrow, and I know He watches me. His eye is on the sparrow, and I know He watches me.*"

Like most farm girls, Holly was at home in nature, even in potentially dangerous situations.

"Come on in," my father called. "Let's sing grace and eat! You're going to love this walleye."

"Okay," she said. "I'm coming in."

Above the golden birch trees on the far side of the lake, a flock of geese came into view. Holly jumped up and waved her paddle. "Fly over here, you geese! Honk, honk, honk! Fly over here!"

My father shouted, "Holly, sit down!"

Her eyes locked onto his eyes for a moment as if to apologize while she lost her balance and fell. Her head smacked against the side of the canoe, and then she hit the hardness of the lake.

The impact jostled the unzipped lifejacket away from Holly's body. Facedown in the water, my sister began to drown. In a panic, my father ran to her rescue, splashing and wading up to his chest. It was only then that he paused, realizing that he needed to take off his heavy boots and wool jacket. For a few seconds he tried to get free of them, but seeing Holly's body floating away, a sense of terrified love compelled him to immediately swim after her.

The cold water made everything heavier; and although my father was an ex-marine and a powerful swimmer, his head went under and he panicked again, thrashing his arms and kicking his legs. Down he went into the frigid depths, coughing up bubbles into the hazy light. His boots soon touched the bottom of the lake. He thrashed and kicked and merely stirred up the sand between the ancient rocks. And he knew there was nothing more he could do. In the swirling of silt and golden sand, he gave himself up for lost.

But Father began to rise. He could never explain how. He just rose, slowly floating toward the reflected clouds and the lighter blue. He broke the surface and breathed again, and found himself within reach of his daughter's pale hand. He pulled Holly close to his side, then rolled her onto her back and tried to breathe into her cold mouth. There was no response, just a sick gurgling of water in her lungs. Weeping and praying and kicking to stay afloat, Father continued to breathe into the blue lips.

Another flock of geese sailed over the water, the reflection of wings beating wildly in the ripples around Holly's face. My father tried to guide my little sister to shore. He kicked and kicked, but he could barely move. Waves caused by his panic swept into Holly's mouth, and Father had to roll her over and try to lift her so that the water could run back out. He could not lift her high enough. The quiet gurgling in her lungs was the most horrifying sound he'd ever heard, including all the sounds of war, and it was even worse when the gurgling stopped.

Finally, Father managed to push Holly's body into the shallow water, his numb feet hitting the glittering rocks. With what little strength he had left, he hoisted her out of the lake and carried her close to the fire. He performed CPR, and breathed and breathed into her.

But Holly was already in the air.

At the southern end of Illinois, I hugged the steering wheel while approaching a strange rock formation. The huge rust-colored rocks seemed to form a gateway, jagged and crumbling. I half expected a medieval guard to appear in the center of the road, sword raised to stop the pink Cadillac. The high-rider accelerated and passed through the gateway. And I entered a different world.

The South.

I rolled down the window. The November air was warm and cool and humid at the same time, tasting of some kind of fermentation. A clay-colored light hung over the land-scape, and it seemed like the tree branches were struggling with a greater pull of gravity.

My gas tank was empty, so I exited the interstate and stopped at a station in a small town. At a self-serve pump, I was approached by a man in a dirty denim jacket, his belly bulging over faded jeans. He motioned for me to roll down the window. "I fillerup for ya."

"That's okay," I said. "I can do it myself."

The guy hitched up his pants, grunted, and stared into my aching eyes. "You tired from paintin' this car?"

"Oh, I didn't paint it. This is my friend's car."

"Hmm-hmm-hmm," the belly man said. "This kinda car getya killed."

"Oh?"

He rubbed his stubbly chin. "Methlabs are springing up in the woods. Fast cash and colorcars commin'outa the woodwork."

"I'm not into the drug scene," I said. "I'm just driving a pink Cadillac because my friend has an obsession with Florida. If people want to hurt me for that, then I guess people will hurt me for anything."

The belly man smiled and pointed at the sign on the pump. "This here is self-serve." He hitched up his pants and hauled himself over to a rusty chair near the station door.

When the Cadillac was full to the brim, I reached into my pocket and pulled out the fat clip of cash. Thumbing the stack, searching for a couple of twenties, all I could find were hundreds. "Grease," I whispered out loud, "you gave me over two thousand dollars!"

The belly man perked up. "Surprised by yerown wealth?"

I walked over and handed him a hundred. "Keep the change."

His reaction was a complex combination of being grateful, worried, and angry. "Thankya, buddy. Now, don't cause no trouble with that stolen Caddy. Ifya cause trouble 'round here, yagonna pay more than a hundred dollars."

"Thanks for the gas," I said, and sped away.

My heart pounded and ached, and I hated being on the run, and I was sure that any plan devised by Grease was doomed to a fate worse than failure. I accelerated down the ramp to the interstate, my eyes darting, searching for possible pursuers. And because fear was clouding my sense of generosity, I failed to stop for a sunburned hitchhiker. In the rearview mirror, he grimaced and waved, his face a dead ringer for Will Bentley, and then he plopped down among the weeds and garbage.

I was too exhausted to discern the spiritual correctness of the moment, and I hoped my decision to leave the hitchhiker behind was okay with Heaven.

Life on earth, even on an easy day, is so exhausting that everyone eventually collapses into a sort of cocoon and dreams for hours and hours before rising again. We are like butterflies and light-loving moths, but without the wings. Or perhaps we do have wings—wild, beautiful, and invisible.

A quick nap was desperately needed, so I pulled into the next rest area, knowing full well that I was risking getting captured. I parked between two semis whose drivers were soundly snoozing, and I caught just enough winks to get me back on the road almost refreshed.

There was the hitchhiker again.

I slammed on the brakes and skidded to a stop. "Get in," I said. "Sorry about passing you by earlier."

The guy sneered like Will Bentley and pointed at the high-rider. "I ain't climbing into that thing! Git away from me."

"Are you sure?"

"Git! And don't let me see you again."

In western Kentucky, at dusk, a spotted pony trotted in a field parallel to the road as if following an invisible hand full of sugar. When the pony saw the Cadillac, he tried to outrun me. I admired his playful willingness to race despite his falling so quickly behind, and I watched the pony gallop in my rearview mirror until he finally stopped at the outer limits of the field, where he reared up at the last second to avoid a collision with the fence.

And I remembered the white fence at Grove Baptist Church, not far from Saint Isidore's, where I once attended a class for "Future Christian Farmers." The only other students were the Samsonov brothers—Mud Eye and Slopper. Our teacher, Pastor Gordon, suffered from a disease that was slowly killing him, but he was a compulsive smiler. And he always said, "Love. Joy. Mercy. Peace."

That dark afternoon, down in the church basement, I raised my hand to ask the pastor a question about farmers in the Bible. But my hand went unnoticed because Mud Eye and Slopper began fighting. In an instant they overturned a table and tossed several chairs.

Pastor Gordon responded by saying, "Love. Joy. Mercy . . ."

Mud Eye and Slopper kept fighting.

Pastor said, "Boys. Let's go outside for our lesson. What do you say?"

"Ya-hoo!" they shouted, rampaging out the door.

"C'mon, Danny," the old smiler said, limping after them. "I need your help to teach those boys a lesson."

The moment we reached the backyard, we witnessed Mud Eye and Slopper hurling sticks at a black-capped chickadee that was perched in the upper branches of a barren oak.

The minister reminded them. "Boys, that bird belongs to God."

The brothers nodded, and hurled more sticks.

The chickadee's feathers were ruffled, but the bird simply sat and chirped, refusing to fly away.

"Mud Eye and Slopper," the pastor said, approaching them with outstretched arms. "I want to teach you about faith. I'm going to close my eyes and let you lead me. I'm going to let you play God. You can lead me wherever you wish."

I exhaled a loud worried breath.

Pastor whispered, "Danny, your job is to watch and not make a sound."

The brothers grabbed his pale hands and led him through a pile of leaves in the yard. Pastor Gordon stumbled but did not fall. Mud Eye and Slopper escorted him toward the church, where in a moment, if they didn't turn, he'd smack his head against the wall. I almost blurted out a warning, but then Mud Eye and Slopper twirled the smiler safely away.

I thought: maybe the brothers have a conscience after all.

They turned and led him toward the pond.

I bit my tongue while the chickadee twittered nervously from its perch in the oak. Pastor Gordon chuckled as if unaware that the brothers were planning on pushing him into the water. Mud Eye turned and gave me an evil grin, and then Slopper gave me an evil wink.

They approached the shoreline, and I couldn't contain myself. "Don't do it!"

The brothers paused, holding their prey.

Pastor said, "Danny. Hush. Your friends are doing fine."

The gray sky reflected darkly on the frigid water, and I was afraid. The fragile man of God, if dunked, could easily catch his death of cold.

"Okay," he said, squeezing the hands of his tormenters. "Let's keep going. Let's finish this."

I leaned forward, ready to rush to the pond. Even if I had to ruin the pastor's lesson about faith, I felt compelled to take action and save him from harm. Suddenly the brothers whirled him around and led him back toward the starting point. The brothers were careful to guide him along the smoothest part of the yard, and safely around the large cross that was planted near the white fence.

So maybe this was a good lesson after all, I thought. Maybe Mud Eye and Slopper really learned something.

As if reading each other's minds, the brothers veered and smashed the pastor into the fence. Either a board or a rib cracked. He bounced back, swaying, but did not fall.

I rushed to Pastor Gordon's side. His lip trembled and he continued to smile.

"I'm okay, Danny," he said, his eyes still closed. "C'mon,

now, just let it happen. Love. Joy. Mercy. Peace. Let's keep going."

I drove the Cadillac deeper into the night and the South, only stopping for coffee and gas or an occasional wash and nap at a rest area. I slept peacefully most of the time, but a few of my dreams had me running for my life through jungles, over deserts, in canyons, and under water.

In the dusty light of dawn, a Tennessee mountain rose up. It made me nervous for some reason, and I slowed the car to a near crawl. A line of vehicles passed me, with drivers and passengers staring at the freak show on wheels. While the pink monstrosity meandered up the mountain, I received looks of fear, rage, jealousy, and admiration. The admirers were mostly children in the back seats, delighted to see the spectacle. The kids grinned and waved and held up their stuffed animals as if they wanted me to bless them. And I could almost hear the children begging their parents to slow down so the thrill of this strange parade would continue on and on, up and up, into the clouds.

Eventually the high-rider hit the peak and descended with great speed, passing all the other vehicles, flying farther and farther down.

About forty miles beyond the mountain, I pulled over at a rest area. The oil gauge was dangerously low, so I raised the hood and gave the pink monster three quarts of the good stuff. Grease had put a whole case in the trunk, along with a scribbled note: "Take good care of my baby. She loves her bottles."

I turned toward Iowa and shouted, "Thank you for the oil! You're a good man, Grease!"

Then I read the postscript on his note. It was barely legible because of the grime. "Send me dirty postcards."

"Shut up, Grease."

Back on the road, approaching Nashville, I turned on the radio and fiddled with the dial and found a station that was playing traditional gospel music. What a wonderful way to fill up the airwaves. And I thought about how those songs had inspired my grandmother when she was a girl and spent a summer with her aunt in Memphis.

Grammy Dorrie, who at her death was hailed in the *Des Moines Register* as "the Ma Carter of the Midwest," had often talked to me about the slave spirituals. "The greatest songs composed on American soil came from the slaves," she said. "Can you imagine the world without 'This Little Light of Mine' or 'Swing Low, Sweet Chariot' or 'Joshua Fit the Battle' or 'Free at Last'? Those songs are eternal."

Passing through Nashville, I remembered my grandmother's love for the Jubilee Singers of Fisk University. They were the ones, after the Civil War, who traveled around and performed the spirituals as a choral group. Of course that style was not how the songs were originally sung, and much of the raw power was diminished, but the Jubilee Singers guaranteed that the spirituals would not be silenced.

"Thank you," I whispered, knowing that the pain I felt was not nearly enough. "Thank you for helping us to be the Gospel Family."

A couple hours later while approaching Chattanooga, I was feeling upbeat and began singing the choo-choo song. A large family in a minivan started singing alongside me, tugging on imaginary train whistles. Choo-chooing, we rolled slowly through town while two lines of cars followed behind us, honk-honking.

That night, driving alone through Georgia, with the universe sparkling above and all around me, I kept getting flashes of a new song. Words arrived that could have been at the beginning or end, words like "creation" and "groan" and "dark days." The words wanted to make music, but I just couldn't fit them together. I had a good melody, but I couldn't find the story line.

When the sparkling universe receded and the sun blazed up, southern Georgia was a jungle. Thick walls of trees, bushes, and billboards lined the freeway, blocking peripheral views. Houses, churches, farms, even large cities may have been out there, but I couldn't see anything from the road. That made me somewhat uncomfortable, because back home you can see for miles and miles. Even if there wasn't much to see in Iowa, at least you could see it.

WE'RE NUTS ABOUT NUTS! a sign proclaimed.

Another sign enticed me to stop at the PECAN EMPORIUM.

Another one proudly boasted: THE GRAND OLD PLANTATION.

Passing by the various tourist traps and southern temptations, I kept flying south. The jungle grew thicker, making the interstate seem like a narrow path between mighty realms of wild animals that in my imagination had no real boundaries—lions, elephants, rhinos, wildebeests, and boars—rampaging for the Lord and praising him in ways beyond human reckoning.

Finally, I reached the Florida border, and the car shuddered as we passed over, as if we actually broke through something. And I recalled breaking through something at the farm.

The morning of Christmas Eve, the year that Holly and Grammy had died, I was alone in my room, reading through *The Chronicles of Narnia.* I'd imagined myself a prince of that world a dozen times before, but now it was time to actually visit.

I jumped to my feet and went to my closet, and then opened the door and pushed through hangers and flannel shirts until my head hit the back wall, causing a Monopoly set to fall from the game shelf. Little plastic houses, hotels, a silver shoe, a dog, and a rainbow of money scattered across the floor.

Dazed and angry, I backed up, bowed my head, and charged forward. The miniature real estate crunched beneath my feet. Flannel caught my face. And I hit the wall again, causing a model airplane to crash to the floor and break into pieces.

Now furious that Narnia might not be real, I backed up and then lurched forward and took a flying leap against the sturdy wall, causing a baseball bat to swing down from the top shelf and smack my head.

Bleeding, I crawled out of the closet with a better idea about how to break into the magic.

With an ax.

Five minutes later, returning from the shed, I entered my mother's kitchen. Still wearing her bathrobe, she was slouched over the counter, doing some prep work for dinner. She turned to face me, her eyes watery from wine.

"Danny, you brought an ax into the house," she said. "Good. You can help me chop some carrots."

She poured herself another trembling glass and spilled some on the cutting board. "And chop some potatoes, too. Please?"

Carrying my ax to the stairs, I said, "Mother, do you remember Narnia?"

"Children's story," she slurred. "If I wasn't so tired, I'd read it to you."

I wanted to kiss my mother's sad wet face and tell her how much I loved her, but I just hurried up the stairs and entered my closet.

Hack! Hack! Hack!

I swung with all of my strength, daring the light of Narnia to come flashing through the splintered wood.

Hack! Hack! Hack!

The games and sporting equipment fell from the shelves.

"Narnia, Narnia," I said, "behold, I stand at your door and knock."

Beautiful mist appeared before my eyes, a sparkling cloud. It was lovely, lovely, and suddenly it became a stream of wild water, spraying me in the face. Cold and invigorating, it made me wonder: is it possible? Is this the water between the worlds?

A few minutes later, everything was soaked, upstairs and downstairs. The magical land of Narnia was nowhere to be seen, but I had broken some water pipes in Iowa.

Father tried to fix the pipes but only made things worse, and ended up calling a plumber. The bill was several hundred dollars, and my father had to beg Tom Jenks to please not cash the check for a while. Jenks was a good man who loved gospel music and farmers. He said, "Okay, I understand. I'll hold the check. How long?"

My father hesitated, agonizing. "Maybe a year."

Jenks whistled. "Things are that bad?"

From where I was hiding, in Holly's room, I could sense my father's scalp burning, the cancer eating him alive. He said, "We should have milk and honey by next Christmas."

Jenks picked up his toolbox with a sigh. "Okay. I'll hold the check."

"Thank you. Here, take this cross as collateral. It's worth a lot."

"Well, I don't know . . ."

"Take it."

"We don't really wear crosses in my family, Pete."

"Take it. You won't regret it."

"Well, my wife won't like it, but okay."

The two men walked into the hallway, where dozens of photographs of our family were hung. They paused beneath the photos, and then Jenks said in a low voice, "I need to tell you something, Pete. And it's not just me saying this."

"What is it?"

"Your boy. Danny."

"What about him?"

"He, well, he doesn't seem normal."

The look I imagine Father had on his face should have told Jenks to shut up, but the plumber continued. "Danny seems to have, well, problems."

"Danny's a good boy."

"Yeah, that's true. Danny's a good boy. But people have

been talking. I just wanted you to know. People think he could, well, do something dangerous. Since the funeral, he's been seen wandering the roads."

"I know."

"Wandering, singing, talking to the birds. It's just not normal."

My father let the word "normal" hang in the air for a while. Then he said, "Well, Danny has a new girlfriend."

Jenks was intrigued. "Oh? Really?"

"Yeah. This girl's from New York. Christian and Jewish, all mixed up and beautiful. I think she can help him."

Jenks laughed nervously. "You talkin' about his mind or you talkin' about sex?"

"I'm talking about his soul. I'm hoping Rachel can help keep it safe."

Florida sounded good in theory, but for all I knew, the place was a hellhole, and perhaps I would do better to turn around and return to Iowa. After all, my brother was a good lawyer and his fiancée was a good lawyer and I was almost innocent.

Something told me: go back home and face the music.

Something told me: at least call Grease and get an update on the situation. Maybe Will Bentley survived.

Something told me: keep on going and start a new life.

Suddenly I was in the middle of a flow of speeding traffic flooding down into Florida. Too many cars, too many people. I felt smothered, on the verge of a panic attack, and took the next exit. I pulled into the first parking lot that appeared, a tourist trap that was managed by a one-armed peddler. HALF OFF, the sign said. There were long tables lined with colorful seashells and ocean-themed jewelry, baskets of oranges and grapefruits, plastic alligators and snorkeling equipment. And to the side of the tables were racks of gaudy shirts, shorts, sandals, wide-brimmed hats, and mirrored sunglasses.

"Half off," the peddler said.

I realized I'd brought no change of clothes and said, "I might need a shirt or two."

He started grabbing things off the racks and tables as if he had six arms, and I ended up with a whole new wardrobe. The peddler didn't have any underwear for sale, but he sold me seven bright Speedos. "That'll get you through a year in Paradise," he said. "Just wash 'em in the ocean."

"Okay," I said. "Sounds like a good plan."

While the peddler jotted a happy amount in a yellow notebook, I pointed at his shoulder stump and whispered, "Alligator?"

He grinned proudly. "Ex-girlfriend."

All I could think to say was, "Wow."

"Yeah," he said. "She wanted the other arm, too."

"Wow."

"Yeah, she was amazing. I'm still crazy about her."

The peddler handed me a bill and pointed his stump at the pink Cadillac. "You work for Mary Kay?"

"No," I said, opening my wallet. "I'm a gospel singer. Farmer. Mailman. I mean, I was all those things. I don't know what I am anymore."

"Whatever," the peddler said, taking my money. "Welcome to Florida."

Eager to try on my new look, I asked the guy if there

was a dressing room. He told me to toss my dirty clothes into the smoking trash barrel and change into my new attire behind a stand of palm trees.

I returned to the Cadillac looking like a jungle parrot, accessorized with wrap-around shades and leather flip-flops. I felt wild in my new plumage, and my breathing was easier, as if I were already getting used to this place. I shifted the convertible into vroom, and away I flew—footloose, wing loose, and fancy free. "Florida," I said to the sunshiny sky, "I'm happy to meet you."

WE DARE TO BARE ALL.

A gigantic billboard blocked my vision with alluring women so enormous that I wondered if they could ever be happy on Earth. The sky-walking strippers reminded me of the daughters of the Nephilim. My brother had told Grease and me about their existence one day in the gravel pit while the three of us smoked cigarettes and leafed through the Bible.

"Relations with angels," Grease said, his face burning. "Man, I love the Old Testament."

My brother snuffed out his smoke in the sand. "Life was different back in the day. Heaven and Earth had a thinner sky between them. Spirits were falling for farm girls and swelling their bellies. And the babies were giants."

I wheezed for air. "Do you take . . . those Bible stories . . . literally?"

"I don't know, Danny."

"Well . . . I believe . . . the whole thing."

"Relations with angels," Grease said with a longing sigh. He rose to his feet and waved. "Hello up there, please send down an angel for me. A *girl* angel!"

The gigantic billboard held no magic over me, and I sailed past the strip club without turning the wheel, descending farther into the kingdom of Florida.

VISIT CHRISTMAS WONDERLAND, the next sign said. Wonderland, I thought. Yes. But how can people celebrate Christmas without winter? What about the cycle of life? Without winter, how can you experience the magic of spring?

I recalled the thawing of the farm, the warm winds and dust clouds drifting over the resurrecting fields. And in the fallows, the greening shoots of grass, goldenrod, and bluestem. And by the rising river, the fluting meadowlark and the redwing gurgling water-music.

JESUS IS LORD AND SAVIOR AT THE CATFISH HOUSE.

So many signs, so many messages, yet I stayed on the road, only stopping for absolute necessities, such as when a thunderstorm forced me to pull over and raise the convertible's top. Flashing in the lightning was a sign for the Magic Kingdom, an impossible castle exploding with fireworks, but I sped through the glittering rain, avoiding Disney and all of its illusions.

Several hours south of Orlando, the sun showed itself again. I was just daydreaming and minding my own business, when a shiny mosquito appeared on my dashboard and gave me a funny look.

"So," I said. "Are you talented or what?"

The mosquito flew over to the passenger-side window. And sure enough, there was an exit.

"Hmm. Shouldn't we keep going to Key West?"

The mosquito buzzed loudly while I passed the exit,

and she began to smash her little body against the window. She flew back a few inches and smashed the glass, again, and again.

With a big sigh, I turned the wheel at the next exit and drove into West Palm Beach.

ORCHID CITY, a sign proclaimed.

Flowers were everywhere, on fire with sunlight. I rolled down the window and breathed deeply. "Ahhh, that's wonderful."

The mosquito repositioned herself on the dashboard while the cars and trucks behind me blared their horns. I quit smelling the flowers and continued onward, driving past what looked like a glass opera house and an Italian-looking chapel. A towering stained-glass Jesus with golden-black skin greeted everyone going east.

The mosquito hummed happily, and I was pleased by how the Florida buildings had a Mediterranean flair, with archways and pillars and warm walls coated with bright colors. I came to a stoplight. It was red and I was glad, because it gave me some time to contemplate my options. To my left and right was a tropical road lined with palms. Running parallel to the road was a great river, smelling of sea salt. The river was as wide as the Mississippi or the Ohio. A sign said INTRACOASTAL WATERWAY.

Straight ahead was an old green bridge, and beyond that was a scene fit for a postcard or a mirage, a lush little town that seemed to be one large garden with a thousand mansions. I wasn't sure if I should cross over, so I looked to the mosquito for direction. She avoided eye contact and then buzzed out the window and disappeared over the water. The light turned green. Cars and trucks honked while I made up my mind where to go. Feeling both intimidated and beckoned, I guided the pink monstrosity over the bridge and across the waterway to a glittering island.

Paradise?

chapter eight

THE CADILLAC RATTLED over the bridge to Palm Beach. Greeted by a giant corridor of palm trees, I entered another world, a place that seemed to have no sense of Iowa, and then I found myself facing one of the most beautiful dead ends imaginable: the ocean blue.

I steered the high-rider south and drove beside the beach. Swimmers and sunbathers, surfers and boaters were out enjoying the sunny November day. The ocean was so blue, but not sad, and my heart was lulled into a pleasant calmness. I pulled over near a white condo building, opened the roof of the Cadillac, and inhaled the sweet salt air.

A skinny boy carrying his surfboard across the street gave me a hand signal. "Nice ride, Pimp Daddy!"

Pimp Daddy is not something I'd been called before, and although it was said as a compliment, the words burned my ears. And I sped away.

Because of my haste, I pulled out in front of a silver Jaguar that sniffed my bumper, so I panicked and made a sharp turn away from the ocean and another sharp turn at the city fountain. The silver Jaguar kept sniffing my bumper until I pulled into a gas station. The Jag paused and then roared away.

The station attendant approached my window. He was a clean-cut young man in a blue button-down shirt. "Gabe" was embroidered over his heart in red lettering.

"Hello, Gabriel. Fill 'er up."

Gabe gestured toward the mainland. "You better cross back over."

"Why?"

He frowned at the pink high-rider. "If a cop sees you, you'll be pulled over. Maybe even jailed."

"Jailed? They have a jail here?"

"Yes. Full of people like you."

"Okay," I said, climbing out of the car. There was a newspaper dispenser by the sidewalk. "Just let me grab a paper and I'll be on my way."

After buying a copy of the *Palm Beach Daily News*, I drove around the block toward the old drawbridge. Reptilian green, its jaws were now open like a giant alligator trying to eat the sky. I was temporarily stuck on the island, so I drove over to the docks, where rows of yachts were tied in the waterway. The sun was setting and haloed pelicans and gulls dozed starboard and aft, gently bobbing on the glowing boats. A manatee and her calf lolled in the lapping waves, and a large gray-striped fish leapt and turned rainbow in the air.

Palm Beach is fabulous, I thought. Nobody's going to send me back over that bridge. I belong on this island.

Opening the newspaper, I checked the classifieds for rental prices on mobile homes, but there wasn't a listing, not even for double-wides. Well, I thought, how about a cottage? Let's see. Here's one for rent. Five thousand dollars! Per month! Man alive, who can afford to live in Paradise? Hmm, there must be something reasonable. All I need is basic shelter, an old shack. Okay, here's a studio apartment above a drugstore. Unfurnished. Some repairs needed. Two thousand dollars per month! For that much money, you should get a big farmhouse.

At the bottom of the page was a listing without a price. The advertisement merely said: DREAM TOWER APARTMENTS. RENTERS BEWARE.

No address or phone number was given. So I drove back to the gas station and asked Gabe if he knew anything about the Dream Tower.

"Sigh," he said. "We're not going to get rid of you, are we?"

"Not if God wants me to be here."

Gabe sighed again and then pointed above the treetops. "There's your Dream Tower, the tallest building in town. It was a brothel-casino back in the day. It's condemned now and scheduled for demolition, but the lady who mismanages the place allows some misfits to live there. She charges by the night."

"Sounds good," I said. "Thanks for the info, Gabriel. You're an angel."

The dusty doors at the bottom of the Dream Tower were unlocked, and I went inside. The old brothel was as quiet as a church, with green vines growing on the corridor walls, partially covering the paintings of naked gods and goddesses.

"Who on earth are you?" an old woman asked, appearing out of the vines. She wore a pink dress and pink hair.

Even her hands were pink. She pointed a fat cigar at my face. "Well, speak up."

"Hi there. I'm from Iowa."

The old woman shook her head. "Never heard of it."

"I'm Danny," I said, extending my hand.

She slapped my wrist, then grabbed it and dragged me through the vines into her office. "My name is Mrs. Concher," she said, leading me to a pink loveseat. "I've lived in this Dream Tower most of my life. I could tell you a million stories about this place. Robber barons, gamblers, pirates, politicians, and monkeys. And the women who love 'em."

"Mrs. Concher, I'd like to rent a room here. If that's still possible. I heard this place is condemned."

The old lady brandished her long pink fingernails. "They better wait until I'm dead before they start tearing down this tower, or else I'll tear them to pieces."

Mrs. Concher puffed her cigar, cackled, and stared into my eyes. "Are you the living dead, sent to drag me down? That's okay if you are. Half the people in Hell owe me money."

I laughed. "No, ma'am. I haven't been sent to torment you. I'm here to start over."

She nodded. "Everyone who comes to Florida is running away from something. Could be the weather, or a bad relationship, or something in your head that won't go away." She reached into her desk drawer and pulled out a rusty key. "Your room is 1201. On the top floor."

"Thanks."

Mrs. Concher held out her hand. "Forty dollars and forty cents. Cash."

My room was surprisingly small and smelled like dead

leaves, rotten roots, and stale incense, but the view was pure blue ocean and golden sky. Yes, I thought, gazing dreamily out the window. This is the place for me. Now I'd better find a job so I can stay here. Grease's money won't last forever.

Having burned my bridges at the post office, I thought about some other job possibilities. Gardener. Lifeguard. Limo driver. Interior decorator. I could do just about anything, I thought. And I wondered: how hard can it be to gather worldly possessions? Many idiots in the history of the world have gotten filthy rich. Why not me?

To enjoy the remaining light, I left my room and climbed the rickety stairs to the steaming roof. What a view! Out east, the waves, rolling in to shore. To the south, the castles, their towers and battlements sinking into the sweltering twilight. Out west, over the waterway, the busy streets of West Palm Beach, packed with commuters heading home after work. And to the north stood the giant rows of palms. The trees were skinny, except in their middles, which were swollen like the bellies of well-fed snakes.

My first night in Paradise, stretched out on the musty bed with moonlight washing over me, I sank into a deep sleep. Rachel was flying above a flock of gray birds, rising into a blue sky that was blazing with red-orange streaks of light. She was in the heavens, and there was a city with glass buildings higher in the sky, and the gray-winged birds became swirls of ashes and the red-orange streaks became fire. And through the New York smoke, Rachel's flying now seemed like falling.

"Danny!" someone shouted from the roof. "Come on up! We're having a party!"

Half awake for a moment, I heard other voices, too,

and music and dancing, all tempting me to the roof. But I sank back into the dream to see if I could catch her. I held out my arms but she never came down.

In the morning, depressed, I crawled out of bed, stumbled into the bathroom, and was disappointed to see no towels. So I threw on a pair of shorts over my Speedo and took the long and shaky elevator down to Mrs. Concher's office. The door was open, and she was sitting on a red-cushioned stool at a breakfast bar, drinking coffee, smoking a cigar, and reading the newspaper.

"Excuse me, ma'am," I said. "Could I please borrow a towel?"

She glanced up from her *Wall Street Journal*. "Borrow?"

"Yes, ma'am. There are no clean towels in the room. And I need to take a shower before going out for interviews."

She shook her head and tsked at my appearance. "Danny. If you want to look like a million bucks at your job interviews, you'll need the proper attire. I'll only charge you a hundred dollars and a hundred cents. And I'll throw in a towel and a shaving kit for free."

"Umm, okay."

Mrs. Concher snuffed out her cigar, slid off the stool, adjusted her pink robe, and then strode over to the wall and threw open a closet that was stuffed with men's clothing. "Oh, the stories I could tell," she said, cackling. "True tales of buccaneers, bureaucrats, and monkeys. And the clothes they left behind."

I stepped forward to take a closer look.

"Danny, let's get you fitted into a navy blazer, white button-down shirt, khaki pants, and brown loafers. That's what high-society men wear. Put on this blazer. Let's see if you can look like a Kennedy. Or a Trump."

"Oh, I don't know," I said while she began to dress me up. "This isn't my style. This blazer feels strange. It feels fake."

A minute later, I was admiring myself in the mirror. And Mrs. Concher was writing a bill of sale.

Back in my apartment, I shaved, took a good long shower, and found myself singing part of the song that I'd begun during my journey. For some reason, a recurrent word was "reverie," and I was almost feeling hopeful about my new life on Palm Beach. But after toweling off, I felt compelled to forego the high-society uniform and put on the gaudy peddler's clothes.

"I'm still a tourist," I said to the macaw man in the mirror. "And tourists don't have to work today."

I put on my shades and left the room and took another scary elevator ride. It was one of those elevator rides that reminds you to pray, and maybe take the stairs next time. I rushed out to the street and was welcomed by the Cadillac glowing in the morning sun. And away we flew to explore the island.

Palm Beach is a thin strip of land, and the beach was soon in view, with beautiful waves and swimmers everywhere. A woman hovered between the water and the air, her hair a scintillating cascade of changing colors while she body-surfed in to shore. From my perch in the convertible, I stared as the woman washed up and stood on the sand. She was dressed in a lily-white one-piece swimsuit. Showing off what God had given her without showing too much, she was perfectly lovely and reminded me of the one who had kissed me.

Out of the surf appeared a handsome boyfriend. He put his strong arm around the woman's waist and kissed her like he really meant business.

And I drove away to explore more of Paradise.

The road along the beach was flooded with light, palm trees dripping with gold and splashes of brightness bouncing off the windows of condos and mansions. My eyes were dazzled in this world of radiance. The road suddenly snaked left, and I almost missed the turn, barely avoiding a giant iron gate.

At the stoplight I turned right, and soon a great castle appeared with two towering towers. A sign said THE BREAKERS HOTEL and I wondered how anyone could stay at The Breakers without going broke.

And had the ocean been sold? God's blue water was nowhere to be seen in this part of Palm Beach. Fences, gates, hedges, and walls blocked all glimpses of infinity. The best use of money, I thought, would be to reveal God's glory, not hide it. The next stretch of road was almost a wilderness, with a dark tunnel of leafy trees that twisted in all directions. Large arches of roots plunged deeply into the earth as if sending a message to the next hurricane: go ahead and gust with all the power of the heavens; your little squalls have no power over us.

The whole island seemed to be one long boast.

Farther up the road, out of the woods and into the light, I rounded a curve—and the ocean reappeared with wilder waves rolling in from the horizon. A minute later the view was again blocked by hedges, fences, walls, and iron gates.

Finally, after another mile or so, the road dead-ended

at an inlet between Palm Beach and another island to the north. The view was spectacular, and I climbed out of the car, despite the warnings.

NO PARKING.

NO VIEWING.

VEHICLES WILL BE TOWED AT OWNER'S EXPENSE.

I walked to the end of the dock and gazed across the inlet. There were fishing boats, sailing boats, yachts, and pleasure craft of all kinds. The gray-aqua tide was rushing toward the ocean, and I tried to discern the change on the surface and in the depths where the divergent waters crashed and embraced. Shadows of large fish ebbed and flowed within my vision, and I was filled with an overwhelming desire to go fishing.

A door opened. A door closed. I turned, and there was a hefty cop standing between his squad car and the Cadillac. The officer glared at me. "You're trespassing."

"I am?"

"Come over here," he said. "Let me see your driver's license."

Reluctantly, I approached the cop and gave him my license.

He frowned. "You're from Iowa?"

"Yeah. I just moved here."

The cop grimaced at my gaudy clothes. "Who are you trying to be?"

"Just me."

"You live on Palm Beach?"

"Yes, sir."

"What street do you live on?"

186 — David Athey

My mind went blank.

"What street?" he repeated.

My mind raced but stayed blank. "I don't know. I don't know where I live."

The officer smirked as if he'd caught me in a lie. "Open the trunk."

"Why?"

"Because you handle a lot of fertilizer up there in Iowa, right? You know how to mix explosive chemicals."

"I know how. But I never did."

The officer touched his holster. "Open the trunk. Now."

"I'm not a terrorist."

The cop unbuttoned his holster. "Listen," he said, "you could be anyone. We aren't taking any chances here. Do you understand? Now open the trunk."

"Okay." I opened it.

The cop dug around and found nothing but coffee cups, water bottles, and empty oil containers.

I asked, in all seriousness, "Does Palm Beach recycle?"

"Get out of here," he said, flicking my license at my feet. "And don't let me see you again."

I picked up the license. "But I live here."

The officer snarled, "What street?"

"I don't know the name, but it's where the Dream Tower is. That's where I live."

"Not for long."

Mrs. Concher, in her pink bathrobe, sat in the lobby, huffing a huge cigar. Clouds of smoke billowed from her nostrils while I told her about my misadventure.

She said, "I should have warned you. The cops are on high alert."

"What are they worried about? The town is surrounded by a moat and an ocean."

"Some of the hijackers were on the island before the attack."

I felt my gut tighten, and made no response.

"Here, Danny. Take this."

She handed me a parking decal. "This symbolizes that you belong here, that you're one of the chosen few. The next time you go for a drive, stick it where the sun shines."

"Thanks, Mrs. Concher."

She held out her hand. "Twenty-five dollars and twenty-five cents."

After giving her the money, I glanced warily at the old elevator and went for the stairs.

When I reached the twelfth floor, I stepped out of the stairwell and paused to catch my breath. Down the hallway, a beautiful woman in a flowery dress caught my attention. She was probably in her early twenties, and she was shouting, "Angelo! Open up!"

I slowly approached the scene.

"Angelo!" the blond woman hollered, pounding her fist on the door. "Let me in! I'm warning you. I'll make your life miserable if you don't open up—now!"

"Good morning," I said, inching closer. "Are you okay?"

The woman ignored me. "Angelo!" she shouted. "Open the door or I'll break it down!"

"Miss, do you need help?"

"I can kick in the door by myself."

188 — David Athey

"Umm, have you been hurt? Should I call the police?"

"Angelo!" she hollered. "I'm not waiting another second!"

The apartment door swung open. A large, bearded man with long red hair stepped into the hallway. He was wearing nothing but cut-off jeans. "Gloria," he said gently, "did you lock yourself out again? Why don't you take a key when you go for a walk?"

She shrugged. "This dress doesn't have any pockets and I don't like purses. So just leave the door open, you jerk. Why do you have to be such a jerk?"

"Excuse me," I whispered. "The world is sad enough. Couldn't you speak kinder words to your husband?"

Gloria shook her head. "He's my father. He knows he's a jerk."

Angelo grinned and rubbed his hairy belly. "You're new here," he said, his eyes showing that I was welcome.

"I'm Danny. From Iowa."

Gloria shuddered. "Talk about cold. Just like our home country. We grew up in snow and ice, too."

"Yes," her father said. "We're from Norway." He reached out as if to shake my hand, then slapped my stomach. "Man, you need some fish fat!"

I took a step back. "What I really need is a paycheck, before I run out of money."

Angelo laughed. "Money? What do you want with that misery?"

"I'd like to buy a castle for the woman of my dreams. But I'd settle for a grass hut. Or just the beach and a ceiling of stars. With love, that would be castle enough."

"Oh my goodness," Gloria said. "You believe in true love?"

"Yes."

"For real?"

"Yes."

"Really?"

"Yes, of course."

Gloria walked over and kissed me. Full on the lips. She tasted like music and tropical fruit.

"Danny of Iowa," she said, "will you take me dancing in the sky?"

Angelo grabbed his daughter's hand and pulled her away. "My apologies," he said. "I'm afraid Gloria has an overactive imagination. Sorry to have disturbed you."

I didn't feel disturbed. A bit tingly, perhaps.

Angelo led his beautiful daughter into their apartment, leaving me standing alone in the hallway, wondering: what is God doing to me now?

The rest of the day, I sat in my living room and stared out the open door, wishing that Gloria would reappear. The sun went down and the shadows came up. Eventually, I quit my vigil, washed my face, and went to bed. My dreams that night were all about the sky and birds and stars. And there was something beyond the stars that I could almost glimpse, but no matter how hard I flapped my arms, I just couldn't get there.

A crash awakened me. It sounded like a bottle busting on the roof, and there were people laughing and dancing.

"Danny!" a voice shouted. "Join us!"

It was tempting, but I rolled over and went back to sleep, rejoining the sky and trying to get beyond it.

At sunrise, I showered and put on my high-society clothes, but instead of pursuing employment on Worth Avenue, I went for a melancholy walk in the opposite direction. It was a beautiful day, warm with a soft breeze whispering through the green and golden palms. My heart pounded and ached as usual. And my feet kept walking north, beyond The Breakers Hotel, all the way to Saint Edward's Church.

There was a woman in a white dress at the top of the stairs. And I wondered: is there a wedding?

"The church is locked," she said with a Boston accent.

"Really? That seems strange."

The lady tugged on the door. "Nobody seems to be on duty. Crud. I need to get in there and confess something. My husband and I just flew down here for the week, and I maxed out the credit card already. This town's a real killa."

She gave the door a kick and then sat on the top step of the church in her new dress. "Crud. I feel really cruddy."

I was disappointed that the church was locked, but I climbed the stairs and sat beside the lady in white and introduced myself. "I'm Danny."

"Hiya, Danny. I'm Velma."

We shook hands and just sat in the light for a while. Eventually, Velma said, "I don't think they're gonna let us in today."

Hating to see anyone suffer, I tried to give the lady some advice. "Why not just return all the merchandise?"

She gave me a funny look. "Return everything? Even the one dress in all of the world that perfectly fits me?"

"Well, maybe keep that dress. You have the receipts for everything else, right?"

"Yeah, I have the receipts. I do this sort of thing all the time."

I paused, thinking that my wisdom had run its course. Offering Velma a smile, I added one thing. "You look lovely. You probably don't need any more clothes."

Velma patted my knee. "Danny, you just keep talkin'. I'll sit right here on the steps and listen all day."

We sat in silence for a while, the sun growing stronger. I could feel myself starting to turn color, but I didn't feel burned. Velma squinted. "What about you, Danny? Did you max out the credit card? What's on your heart, dear, if I might ask?"

During the next half hour or so, I attempted to explain my sins, including what I did at the post office, but the lady from Boston was easy on me. "You're kinda different, Danny. But your heart is pure."

"So tell me," I asked, "what should I do?"

"Keep loving God and neighbor," she said, "and do whatever you feel is best."

"That's my penance?"

"That's it."

It seemed too easy. So I felt the need to protest. "You should give me a penance that hurts."

Velma shook her head. "You got what you deserved. Unless there's something you didn't tell me."

"I feel like I haven't told you anything, because everything is so complicated and mysterious. I could write a whole book."

Velma chuckled. "A whole book! That would be cruel and unusual punishment."

My heart pounded and ached. "That's the penance I want."

"Really?"

"Yes, I need to suffer . . . my story. The whole of it."

"Okay," Velma said with a shrug. "So be it. Your penance is to suffer the writing of your life. And if your book is published, I'll buy the first copy."

"Thank you," I said, rising. "I feel better already."

I bounded down the steps of the church and rushed around the corner to the drugstore to buy some spiral notebooks and pens with blue ink. And then I hurried back to my room in the Dream Tower and sat at the window with its view of infinity. And I began my story.

We played our first concert by torchlight near the river. Free of charge, our old-fashioned act attracted a crowd to the hymns and spirituals that most people know by heart.

That night, there was another party on the roof. A band was playing amazing melodies, but nobody was singing. I thought: eventually I'll have a song to share with them. Eventually I'll have all the words.

The parties on the roof continued day after day, week after week, and I was tempted to go up there and sing, but I never strayed from my room.

Gloria knocked on the door every morning and asked if I was okay and left some food for me to eat. Sometimes I would speak with her for a minute or two and express my appreciation for her graciousness, but I was careful not to flirt. The last thing I needed while doing my penance was to feel all tingly.

Mrs. Concher, every afternoon, scratched on the door with her pink fingernails and warned me against becoming one of those people in Hell who owe her money. If she scratched long enough, I came to the door with a wad of cash that was growing smaller.

The week before Christmas, Mrs. Concher entered my apartment and blew smoke in my face. "You need to get a life, Danny."

I choked on the haze. "I'm working on it."

She gestured emphatically, sprinkling me with ashes. "You should be doing things, not scribbling things."

I brushed off my shirt. "Mrs. Concher, may I ask you a question?"

She aimed her cigar. "Shoot."

"Would you say that you have a normal happy life?"

The worn old woman took a deep drag, her eyes narrowing while she considered the question very carefully. "No, Danny. I don't have a normal happy life. But at least I'm trying. You need to try, as well, especially since God has put a mark on you."

"A mark? What do you mean?"

Mrs. Concher reached out with her smoke-free hand and touched my heart. "It's written all over you, Danny. A romance. Now get busy loving."

The tears trickled into my whiskers. "I do love. You'll understand when you read my penance."

That night the denizens of Dream Tower laughed and danced and broke bottles above my head while I suffered my life story. After filling up another spiral notebook, I closed my eyes and concentrated on the music. Some lyrics floated to my tongue, and I lifted my head and sang in a loud voice, "If you sing your life, you pray it twice, through the dark days and the sun-filled nights."

The revelers heard me, and answered, "Danny, come up here and join us!"

Not yet, I thought. Not until my life story gets to where I am.

Three nights later, I had written myself all the way to Florida, all the way to the Dream Tower. To celebrate the suffering achievement, I got all dressed up in my blue blazer. My head was swirling with exhilaration as I left my room and climbed the rickety steps. At the top of the stairs, I paused, took a deep breath, and opened the door. Two coconut-topped women with mermaid bottoms were swinging their hips with joy. Behind them, a plump pirate with a peg leg grinned and drank his grog. And a thin man in a flamingo mask flapped his arms and screeched.

Near the barbecue was a laughing group of surfer boys and girls in bathing suits. Slabs of ribs, the apparent feast, sizzled and smoked. Behind the barbecue was the band, including a guitar player, a bongo player, and a shell blower. And towering above them was a giant with a three-pronged weapon. A trident.

I wondered: what if this party is some kind of cultic ritual? What if the cult needs to sacrifice an Iowan to appease their tropical gods?

A shadowy figure in a chair struck a match. The pink face of Mrs. Concher appeared. She cackled and pointed her cigar in my direction. "He's come out of his cave! Look at that beard!"

The giant strode toward me as if he were the guardian of the party. I extended my hand to greet him. He poked his trident into my chest, nearly breaking the skin. It was Angelo. He had seaweed and shells in his hair, and fish skin wrapped around his legs. "Hello, Danny," he said. "What do you want?"

"I'd like to join your party. And I'd like to sing some lyrics for the band."

"Ha!" Angelo said, poking me with the trident. "Ha! Ha!"

Mrs. Concher cackled. The mermaids giggled. The plump pirate tapped his wooden leg. The flamingo-man flapped his arms and screeched.

"Okay," Angelo said, pulling back his weapon. "You can join the party. Why not? It's almost Christmas. We'll let you have this present. But you can't sing with the band. At least not tonight."

"Why not?"

Angelo's face grew solemn. "Maybe tomorrow night."

The music began to play and the dance resumed. I looked around for Gloria.

Angelo spoke gravely into my ear. "Danny, there's something you should know about Gloria."

"Here I am," she said, whooshing out of the shadows from the other side of the roof. She was dressed in a white ball gown and her tiara was filled with moonlight.

"Goodness," I said, "you look so real."

"What do you mean, 'real'?"

"I mean, like an actual princess. The gown really suits you, like it was designed special, like you're really from a royal family."

Gloria curtsied. "I'm glad you came up, Danny. I've been inviting you every night."

"I know. I've been busy trying to create my life. I mean—"

"Danny, let's talk in private."

Gloria smiled a pert good-bye to her father and then took my hand and led me away, back into the shadows from whence she had come. "Let's sit here on the ledge," she said. "I have to tell you something."

The air was sultry and my head was swimming.

"I had a dream about you," Gloria said, staring out at the wall of royal palms. "It was back in October. You appeared in my bedroom at dawn. And you kissed me."

"I kissed you?"

"Did you ever."

My cheeks burned under my whiskers and I turned away and looked up at the stars. The Big Dipper was pouring, hopefully a blessing.

"C'mon, Gloria," I said, standing and taking her hand. "Let's join the dance."

"Oh, yes."

We waltzed over to the other side of the roof, where Angelo immediately assailed us and broke us apart.

"Stop that!" he shouted.

And the music stopped.

Gloria stamped her foot. "Father!"

"Danny," Angelo said, "come with me." He handed his trident to a mermaid and then led me to the eastern ledge of the roof. "Look out at the ocean. What do you see?"

"Nothing."

Angelo pushed me, and I almost toppled. "C'mon," he said, "can't you see the light in the ocean? Can't you see it swimming out there? Can't you see the king?"

"No. I can't see anything out there."

Mrs. Concher came up behind me in a cloud of smoke and pushed me farther out, gripping my blazer with her fingernails. "Can't you see the king?"

"No. I can't."

"Well, that needs to change."

She suddenly released me, and I flailed backward into the arms of a mermaid.

The mermaid hugged my body against her coconut bikini and announced, "This boy's a keeper!"

Gloria smiled and took me by the hand and led me away from the crowd while the music resumed.

"Who is the king?" I asked. "Do I need his permission to sing with the band?"

She rolled her eyes. "It's just a game we play."

"A game?"

She shouted at Angelo. "For pity's sake, Father, the end of the world could come at any second. Why don't you let Danny sing? We've all heard his voice. He's wonderful."

Angelo grabbed his trident and strode toward us. "Danny, you have to go now!" He pointed the weapon at my chest. "I'll meet you in the hallway tomorrow morning. We'll go out in my boat. And if we don't sink, and if you catch the king, then you can sing with the band."

"Okay," I said, backing toward the door. "It's a deal. But what if I don't catch a big fish? What if I catch a little one?"

"We don't need a trophy to hang on the wall. Catching the fish is not about size, it's about wild beauty, strength, and grace. And you have to be very careful about eating mercury-flesh. The bigger the king, the more mercury in your blood."

"So what's good? Twenty pounds? Thirty pounds?"

Angelo poked me gently in the heart. "I'll tell you what's good, Danny. Getting out on the water and searching for the king. That's really good."

"And what if I don't catch him?"

"We'll just go out to the deep. And take it from there."

Gloria blew me a kiss, the mermaids waved their hips, Mrs. Concher blew smoke, the pirate tapped his wooden leg, and the pink flamingo flapped his arms and screeched.

At first light, I was already in the hallway when Angelo stumbled out of his door and laughed at my clothes.

"You look like a tourist in that rainbow shirt," he said. "The kind of tourist that drowns."

"Well, look at you."

Angelo wore cut-off jeans. That was it. No shoes, no shirt, no hat. He wiped his bleary eyes and yawned. "You drive, Danny."

"Drive? The docks are just a few blocks away."

Angelo laughed. "You think I can afford to keep my boat on Palm Beach?"

We went down to the Cadillac and drove away from the island, across the alligator-green bridge, and up the road for a mile or so, and then Angelo told me to get on the interstate and go north. Traffic was frantic, and a silver Jaguar seemed determined to sniff my bumper, making me swerve.

Angelo said, "Danny, you're a lousy driver."

Fortunately, I was able to avoid several accidents as we approached Blue Heron Boulevard.

"Exit here." Angelo wiped some of the sweat from his face. "Go east, under the bridge. Watch out for that jogger! Man, what's wrong with your eyes? Okay, there's the entrance to the marina. See it?"

"Yes, Angelo. Relax."

"Watch out for the baby manatee!"

"What? Where?"

"Ha! Just kidding."

I parked the high-rider between a shiny red pickup and a shinier yellow Corvette, and we climbed out.

Near the waterway was a grizzled fisherman with a pole over his shoulder. He stood near a shack with a sign above the entrance: FISH R US. The old man looked in our direction and shouted, "Good morning, Angelo!"

"Good morning, Jig. Do you have any sardines?"

"I've got sardines swimming out of my ears."

"Ha!"

Jig staggered toward the shack and shouted over his shoulder, "You want a six-pack of beer and a couple of sandwiches?"

Angelo smiled. "We sure do. Put everything on my tab."

"No, let me pay," I said, reaching for my wad of cash.

Angelo waved me aside. "It's all on me."

The late-December sun was rising more furiously than one would expect. It would be a scorcher. "What a beautiful day," Angelo said, strolling toward the dock. His red hair was a tangled mess of fire, and the freckled blotches on his back were like countries on a leather map. "It's a perfect day to catch the king," he said. "What do you say, Danny?"

"I'm game."

"Good boy."

Angelo walked between the rows of boats. I followed, wondering: which one is his? The old sailboat? The old skiff? None of the vessels were like the polished yachts on Palm Beach. The boats in this marina were covered with a paste of algae, dirt, and oil.

My heart sank when Angelo walked past boat after boat, that seemed barely seaworthy. Finally, at the end of the dock, he disappeared as if he had walked the plank.

"Where did Angelo go?" Jig said, staggering toward me with a cooler and a bucket of bait. "Did he fall overboard already?"

I stepped forward and peered over the end of the dock. And there was Angelo, sitting in a small brown dinghy. It was hardly bigger than a canoe. It looked like a coffin built for two.

"We're not going out in that, are we?"

"C'mon," he said. "It'll be fun."

"Fun? I don't think so. We're going to need a smaller ocean."

"Don't worry. It's going to be a calm day."

"Perfectly calm?"

"Yes, Danny. I know what I'm doing."

"But what if there's a sudden storm? What'll we do?"

"We'll flap our arms and fly above it."

"What?"

Angelo sighed. "Danny. Do you want to sing with the band?"

"Yeah."

"Do you want to catch the king?"

"Yeah."

"Do you think God brought you to Paradise in order to kill you?"

"Maybe."

"Really?"

"I don't know. I don't know what God is thinking."

Jig pushed me into the boat. The vessel wobbled but didn't tip.

"Bon voyage," Jig said.

With the help of a twelve-horse motor, Angelo and I sailed down the waterway. Angelo maneuvered the dinghy toward the inlet while a dozen bigger boats nearly swamped us. I had a bad feeling about this fishing trip, and my mind flashed back to Holly and the time her innocent face had begged me to go to the Boundary Waters with her, and I hadn't the strength, and Jon was lost in a cloud of smoke, and we all let her down.

A few minutes later, Angelo and I were at the mouth of the inlet, gliding into the welcoming ocean. It smelled like the first day of planting season in Iowa, or maybe like the first day of creation. Sunlight danced along the surface and dove down into the deep. Blue sparks shot up.

"Flying fish!" Angelo said as a scintillating flock filled the air. Flapping their fins like wings, as quick as hummingbirds, they flew for a hundred yards or so and dropped back into the brine.

Angelo smiled. "This is the life. Hey, look over there."

On the starboard side were two sea turtles. They swam side by side into the great blue, instinctively devoted. The turtles seemed out of place and perfectly at home, just swim-plodding along. I turned around to watch their gracefully

awkward movements, wishing them well as their glisten-
ing shells became tiny specks of light, trailing far behind
us. I wasn't sure if the sea turtles were a sign or a wonder.
All I knew was that I loved them. And I thanked God for
creating them.

Angelo guided the boat southeast toward the sun, and
then eventually cut the engine. "We're a mile out," he said,
"in ninety feet of water. This is where you'll catch the king,
if you're meant to catch him. See that tarp by your feet?
Unwrap it. There's your fishing rod. Hand it to me, Danny,
and I'll bait your hook."

"Angelo," I said, laughing, "I've been fishing before. I
can bait my own hook."

When I was seven and Jon was ten, we went fishing for
Adam the Catfish. We had heard about Adam ever since
we had ears, because all the farmers, including my father,
talked about having hooked him at one time or another;
but nobody had landed the fishy beast.

The summer morning was green and golden and full of
birdsong, and on my first cast into the pond behind Grove
Baptist, I hooked something that nearly tugged me into
the water.

"It's Adam! It's Adam!"

And when I pulled the great fish in to shore, Jon said,
"Congratulations. You've caught Walt."

It was just an average ten-pounder. Jon patted me on the
back and helped me carry Walt home to Grammy Dorrie,
who said, "You're a born fisherman, Danny." And she cut the
meat into thick chunks and spiced them and smoked them
in a covered barrel. After the fish was smoked and cooled,

Grammy took the chunks into the kitchen and dipped them in a golden wash of eggs and cream and honey, followed by a coating of fresh bread crumbs. Then she placed the succulent morsels into a skillet and fried them in butter, turning each piece over and over until perfectly crisp.

That night, we ate dinner on a picnic table covered with a checkered tablecloth. Father said the catfish was the best thing he'd tasted in weeks, except for Mother's lips.

Holly, with bread crumbs all over her face, said, "Danny, catch more Walt!"

Angelo watched carefully while I baited my hook. "Okay," he said, "let out your line, one arm length at a time. Count out thirty lengths and you'll be down in the realm of the king."

I did as he said. Very carefully, I let out the line. The sardine sank, glowing brightly and then softly until it faded into the depths.

"Keep your hands relaxed," Angelo said, "or they'll cramp up during the course of the day. It might take hours and hours for the king to bite. Relax. Be patient."

Although the ocean appeared calm, there was a rhythm of rising and falling. Rising and falling. Everything felt free and yet perfectly connected. Me to the boat, the boat to the water, the fishing line to the deep, and the deep to the heavens.

Above us a pelican mulled over the phosphorescence of the sea. The bird mulled and mulled, and then descended fast. She hit the water with a crashing splash, and I thought: how can she survive that? The poor bird will be dazed, and easy prey for sharks or other predators down there.

The pelican resurfaced near the boat, her bill brimming with life.

Angelo grinned.

I asked, "Aren't you going to fish, too?"

"I don't think so. This is your day."

For the next hour or so, we kept our thoughts to ourselves, watching my line and taking in the sun. No matter which way I turned, there was no escaping the light from above and all around. It seemed like the whole world was on fire. My sunglasses were almost useless.

Angelo cracked open a beer. "Want one?"

"No thanks. Got any flaxseed oil and yogurt?"

"Sorry."

"Anything other than beer?"

"Yeah. Jig packed some water. Here. Catch."

"Thanks."

I opened the bottle and took a long drink. "Ahhh, that's good spring water."

"It probably came from a swamp, Danny, or from Lake Okeechobee, which is full of alligator pee."

"Hmm," I said, draining the bottle. "I like it."

"You can have it," Angelo said, sipping his beer.

We fell silent again, bobbing gently in the blue. I had forgotten how wonderful it was to simply spend time fishing.

After another hour of nothing, I asked Angelo, "Is that your real name?"

He shook his red head, scattering droplets of sweat. "No. My real name is Olaf."

"So you're really a Norwegian?"

"One-hundred percent."

"What about Gloria's mother?"

A faraway look filled his eyes. There was a depth of emotion welling up that I hadn't yet seen. Olaf had to clear his throat several times before he could speak. "My wife's name was Marian. She worked for Nordic Fillets, a large fishing corporation. One day she called home very late—I was already asleep—and she left a funny message on the machine. 'Holy mackerel, I've convinced the haggis-loving Scots to eat more fish. A million pounds sold, Olaf! Fluff the pillow, honey, I'm coming home.'"

Olaf fought the tears and continued. "Marian was a safe driver. In fact, she said it was a serious sin to risk other people's lives by driving recklessly. So I'm sure she was being careful on the way home, when she got hit head-on. The airbag didn't deploy. And she was killed."

"I'm so sorry."

Olaf wiped his eyes. "During the funeral, Gloria began having panic attacks. She saw devils flying in the air. It was horrible. She couldn't stop the hallucinations."

"Maybe they weren't hallucinations."

"During the next several years, I took Gloria to doctors, psychiatrists, all sorts of specialists, but they didn't help. All they did was dope her with drugs. So we started moving around. Denmark, Holland, France, but the devils and panic attacks followed us everywhere. Gloria would be fine for a month or two and then suddenly start trembling. She would fight the fear as best she could and then begin crying uncontrollably. Day after day, she'd suffer the devils and the attacks. She wasn't able to attend a university, even though she's brilliant. Finally, we moved to the States. To Palm Beach. For three years now, the devils have been gone from her mind. It seems like Gloria's been healed. I mean, she still lives in a world of make-believe in which I'm her guardian angel named Angelo and she's a princess, but that's better than living in hell."

I gave Olaf a knowing nod and said, "There are some things that are make-believe, and other things that make you believe."

Olaf wiped his eyes again and smiled bravely. "Gloria's beginning to fill out applications for universities."

"What does she want to study?"

He laughed. "The history of love."

"Who offers those courses?"

He shrugged. "I don't know. Maybe Gloria will devise her own major."

Being out on the ocean with infinity in every direction seemed to make our souls more kindred. I began to see Olaf in the light of my father, so amazingly strong—a king of creation—and so utterly fragile. I whispered, "Have you had the chance to mourn for your wife?"

He shook his head and took a deep breath. "I let God do the mourning. Marian and I weren't good about going to church, but I know she had a great devotion to Jesus. Some people at the fish company made fun of her sometimes."

Olaf glanced at the sky, and I wanted to ask him about his own devotions, but he suddenly asked, "Danny, have you ever lost anyone?"

I stared at the water. "I've lost almost everyone."

"Parents?"

"My father died of cancer. And my mother . . . fell."

"I'm sorry. Do you have brothers and sisters?"

"One older brother. Jonathan."

"Just the two of you?"

"We had a wonderful little sister. Holly. The best sister in the world."

"What happened to her?"

"She drowned."

"Danny, I'm so sorry."

"Me too. I'm always in mourning, even when I'm happy."

Olaf was quiet for a while, staring at my fishing line, and then he continued to search out my soul. "Do you have a girlfriend?"

I shrugged. "I'm not sure."

"What do you mean?"

"I had a fiancée. Rachel Golding."

"Pretty name. What happened?"

"I lost her."

"She died?"

"I don't think so. But I haven't been able to contact her since the attack. Rachel lives in New York, and she didn't call me, even though 9/11 is our shared birthday. She always calls on our birthday. I tried to call her a hundred times, but there was no connection. Do you think I should drive to New York and try to find her? I don't even have her address."

Olaf spoke in a fatherly voice, deep and calm. "I'm sure Rachel's fine, Danny, but you need to give her space. Everyone in New York is probably taking stock of their emotional lives. Rachel's going through a very difficult time, and you have to wait for her to get through it."

"I know."

"And, Danny, you might have to accept the fact that she'll never contact you again."

I shook my head. "Rachel and I love each other, even if we never get married."

"Well, that kind of love is possible. But Danny, she may not be the same person anymore. Who could be?"

"Yeah, I can understand that. But I still believe she'll call. Maybe she's called me already. If I weren't such an idiot, I'd know how to check my home phone messages."

We sat still for a while, and I reeled in the line to check the bait. The sardine was gone. I started to put on another, and Olaf reached around and did it for me. "Here, Danny. Hook it like this."

I replied half jokingly, "Thanks, Dad."

He smiled. "You're welcome."

I lowered the line again, and we patiently stared at it. We blinked and rubbed our beards and contemplated the depths as the time slipped by. My mind drifted from random memories of the farm and the Gospel Family concerts to the scene of Will Bentley and me falling from the pool table, and it suddenly occurred to me that I should have prayed for Will before we hit the floor. Better late than never, I thought, or maybe there is no late or never when it comes to prayer. "Our Father, who art in Heaven, hallowed be thy name. Thy kingdom come. Thy will be done. . . ."

Olaf cleared his throat. "Nothing seems to be biting. Oh well, we can try again another day. You know, Danny, I was just thinking about you and Gloria. Perhaps the two of you—"

The line twitched, just enough to catch my attention. "Is that a kingfish?"

Olaf shook his head. "I don't think so. The king doesn't nibble. He strikes."

Suddenly the rod lurched forward and bent into a perfect arc of tremendous weight.

I shouted, "Does that count as a strike?"

"Ha! Good boy, Danny! Reel him in!"

I strained, but the fish refused to budge.

"Pull him up! Reel him in!"

The fish would not move.

Olaf huddled beside me. I thought he might take the rod, but instead he began to lecture. "It's not enough to catch the king. You have to land him, Danny. And eat him. He has to swim in your blood. Then you can join our band and sing."

My arms were trembling, my lungs gasping for breath. "Angelo, why don't you take over for a while?"

He laughed. "The mermaids on the roof have caught the king a dozen times. Mrs. Concher has caught him a hundred times. I've witnessed a nine-year-old girl reel him in, and now she wrestles alligators. Come on, Danny, get a life."

I gritted my teeth and pulled. The fish budged. I pulled and pulled, and the king was moved. I reeled him in, slowly, my arms aching, my brow dripping sweat.

"You're making good progress," Angelo said. "Now, don't make a mistake. Keep steady. What are you doing? Don't stand up!"

"I've got him, I've got him, no problem."

The king lurched, making a run for deeper water, and he pulled me right out of the boat and into the blue. Down, down, the fish dragged me as if I were nothing. I kicked at the water and tried to rise but only lost my sandals. In less than a minute, I must have been halfway to the bottom of the ocean, still trying to reel in the line.

The fish turned and was now shooting up from the depths. He swam to my eye level and I could see why he was such a prize. The king circled around, showing off his fiery skin of red, green, and blue, flickering and flashing. I let go of the rod and reached out to touch his side, and he swam away in a swirl of sparkling bubbles.

He swam away with Angelo on his tail.

I laughed. It was uncontrollable. Seeing the fat red-haired giant chasing a fish in the ocean was the funniest thing I'd ever seen in my life. I gagged on the salt water, my lungs burning, and down I went, choking and drowning.

How could God allow me to die when I hadn't yet finished my penance, the writing of my life story? Drowning in the waters of Florida was not the ending I'd imagined. My story had to end in Iowa, where it began, with a song.

I gave the ocean a kick. And another kick. And one more.

And I began to rise. Slowly, I began to ascend from darkness to blue. I was rising, but too slowly. I had no energy left to save myself, and it felt like a cruel twist to be rising into my death. I began to see stars, or just one star bursting, and then darkness again.

When I awoke, my eyes opened to a blinding light. I was lying on my back, my outstretched hands touching the wooden sides of what I was sure was a coffin. A dull droning filled my ears and I could smell the stench of blood. And fish. I turned my head and saw the king lying beside me. Dead, but still shimmering, and staring into my face.

"We caught him," Angelo said from the back of the boat. "It was a crazy fight, but we caught him."

I sat up and shielded my eyes. "Where are we?"

"Near the marina. How are you feeling?"

I coughed. "Salty."

He handed me a bottle of spring water. "Drink it slowly."

We didn't speak again until we made it to the dock. Jig was there waiting for us, swigging a beer. "Well, well," Jig said, looking at me and talking to Angelo. "Did our boy catch the king?"

Angelo reached down and grabbed the colorful fish. He hefted it chest high.

Jig was impressed. "That's a good one."

"Yes," Angelo said. "With this king, Danny will be the star of the party tonight. It'll be a feast and everyone will get a good taste."

Jig clapped his callused hands. "I'm gonna eat, drink, be merry, and dance with Mrs. Concher. And if the spirit moves me, I'm gonna propose marriage!"

We all laughed. And then we lifted the fish out of the boat and marched down the dock, our three hands working together to make the king almost weightless. There were whispers and pointing among some tourists standing near the FISH R US sign, and one young woman said, "That fish isn't so great. It doesn't need three people to carry it."

The afternoon sunlight filled the king with more shimmer, and we carried him to the parking lot and tried to fit him into Grease's cooler. The tail stuck out as if the fish were diving down.

Jig said, "Hurry home and keep him on ice. Don't cut him up until just before the meal."

"Okay," I said, trembling.

Angelo grinned. "The grand hotels and mansions of Palm Beach will be hosting parties tonight. The Season is in full swing. The rich and famous will be all dressed up for their charity balls and fancy shindigs. And we'll be having the greatest time on the roof of a condemned building."

"Cha cha cha!" Jig said, slapping me on the back.

"Go easy on him," Angelo said. "Danny has to sing tonight."

Jig's crusty old eyes suddenly grew wistful. "Sing lots of love songs. I want Mrs. Concher to get in the mood for marriage. Inspire her to become Mrs. Jig."

Angelo bellowed with laughter.

Jig was totally serious. "I had a ring made out of my lucky hook. With the barb removed."

I said, "Lovely," and Angelo bellowed again.

We hoisted the king into the trunk of the high-rider and then drove back to Palm Beach in silence, except for when Angelo shouted insults at my excellent barefooted driving. "Slow down! Stay away from that Jaguar! Here's the exit! Don't hit the bridge! Watch out for Jimmy Buffet!"

Eventually, I screeched to a stop in front of the Dream Tower. The shadows of the swaying palm trees were growing long in the late afternoon, snaking their way toward the ocean.

Angelo and I climbed out of the Cadillac, our muscles

stiff and our skin sunburned. The giant stretched. "That was a good day of work."

His deep voice reminded me again of my father. I felt like a little boy as I helped Angelo retrieve the cooler from the trunk of the car. We lowered the king to the ground and Angelo nodded with pride. "Well done, Danny." Then he gave me a big sweaty hug soaked in fish blood, sweat, and brine. I was feeling very emotional, probably on the verge of blubbering, when Angelo stepped back and poked me in the ribs with three fingers. "Ha! We're gonna eat your king tonight."

"You mean *our* king."

"That's right, Danny. It was amazing teamwork."

After I'd shaved off my beard, showered, and gotten dressed, Gloria invited me to her kitchen to prepare the fish. Angelo had already cleaned the king and carved out two huge fillets. I cut the meat into single-portion chunks, spiced them, and dipped them in a golden wash of eggs, cream, and honey. Gloria had a sack of flour in the kitchen, but no bread crumbs. I said, "Well, that's all right. My grandmother would love you anyway."

"Your grandmother?"

"She always used bread crumbs."

"We could run to the store real quick."

I kissed Gloria lightly on the cheek. "This will be our special recipe. What else should we add?"

She smiled. "I sometimes make an almond crust for fish. Angelo loves that."

"Perfect."

We fried the fish chunks in olive oil for a few minutes,

let them cool off, and then added more of the wash and the almond crust. Then we baked the fish for a secret amount of time at a secret temperature. It smelled heavenly.

Gloria and I stood near the stove, talking quietly about simple things, and then I felt a twinge of panic. "What about side dishes? Should we make mashed potatoes or something?"

"Don't worry, Danny. The others will bring rice and beans. And they'll have the grill going with wonderful skewers of veggies."

"And drinks?"

Gloria laughed. "Nobody ever thirsts up there. That's for sure."

We stood reveling in the sweet scent of the kingfish. And we just kept looking into each other's eyes, and looking away, and talking quietly about simple things, even though it seemed certain that important things were happening.

"Danny, are you ready to sing tonight?"

I leaned back against the kitchen counter. "I'm almost ready. A song's been swimming in my head. I just need a few more lines to finish it."

Gloria reached out and took my hand. "You better figure it out soon."

Our fingers intertwined. "I know."

"And Danny, my—"

She almost said "love."

"Yes?"

Gloria looked far away into my eyes. "I hope it ends happily."

I squeezed her hand. "Me too."

It was time for a really good kiss, but Angelo appeared

from his bedroom, which must have doubled as a prop room. He was dressed up in fish skin, seashells, and wings. "I'm going up to the roof," he said. "Sounds like the restless natives have already started the festivities."

Sure enough, there was a tap, tap, tap of a peg-legged pirate.

Gloria let go of my hand and went over to hug her father, wrapping her arms around the feathers. "Papa, you don't wear these very often."

Angelo nodded. "It's a special night. Danny is going to feed us the king. And sing."

I shrugged. "It might be a short song."

"But sweet," Gloria said.

Angelo kissed his daughter on the forehead and then turned and strut-fluttered away, almost knocking a photograph from the living room wall. He immediately straightened the picture, which I'm sure was his wife, Marian, smiling down.

Gloria and I put the finishing touches on the kingfish, sprinkling fresh parsley over the golden morsels on the platter.

There was more tap, tap, tapping above our heads, and shuffling footsteps.

I said, "I can't believe they're dancing already."

Gloria looked up. "They're probably just rushing to the buffet line. We'll give them another few minutes or so to load up the side dishes. And then we'll wow them."

The roof eventually became quiet. The partiers were now seated at their respective tables, awaiting their gifts.

"Now," Gloria said, lifting the platter and placing it in my hands. "It's time to make your appearance."

We climbed the stairs and stepped out into moonlight, starlight, and the glow of candles. There were five tables full of people. The mermaids, the pirate, the flamingo, and another flamingo. The band. The surfers. Mr. and Mrs. Santa Claus and some elves that were probably children. Angelo, Jig, and Mrs. Concher.

Gloria whirled away in her princess dress and took a seat next to her father. And I began to serve each table. Everyone was perfectly silent, except for the polite "Thanks" and "Thank you" and "Please" and "Good job, Danny" and words like that.

When every table had been served, Angelo stood, his wings reaching above the Dream Tower.

"Grace," he said.

And we ate. I sat next to Gloria and was very pleased when she said, "Danny, this is the best meal I've had in ages—the food and company combined."

The meal began quietly, and then the tables got louder and louder, the mermaids telling stories about pool parties they'd attended in local mansions, the pirate telling stories about adventures at sea, and the flamingos screeching with laughter.

The band ate quickly and rushed to their instruments, the surfers expressed their happiness with weird words and bizarre inflections, Mr. and Mrs. Santa Claus pulled on each other's red suspenders and made the elves giggle, Angelo cleaned his plate and grinned proudly, and Jig whispered something into Mrs. Concher's ear that made her blush.

Suddenly the band struck up a melody that was impossible to place, sort of a Calypso-flamenco-Mediterranean free-for-all, and everyone got up and started dancing. Gloria and I started out with a formal embrace and a one-two-three, one-two-three pattern, and then started whirling and twirling all over the roof. She was all joy, and so was I, and we danced together most of the night, with just a few interruptions. Gloria danced a number with the pirate and one with her father. I found myself for a while in the arms of Mrs. Santa Claus, and then I did a jig with Jig and Mrs. Concher, and we all blushed happily.

The band was relentless, never taking a break, playing the most amazing melodies while everyone tore up the roof like there was no tomorrow.

And then it was time for me to sing. Angelo stood in front of the band and said, "Excuse me. Listen up, everyone! Quiet! As you know, we have a visitor here, Danny, who is not so much a visitor anymore but a dear friend. One of us. He's a very talented young man, and we're going to ask him to join the band now and bless us with some gospel music."

There was a nice round of applause and cheering, and it suddenly occurred to me that I should finish the song I'd been working on. I needed another few minutes, so I went over to the surfer table and asked the boys if any of them had deep voices. Being boys, they each proclaimed, "YES, I HAVE A DEEP VOICE."

"Good," I said, and I whispered lyrics into their ears.

Then I asked the surfer girls, "Can any of you sing mid-range to high?"

Being girls, they each said, "I can sing a little."

I laughed. "You've probably had professional lessons."

Several of them nodded, and I whispered lyrics into their ears.

The people at the other tables were getting impatient, clamoring for my song. I hadn't quite finished writing it in my head yet, so I stalled for more time by saying to Jig, "Does anyone have any announcements before we proceed?"

He nodded crazily and exclaimed, "Mrs. Concher and I are getting hitched to the ocean of love!"

She dropped her cigar. "Are you serious? Do you mean it? Marriage?"

Jig nodded crazily. And then Mrs. Concher kissed him a yes, and another yes.

The hearty laughter and congratulations that ensued gave me enough time to give the band their instructions, just as the last lyrics floated into my soul.

The tables hushed, and the a cappella song began with me:

If you sing your life, you pray it twice, through the dark days and the sun-filled nights.

(Boys:) ALL OF CREATION GROANS.
(Girls:) And everywhere there's a reverie.
(Boys:) ALL OF CREATION GROANS.
(Girls:) And everywhere there's a reverie.

Singing in the fields, shimmering seas. Beneath canyons and above the trees.

ALL OF CREATION GROANS.
And everywhere there's a reverie.
ALL OF CREATION GROANS.
And everywhere there's a reverie.

Prairies, mountain tops, and deserts bare. Solar sys-
tems, molecules, and angels in the air.

ALL OF CREATION GROANS.
And everywhere there's a reverie.
ALL OF CREATION GROANS.
And everywhere there's a reverie.

Everybody's family, everybody's friends. So many
burdens and so many amends.

ALL OF CREATION GROANS.
And everywhere there's a reverie.
ALL OF CREATION GROANS.
And everywhere there's a reverie.

Now the band started playing. A heartbeat of bongos
rising into a fullness of music.

If you sing your life, you pray it twice, through the
dark days and the sun-filled nights.

ALL OF CREATION GROANS.
And everywhere there's a reverie.
ALL OF CREATION GROANS.
And everywhere there's a reverie.

O JERUSALEM . . . and everywhere there's a reverie.
O FLORIDA . . . and everywhere there's a reverie.
O AFRICA . . . and everywhere there's a reverie.
O IOWA . . . (laughter) . . . and everywhere there's a
reverie.

HOLY TOLEDO . . . (laughter) . . . and everywhere there's a reverie.

NEW JERSEY . . . (some playful boos and more laughter) . . . and everywhere there's a reverie.

NEW YORK CITY . . . (respectful silence) . . . and everywhere there's a reverie.

The band stopped playing. All eyes fell on me.

Sometimes out of time, sometimes out of place. Ring around the graveyard, Paradise through grace.

ALL OF CREATION GROANS.
And everywhere there's a reverie.
ALL OF CREATION GROANS.
And everywhere there's a reverie.

If you sing your life, you pray it twice, through the dark days and the sun-filled nights.

When the song was finished, the only sound was a slight rustling of wind down in the palm trees. The revelers were motionless, just looking at me. It was difficult to interpret the expressions on their faces. I was worried that my song hadn't touched their hearts, because people had always applauded when I sang with the Gospel Family.

The silence continued, and then I realized that the revelers' hearts had been touched, and their glowing faces were like those you see in church during a candlelight service, reverent and prayerful.

"Amen!" Jig shouted.

And his fiancée, Mrs. Concher, said, "That was very

beautiful, Danny. The most wonderful sound this old building has ever heard."

Winged Angelo agreed. "I loved it."

And then the mermaids, the flamingos, the pirate, Mr. and Mrs. Santa Claus, and the elves started talking all at once, and some of the surfers began singing again, trying to remember the whole song, while Gloria sat peacefully at the table, smiling at me.

That was a perfect moment in Paradise, and I was tempted to reach out and grasp with all my might and never let it go. But I wasn't about to fool myself. The little island of Palm Beach in the kingdom of Florida was not really Heaven. Not even close. And it would not last forever.

I walked over to Gloria and took her hand. "You have to trust me," I said. "And forgive me."

She nodded. "I knew you'd be heading back to Iowa tonight."

"You did?"

"Of course. All of your unfinished business is there."

I leaned toward her face and gave her a soft kiss. Then I whispered, "It's all up to God."

Gloria whispered, "Yes."

We kissed again, through the tears. Then I turned and hurried down the stairs, went into my apartment, and packed up my spiral notebooks and a few other things. I placed some folded pages on the table beside the lamp. Mrs. Concher received a gratuity of two-hundred soggy dollars. And two-hundred cents. "And a million THANK-YOUs for your hospitality. May you and Jig always be dancing."

To Angelo I wrote, "Thanks for risking my life and saving it."

For Gloria, I left my address and phone number and the following words: "I hope our connection lasts forever. That's what I can offer you now. Love, Danny."

A few minutes later, with creation groans and reverie still ringing in my ears, I was speeding away in the high-rider, looking askance at the moon. It hung low like a great circular promise over the edge of the Everglades.

I hoped I could make it home in time for my brother's wedding.

chapter nine

CLIMBING THE CONTINENT toward home, my sense of distance seemed imaginary—with the miles flying by—and excruciatingly real, every moment feeling like a great failure to get to such a simple place. I remembered reading about saints who had the gift of bi-location, the ability to be in two places at the same time. I tried to imagine what it would be like to have a heart in two places, with double the love, and twice the breaking. I would never pray for such a gift, and would only accept it as suffering.

Out of the kingdom of Florida, the high-rider passed through a cloudy Georgia, a misty Tennessee, a rainy Kentucky, and a snowy Illinois. The gas-guzzling, oil-burning chariot climbed higher and higher and crossed the border into Iowa on the morning of Christmas Eve.

The whitened cornfields were tinted ocean-blue, with a wind-swept crow reminding me of a seagull, disappearing into the southern horizon. Winter is always an in-between world in my mind, the landscape seemingly locked between few possibilities. The frozen ground and frigid sky whisper to the warm blood that keeps me awash in this life, in this world, where the bleakness of Iowa snowfields resonates with my longing for infinite earth . . . and infinite heavens . . . .

The crow wheeled and returned into sight again, wings flashing brilliantly in the wintry air.

I whispered, "*I got wings . . . you got wings . . .*" and kept on flying between the fields.

The pink Cadillac attracted attention among the humble cars, pickups, and semis that crawled along I-80. Upon seeing the speeding high-rider, several people began dialing their cell phones. I was worried that my arrest was imminent, and yet I just kept on going because I honestly believed that it wasn't my will that was being done.

Taking the exit into Iowa City, the Cadillac flew into town as if invisible and made it safely to the trailer park. Pulling into the driveway, I saw something I didn't want to see. Footprints all around my place. And a yellow CAUTION tape across the door. I jumped out of the car and climbed the stairs and ripped down the tape, wondering if any neighbors were watching. I whispered, "What's been going on here?" and I unlocked the door and hurried into the house. Like a thief, I crept through the kitchen and down the hallway and into the bedroom. I paused in front of my dresser and then reached out and opened the sock drawer in slow motion, as if my slowness could somehow change the past. But no. It had already happened. The evidence was taken, and my secret was out.

The red light on my answering machine was blinking. With dread, I pressed the button.

"Danny, this is Esther Henderson on your mail route. Young man, I knew you were up to something when some of my mail went missing, but I had no idea how far you would go."

"Hey, it's Plain Jane. Give me a call."

"Danny. Listen. Marta and I and the partners can help you. We've already contacted the post office. Let's get this settled before the wedding. I hope you've decided to be my best man."

"Yes, this is Mr. Grime calling. Do you understand? Grime. Sort of like Grease, but it's not Grease. It's Grime. This call is to alert you to some interesting news regarding your car insurance or something. Please contact Mr. Grease—I mean Grime—at your earliest convenience. Or stop by the gas station. Umm, any old gas station will do."

"Yeah, okay, so listen to this. I wanted to apologize before I fly out to boot camp. My head is much better. It was just a concussion and a cut. Twelve stitches and a really cool scar. I'm ready for the Middle East, but is that sandbox ready for me? Anyway, it's all bygones between us. Later."

"Hey, it's Jane. Give me a call."

"Good day, sir. This is Mr. Grime returning the call that you haven't made yet. Please remember to change the oil in your Cadillac. That is, if you have a Cadillac. You probably don't, but you never know. This morning I changed the oil in a Chevy pickup. Not that anyone is hiding a Chevy for anyone."

"Jane again."

"Brother Paul here. I'm worried about you, Danny. Call me back. Where are you? I have a letter for you."

"Danny Gospel, you did strange things with the mail. But the new letter carrier is even worse. He never eats the brownies that I make. I would appreciate a return call. 555-6382."

"Call Jane."

"Hello? Is this thing on? Hello? Oh dear. This is Mrs. Lindgren. When the federal agent came to my house and explained what you had done and said that you might face prison, I told him to tell President Bush that you deserve a medal."

"Hey there, Iowa Boy, are you gonna kiss me again? Your kingfish was delicious. And I loved your song. See you soon, Danny. And that's not just a hint."

I was amazed to have a message from Gloria, because it seemed like my Florida adventure had already drifted away like a tropical dream. Gloria. I don't know how she made me feel so tingly, but she did.

Suddenly I heard sirens and stopped the machine. I thought the sirens might be coming from the McCuskeys' TV, but when I went to the window, I was surprised to hear laughter and music over there. My neighbors were watching It's a Wonderful Life, the final scene where the angel gets his wings.

The police sirens were fast approaching the trailer park, and I had to think quickly. I wanted to play the rest of my messages, but if I didn't escape now, it might be too late and I'd miss the wedding. I hit the red button, and an excited voice said, "I'm calling from corporate headquarters to inform you that Spitzoclean has received a government patent and will soon be trademarked by Grease Industries International. Wanna invest?"

While the messages played on, I ran outside and climbed into the high-rider and escaped through the trailer park's back entrance.

Although my instinct was to drive toward farmland, something compelled me to race into the maze of one-way streets in the downtown area. The sidewalks were bustling with last-minute shoppers wrapped in colorful scarves and bundled in thick wool coats. A Christmas carol resounded from loudspeakers, and some of the shoppers were singing along.

The sirens blared over the music while I raced up and down the snowy streets, searching for a hiding place. How pleasant it would be, I thought, to recline by the fireplace in the Cottage Deli, sipping hot cider and casually enjoying the spirit of Christmas with friends and family.

The sirens were relentless, so I whirled around the block.

For a moment I glanced at the front window of the Hamburg Inn and saw a man dripping with ketchup, relishing his simple lunch. He swallowed and smiled. He seemed normal and happy.

Why not me?

The sirens and flashing lights were on my tail.

At Pearson's Drugstore, I turned left against the one-way traffic on Jefferson Street. Barely avoiding some iffy drivers, I turned left at the Foxhead Tavern, and left again into the alley by Murphy-Brookfield Books. The sirens wailed, and the Cadillac backfired and skidded around the block and slid down the entrance to the Newman Center parking garage. I cranked the window, reached out and pressed the button, and the garage door opened and closed behind me.

The sirens faded while I descended into sanctuary.

I parked in a dark corner and got out and hurried down the corridor, deeper into the Catacombs. The place was perfectly quiet, and I snuck into a study chamber, a cave with white cement walls and a brown plastic table surrounded by orange plastic chairs. I collapsed into a chair, rested my head on the table, and tried to think.

Footsteps sounded in the church above.

In a panic, I stood and closed the study-room door, a bit too loudly. I tried to hold my breath and hoped that whoever was upstairs was just passing through the church for a quick prayer and a splash of holy water.

The footsteps padded down the stairs.

Stay calm, I told myself. It's just one person.

The footsteps quickened, getting closer.

I was weak from lack of sleep, but I readied myself for an attack. And I prepared myself for surrender. It all depended. "God, please help me," I whispered.

The footsteps found the threshold of the study. A man's voice, nervous and edgy, called out, "Is anybody here?"

I thought: do I know his voice from somewhere?

The door swung open.

Punch and kick, something told me. Hurt him before he hurts you. Don't take any chances.

A large man in a green suit leaned in and saw me behind the door. "This is very odd," the man said, rubbing his bald head. "Or perhaps this is merely a statistical probability, with all things taken into account, considering your habitual proximity to places of worship."

It was the physicist from the gravel road, the Atom Smasher who had wanted to stone me.

"Oh, I'm glad it's you," I said. "Welcome to the Catacombs."

"My, my, my," he said, rubbing his scalp. "You say the strangest things."

"Yeah. Or maybe the strangest things say me."

"My, my, my . . ."

The physicist sat at the table. I sat across from him and asked, "How are you? Are you doing all right?"

"Well, actually, that is very difficult to quantify."

I nodded in agreement.

He said, "I suppose one should keep certain difficulties to oneself, but of all the possible listeners, you may be the best for this sort of thing. You see, the thing is, I am having some issues."

"Issues? What do you mean?"

He pointed at the floor, and then at the walls and the ceiling and beyond. "There are things all around us that are beginning to bother me."

"What do you mean?"

The Atom Smasher slouched in his chair and rubbed his scalp. His bushy eyebrows went up and down. Surprised. Sad. Surprised. Sad. "Right now," he whispered, "a great cloud of neutrinos is passing like a ghost through this building, through our bodies, through the whole earth. There is no escape."

I looked around. "Really?"

"Danny, we are open doors to the forces of the universe. And there may be powers more invasive than neutrinos."

"Open doors?"

The Atom Smasher rubbed his eyebrows as if trying to erase them. His eyes were wild with light. "It is impossible to feel neutrinos, but I can feel something moving inside of me. And I cannot bear it much longer."

I wanted to help him, but I wasn't sure what to do. I folded my hands under my chin and rested my elbows on the table. I took a deep breath, hoping the right words were in the air, and offered, "Why not embrace your blessings?"

He scoffed. "What blessings?"

"It's obvious that Heaven loves you. Why not love Heaven in return?"

The blood vessels on the Atom Smasher's forehead throbbed.

I reached across the table and touched his hand. "It might not be a cloud of neutrinos that is after you. It might be angels."

The Atom Smasher yanked his hand away. "That's nonsense. Do you have any evidence? You see, I have proof of the cloud of neutrinos. How can you prove your angels?"

"I can't prove them. I can only live with them."

He squirmed in his chair. "So we are stuck."

There was a chilly silence in the cement room.

Finally, I asked the Atom Smasher, "Can you sing?"

"Pardon me?"

"Can you sing?"

"Why do you ask?"

"Because singing helps."

The scientist shrugged. "I can hit most notes."

"Okay," I said. "Good. Did you ever go to camp?"

The Atom Smasher stared at the north wall. "I loved summer camp. I loved the lakes and rivers, the games and the bonfires, and especially the sing-alongs. That was the last time I remember being completely happy."

I reached across the table and took his hand, and began to sing, very quietly, *"Kum ba yah, my Lord. Kum ba yah."*

The physicist gave me an embarrassed look and tried to escape my hand.

I held on tightly. *"Kum ba yah, my Lord. Kum ba yah."*

He blinked, as if holding back tears, and kept his silence.

I continued. *"Kum ba yah, my Lord. Kum ba yah. Oh, Lord, kum ba yah."*

The Atom Smasher allowed a tear to roll down his face.

I said, "Do you know the history of that song? 'Kum ba yah' means 'come by here.' That was the slaves' invitation to God to visit them on the plantations."

Brother Paul entered the room, wearing a festive green robe. He pretended not to be surprised to find me back in Iowa City, holding hands with a singing physicist. The Atom Smasher, embarrassed, pulled his hand away.

"I heard the music," Brother Paul said. "I knew it was Danny's voice. And I thought I'd step in and say hello."

"Hello," I said.

"Hello," the physicist said, looking sheepish.

We paused for a moment. It was a very awkward situation. Strangely enough, the Atom Smasher picked up the song again, and we joined him. *"Someone's singing, Lord, kum ba yah. Someone's singing, Lord, kum ba yah. Someone's singing, Lord, kum ba yah. Oh, Lord, kum ba yah.*"

That song can be sung for hours, but after a few more verses, we allowed it to fade into the walls of the Catacombs.

Then Brother Paul invited the scientist to return later for the service. "C'mon, join us. Everyone loves Christmas music."

"I appreciate the offer, but I'm not very good at going to church."

Brother Paul confessed, "Neither am I."

And I had to admit, "Neither am I."

We all laughed, and then the Atom Smasher and I stood to say our good-byes.

"Hey, wait a second," I said. "I don't even know your name."

He paused. "You might not believe it."

"Oh, I'll believe it. I'm an easy believer."

The Atom Smasher grinned. "My name is Paul."

I glanced at my friend in the robe. He seemed delighted by the providential coincidence.

"Brother Paul," Brother Paul said. "It was wonderful to sing with you."

"Same to you. And same to you, Danny."

"Sorry about holding your hand," I said.

"Oh, that's okay. It felt better than a handful of neutrinos."

The Franciscan raised an eyebrow. "Neutrinos?"

The physicist shrugged and chuckled, and then shuffled out into the hallway and up the stairs. "Merry Christmas," he said.

"Merry Christmas," we answered.

Then Brother Paul sniffed the air around me and frowned. Being the son of a garbage man, he had a strong immunity to odor. It took a lot of stink to wrinkle his nose. "Ugh. Danny, you can't go to Jon's wedding reeking like that. Quick, we need to get you cleaned up, into a more formal suit and on the road."

"Okay, but I'd like to see Doggie first."

"Don't worry about Doggie. He's fine. I found a good home for him. A woman named Melissa took him in. She owns an antique store out in the country."

"You know Melissa?"

"Yes, she and her fiancé came in for counseling."

"Counseling?"

"Yes. Marriage counseling."

"She's back together with Ethan?"

Brother Paul nodded. "Ethan has a funny head on his shoulders. I think he and Melissa will have an interesting life together."

"It'll be a circus."

"It'll be just fine."

Brother Paul grabbed me by the collar of my wrinkled Palm Beach blazer and dragged me out of the room. "C'mon now, Danny. You need to be presentable."

A short time later, I was clean and shaven and wearing a fine light-blue suit.

Brother Paul escorted me through the Catacombs toward the Cadillac. "Danny, your brother will be very happy to see you."

But would I be happy to see him? I kept that thought to myself.

"A letter came here for you," the Franciscan said, reaching into his green robe. "It's from a law firm."

My hand trembled as I reached out. "Brother Paul . . ."

"Yes?"

"Have you heard anything about Rachel?"

"No, Danny. I'm sorry."

"Do you think I should start my life over?"

"First do your duty to your brother. Be the best man. And don't forget to celebrate. That's a Christian obligation."

"Okay."

"We'll talk after Christmas."

"Okay. See you later, Brother Paul. Thanks for helping me. And thanks for no longer wearing horns."

He laughed. "See you later, Danny."

I climbed into the Cadillac and drove to the garage door, and paused. Feeling overpowered by curiosity, I ripped open the envelope. In the dim light, I began to read the first page of the contents. It was a letter from Shelby Williams.

1 December 2001

Dear Danny,

On Thanksgiving Day, my brother opened his eyes and whispered, "Gospel woke me up."

I haven't been religious in ages, Danny, but I reached down and touched my brother's forehead and said, "If Jesus is calling you, Jack, you better go to Him." He smiled peacefully, closed his eyes, and spoke his final words: "Can't remember Danny's poem. Give him the farm instead."

Danny, you have to understand that I'm a businessman, and businessmen don't give away valuable Iowa farms. Plus, I still have an emotional attachment to the land where I grew up.

So here's the deal. I'm giving you the house and other buildings, the equipment, and two-hundred acres, half of them tillable. If you want the rest of the acreage, you may rent from me. Contact my representatives at your earliest convenience. The phone numbers are listed below. They can answer any questions you might have about this transaction.

Sincerely yours,

Shelby Peter Williams

Along with the letter were several signed and notarized papers, and a house key.

Just like that, I could be a farmer again. Hands shaking, I put everything back into the envelope and prayed, "Forgive me, God, but I'm not sure if I can farm a place that isn't home."

Leaving the Catacombs, I drove the high-rider into the light of Christmas Eve afternoon and lit out for Des Moines. To avoid anyone who might be looking for me, I drove forty miles on a country road that ran parallel to I-80. The high-rider kicked up snow and gravel and I lost some time during that part of the journey, but I made up for it during the second part, when I braved the interstate and allowed the pink monstrosity to roar at seventy miles per hour, flying through the spiral galaxies of snow, dust, and salt.

Here and there, a hill bulged up in the fields. And I thought about my bulbous friend Grease. We usually spent Christmas Eve together, with ham, church, and presents. Hoping my friend would be okay by himself, I made a mental note to phone him between the wedding and the reception.

"Oh no! Oh no!"

I began having a panic attack, realizing that I had no directions to the church. My mind and breath started racing each other, neither one of them willing to pause long enough for me to think clearly. It would have been easy enough to take the first exit and find a phone and call Jon's cell, but no, the panic didn't want anything to be easy.

There were multiple exits into Des Moines, but I just kept driving past them, racing within myself, not sure what to do. And then I noticed that the gas gauge was on empty. Beyond empty. However, instead of feeling more panicked, I felt a sense of peace, because now I had an easy decision. I simply took the next exit and found myself driving into a quaint neighborhood that was sparkling with Christmas lights. Festive decorations warmed the houses, and nativity sets graced the yards. The pink Cadillac sputtered down the street and eventually rolled into a glowing gas station.

A group of old ladies was gathered in the parking lot, sipping from steaming cups. I climbed out of the car and felt a cold wind at my neck and said, "Nice weather for hot coffee."

A lady in a polka-dot parka answered, "Don't spit on our graves yet, sonny. We're drinking eggnog."

A lady in a long green coat flashed a leather cask. "We've just been to the Wise Men of the East Festival in the park."

I ran my credit card without thinking, forgetting that it might be monitored. "Wise Men of the East?"

"Oh, you know," a third old lady said. Her puffy gray hair was held down with a hand-knit purple hat. "You know the story. Magi and shepherds and the Savior born in a barn."

I began pumping gas, my hand already freezing. "Born in a barn? You mean in a stable?"

"No," the flask bearer said. "They brought a real barn into the park. With a real baby. Would you like to see him?"

"Yes, of course, but I'm late for a wedding."

The flask bearer beamed. "Oh, the Christmas wedding. We were invited to that."

"Really? Do you know the location of the church?"

The lady with the purple hat nodded. "It's our parish. Holy Family. It's just beyond the city park." She pointed at the steeple above the trees. "Apparently, everyone was invited, but we didn't believe it. Inviting everybody would be crazy."

I laughed. "It's my brother's wedding. Craziness runs in the family."

The flask bearer turned to her friends. "Hilde? Gladys? What do you say?"

Hilde was the one with the purple hat. She grinned a big gummy smile. "I say we do."

Gladys was ready to burst out of her polka dots. She said, "The merry widows are going to a wedding!"

And away we went. The widows all sat in the back, balancing my seven notebooks, my life story, on their laps while sipping eggnog and singing between sips:

"Here we come a'wassailing among the leaves so green. Here we come a'wandering so fair to be seen. Love and joy come to you, and to you your wassail too. And God bless you and send you a happy wedding. And God send you a happy wedding."

The city park was illuminated with lights shining like bright stars through the snow that was just now starting to fall. Families were huddling around a carnival booth, or skating on a silvery rink, or admiring a display of freshly cut ice sculptures, or waiting in line to visit the Savior and the Wise Men in the barn.

The pink Cadillac received smiles, waves, and cheers

as if leading a parade through the park. The widows and I smiled and waved back, especially at the children, but my mood became somber when I drove around the block into the parking lot of Holy Family. The lot was full. That meant everybody was already inside. That meant I was late. That meant the best man was a bad brother.

With no place to park, I thought: just forget it. There's no sense going inside that church. I would only be a distraction in the middle of things, a freak show. Forget it. Jon will have a better ceremony without me.

"Get out!" Hilde shouted. "I'll take care of the Cadillac. I'll park it in North Dakota if I have to. Now get out!"

You don't argue with ladies who wear purple hats.

"Yes, ma'am," I said. And I scrambled out of the car and took Gladys and Pearl by the arms and escorted them, slipping and sliding, into the back of the church.

At the altar was my big brother in a perfect tuxedo, joining hands with a radiant woman in white. I had imagined Marta to be a nervous anorexic like the lawyer girls on TV, but Marta was calm and voluptuous, smiling at Jon as if they were truly made for each other.

The elderly priest squinted over the pews that were overflowing with Marta's family and friends and what appeared to be a hundred migrant workers. I wondered: did the migrants stay beyond the harvest just for this wedding?

"Dearly beloved, we are gathered together—"

Pearl stomped the snow from her boots while Gladys loudly unzipped her parka. The elderly priest, who should have been immune to such interruptions, halted the ceremony.

My brother's eyes turned from his bride to see me fidgeting near a font of holy water. Without hesitation, Jon motioned for me to join him at the altar. Marta had a maid of honor beside her, and my presence would have created a perfect symmetry; but I hesitated.

Marta, realizing who I was, gestured emphatically, her arms a whirling welcome of beaded white.

Every head turned.

It was one of those moments when it seems like every person in a story is on the same page except for the one idiot who is lost somewhere in a previous chapter and can't find the courage to get caught up. I shuffled backward, attempting to escape.

Pearl and Gladys reached out and held me fast. Just then Hilde burst through the door, having found a parking place closer than North Dakota. She and her purple hat crashed into me and launched me forward, and down the aisle I went.

Jon whispered something to the befuddled priest, who eventually understood and happily announced, "The best man has arrived."

The congregation murmured their pleasant surprise.

Jon winked at Marta. She winked back. The priest squinted at his holy book and continued with the holy words.

When it came time to exchange the rings, Jon handed a small black box to me. I opened the box with trembling fingers, took out the shimmering golden circle, and handed it right back to my brother. Jon's face was joyful, serious, and devout. Very gently, he took Marta's hand and placed the ring upon her finger. The vows were exchanged. A perfect kiss was shared. And a wonderful husband and wife were applauded by the witnesses, applauded so graciously that it may as well have been for Adam and Eve in the first blushing of the Garden.

Pearl, Gladys, and Hilde blubbered in the back of the church. Tears were the only gift they had brought to the wedding, so they drenched their faces and blew their noses with great generosity.

At the reception, seated at the high table, I was asked by Marta to give a speech.

Part of me wanted to politely decline. Part of me wanted to flee the room. Something prompted me to stand like a gentleman, raise a champagne glass, and say, "Jonathan and Marta, may you always be each other's most beautiful dreams."

That was it. One simple sentence and everybody was happy. We lifted the bubbly to our lips, and some people drained their glasses, and some people sipped.

Jon put his arm around me and said to the room, "Some of you know about the Gospel Family. Most of you are meeting us for the first time. Let me just say that Danny and I have a history of biblical proportions."

The crowd laughed. They had historic families, too.

Jon paused, nodding reverently at his guests. "I want everyone to hear something," he said, "a sound that never should have stopped. I want everyone to hear me sing. With my brother."

Talk about pressure. There I was at the high table, standing before Marta's relatives and friends, lawyers, a hundred migrant workers, three blubbering widows, and one squinting priest.

Could I simply clear my throat of years of sorrow and anger and somehow find it in my soul to sing sweetly? Could I suddenly harmonize with someone who had ruined my dreams? Jon had sold the farm, leaving me with absolutely nothing to offer to Rachel. At least, that was the pitiful mythology that I'd constructed to turn my brother into a sort of enemy.

However, in reality, down in my heart, in that place where nothing lives except God's forgiveness, I still loved my brother. Very much.

"Jonny Gospel," I said, putting my arm around him, "what do you want to sing?"

He whispered, "Holly's favorite song."

Those words were so charged with emotion that I almost broke down. My lungs hollowed, my knees buckled. Jon tightened his grip around my waist, but what really saved me from falling was some chaos in the back of the reception hall. It was purple-hatted Hilde knocking over a chair to get at the piano.

All heads turned, and some mouths murmured, and some tongues tsked, giving me a few moments to regain my composure.

Hilde shouted, "What song are you boys going to sing? I'll play for you!"

Jon answered, "'Angels We Have Heard on High!'"

"Wait a second," I said. "Wait."

My brother's face went pale as if he felt I was going to back out. But actually, I wanted to recruit more voices.

"The Gospel Boys will sing a verse," I said, "and then everyone will join the chorus. Feel free to clap your hands and stomp your feet."

A room full of Christmas faces lit up.

Hilde raised her hands above the keyboard and then pounded out a joyful introduction. Jon and I, as if we'd never been out of practice, hit the first note in harmony.

"*Angels we have heard on high, sweetly singing o'er*

the plains! And the mountains in reply, echoing their joyous strains!"

And then there was clapping, stomping, and elated wailing with the "GLORIA" that seemed to go on forever and ever, until finally ending, "in excelsis Deo!"

After the song, everyone applauded for everyone, and then the maid of honor stood to make a toast. Marta's best friend was tall and dark with the brightest brown eyes. She was so pretty in her Christmas-red dress that I had to turn away and focus on the least sexy face in the room.

It was Grease, appearing between Pearl and Gladys. He waved a grimy hand, and I nodded my recognition. It looked as if Grease had left his garage in a hurry, still wearing his overalls, and I wondered if he had important news for me.

The maid of honor spoke eloquently about Marta and praised her many accomplishments. She ended her tribute with this remark: "Marta, you were great without Jon. And now, joined with him as a partner at work, home, and church, the two of you will establish a legacy that will inspire others to live lives devoted to the love of God and neighbor. I want to congratulate you and Jon, and your firm, for dedicating yourselves to agricultural reform. Your hard work is God's pleasure. But also remember, while working for the benefit of others, don't ever forget the kindness, warmth, and special graces reserved for yourselves. Okay?"

The champagne glasses went ting, ting, ting, and the newlyweds stood and kissed, much to the delight of the crowd.

After her public display of married affection, Marta addressed the room. "Christmas Eve is a strange date for a wedding, but Jon and I wanted our marriage to be a gift. We requested no presents. However, the Christmas tree by the window is surrounded by wrapped boxes. Those are presents for you. In return, Jon and I ask for your prayers so that our marriage will be joyful and productive. And Danny, I want to welcome you to the Buenaventura family. Our hearts and homes are open to you. Don't be surprised if a dozen kids call you 'Uncle' tonight in one language or another. We are a fun-loving, crazy family. And from what I hear, Danny, you will fit right in. Okay, that's enough speeches now. It's time for Father Glen to give us a dinner blessing."

The elderly priest responded well to his cue. "In the name of the Father, the Son, and the Holy Spirit, let us continue the celebration with blessed food and music."

Dinner was served—a choice of pork tenderloin or gourmet chicken fajitas. Jon and I chose the fajitas, and then we talked for the first time in a couple of months. Marta gave us some space, chatting away with her maid of honor.

I was nervous, worried that I might say the wrong thing, considering the years of bad blood.

"It was a wonderful wedding, Jon."

"Thanks for being here, Danny."

"So. How did you find such a beautiful bride?"

Jon shrugged. "I don't know. She just crossed my path one day, and kicked my butt in the courtroom. Marta's amazing. She's the smartest person I've ever met."

"That's an interesting coincidence," I said. "Rachel was the smartest person I'd ever met."

Jon acknowledged the pain in my voice. "Danny, I hope this wedding isn't pouring salt in your wounds."

I sipped some water and played dumb. "What do you mean?"

"After Marta and I had planned every detail of our

Christmas wedding and made the announcement and sent out the invitations, I realized that the date of our event was not an original idea."

"Oh really?"

"Danny. You wanted to marry Rachel on Christmas Eve."

"I did?"

"I'm sorry. When I remembered, it was too late. Marta's grandmother and some aunts had already made plane reservations from Mexico."

"It's okay," I forced myself to say. "Life goes on."

Jon nodded nervously, not sure what to say next. "Say, Danny, isn't Marta's wedding dress the most beautiful thing you've ever seen?"

My response was a hiss. "Someone once scorched a dress."

Jon shifted uneasily in his chair. "What are you talking about?"

"You know. The heirloom. Grammy Dorrie's wedding dress. The one Rachel was going to wear. The one Holly was going to wear."

My brother shook his head. "That old dress was never going to be worn by another bride."

"Why do you say that?"

"Danny, did you ever look at the dress?"

"Of course I looked."

"And did you see? It was moth eaten and full of holes. Didn't Rachel tell you that after she tried it on?"

"No. Rachel spoke of the dress as a lovely thing, a heavenly thing. If it was actually a ruin, she pretended otherwise."

The celebrants went ting, ting, ting on their glasses, calling for the bride and groom to kiss again. Jon smiled boyishly and gave Marta a passionate smooch. The crowd applauded and cheered. Adding to their happiness, chocolate cheesecake appeared in large quantities. With chocolate sauce. And a white chocolate candy stick. And coffee and hot chocolate.

The DJ, near the Christmas tree, was eager to get the dance started. His legs were dancing in place, but he controlled himself and put on a mellow CD. The song was another of Holly's favorites. She and Mother loved to sing it together.

"It came upon a midnight clear, that glorious song of old, from angels bending near the earth to touch their harps of gold."

Jon sighed heavily and whispered into my ear, "I feel like I killed her."

I knew what he was confessing. "No," I said. "You can't take all the blame for that."

"Danny, I should have been in the Boundary Waters with her. I should have saved her. But I was too busy raising hell and wasting my life."

"I'm sure she forgives you."

Jon nodded. "I'm sure she does. But I still have to make amends. If I ever have the chance again, I need to save somebody's life."

I was just about to ask him about my trouble with the post office when Marta stood and announced, "It's time to get your presents! Line up!"

The children squealed, as did the merry widows and the auto mechanic. Even the lawyers seemed to have the Christmas spirit. Everyone rushed to form a line in front of the tall tree.

Marta recruited Jon and me and the maid of honor to

help distribute the gifts. Mistletoe dangled from a branch, and the maid of honor in her red dress gave me a warm smile. "I'm Rosalita."

"I'm Danny."

"I know."

I pointed. "That mistletoe is nothing but trouble."

"Don't worry. You're safe."

I stood beside Rosalita and handed out brightly wrapped packages to everyone in the reception hall while music filled the air and smiles adorned every face.

At the end of the line was a family of eight. Rosalita whispered in my ear, "Migrants. Tragic story. Give them everything that remains."

There were only seven gifts remaining. One short. Jon and Marta had estimated the guest list correctly but had not figured in how generous Rosalita and I would be. Many people had received more than one present. In fact, some of the kids earlier in the line had received armfuls.

The migrant family consisted of a tired-looking mother, a work-weary father, and three boys and three girls. The children were aged from teenagers all the way down to a toddler.

When it became obvious that we were lacking a gift, the father insisted that he go without.

Marta said, "Don't worry, we'll find something for you."

Jon said, "I think Grease got two packages. Wait here. I'll retrieve one."

The migrant father stared at the floor, his eyes full of shame. One of his daughters, six or seven years old, had already opened her gift. It was a picture book with Moses on the cover leading his people through the Red Sea. The little girl grinned and showed the book to her father. The weary man, with a strength of spirit I will never forget in this life or the next, gently touched his daughter's face. "Beauti-ful," he said in broken English.

Marta began to cry and rushed off to find Jon. I reached into my pocket and pulled out the deed to the Williams farm. Why not give it to the migrant family? Why shouldn't they have a chance at their dreams?

Rosalita was watching me. She whispered, "Danny. No. That deed is for you."

I whispered back, "You knew about this?"

"Yes. Jon was involved."

"My brother was involved in my receiving a farm that I didn't really want?"

Rosalita shook her head. "Danny, you don't understand. But you will. Now, please put the deed back into your pocket."

"Okay," I said. "But I'm giving them something."

I whirled around to a table and found some discarded wrapping paper, and stuffed my remaining cash into the shiny paper and folded it as neatly as possible.

"Merry Christmas," I said, handing the present to the migrant father.

He opened the gift while I prayed that he wouldn't be offended. His eyes watered. "Gracias," he said. "Gracias, padrino de la boda."

"You're very welcome."

He hugged his little daughter who was hugging the Moses book, and exclaimed, "Feliz Navidad!"

Rosalita smiled and gave me a mischievous look.

I whispered, "What is it?"

"Every good work is rewarded, Danny, one way or another."

"What do you mean?"

She shrugged. "You'll find out when you get home."

Home?

The DJ could not wait another moment. He just had to start playing some disco. A gaudy ball descended from the ceiling and began casting colorful glimmers from wall to wall. And the floor filled with dancers.

Grease was out there with the merry widows, flailing and shaking and making them laugh. And the migrants were out there, too, mixing it up with Jon and Marta and the lawyers and Father Glen and the whole Buenaventura family, everybody dancing with joyful abandon.

Except for me.

I was suddenly overcome with an urge to leave the party.

Knowing the widows could catch a ride with Grease, I snuck outside into the swiftly falling snow, hoping Jon and Marta would not be offended by my early departure. I didn't mean to be rude. It's just that something seemed to be calling me. And I had to answer.

I didn't have any gloves, hat, or overcoat, and I shivered while tromping through the winter wonderland, looking for the buried Cadillac. Since the parking lot was full when we arrived, I searched the side streets near the church, with the north wind briskly tickling my ears. And then I heard an amazing sound—jingling and jangling in the wind—what seemed to be sleigh bells. Was it possible? Was it Santa Claus?

It was Grease, trudging into view, shaking the car keys.

"Danny! I saw you sneak out. But you won't get far without these. Hilde gave them to me."

My friend tossed the keys into the air and I caught them.

"Grease, you're the greatest."

He grinned. "I'm in the top ten, that's for sure."

I laughed. "Now if I could just find the car."

Grease kicked the snow. "I wish you wouldn't leave yet, Danny. The party's just getting started. You should see me dancing."

"I saw you, buddy. You've got some amazing moves."

He nodded proudly and tried to do a spin, and almost fell.

"Remember to go slow," I said, "when you drive those widows home."

"What do you mean, drive 'em home? You think I'm a taxi service?"

"I think you're a saint, almost. So don't drink and drive. Get those ladies home safely. And do you remember what the Canadian voice said about strip clubs?"

"Don't go there."

"That's right, buddy. Now help me find the car."

He pointed. "It's that giant mountain in front of your face! For a Gospel boy, you sure are blind."

"Shut up, Grease."

He laughed and slapped my shoulder, sending a cloud of snow flying. "Danny, Iowa hasn't been the same without you."

"I missed you, too, Grease."

"Did you know that Will Bentley is okay? Did you know that you're not in trouble anymore?"

I was still in trouble for other things, but I said, "Thanks for telling me."

Grease was beaming. "Danny, did you hear about . . ."

"Hear about what?"

Grease bit his tongue. He really bit it. "Ouchth. Never mind."

"Hmm. You know something. Spit it out."

"Well . . . okay," he said, his eyes sort of wild. "I don't know if I know anything or not, but I was wondering if you could possibly help me."

"How?"

Grease stared at the snowy mound of Cadillac. "Danny, can you bring the high-rider to a secret location and make a switch?"

"A switch?"

"I have your truck hidden away."

"Where?"

Grease glanced around and then whispered the secret into my nearly numb ear.

chapter ten

THE BLINDING SNOW made the journey a dangerous trip, but I traversed a center path between the two lanes on the interstate. Winter roads claim many souls, and one wrong turn of the wheel can result in a last-ditch effort to keep from rolling over. I enjoyed the challenge of snow blindness, feeling like a bold explorer at the top or bottom of the world. After several hours, my mind was wandering from memory to memory and face to face. And I began to wonder about dreams and the places they take us and the places they make us stay.

Why did I never dream of moving to New York? Why did I never imagine that the Big Apple was an appropriate place to make music, be in love, raise a family, and have a normal happy life? Why couldn't New York be Heaven on earth for me? After all, in the Revelation of Saint John, Heaven is envisioned as a great city: the New Jerusalem. Not a garden. Not a farm.

In the whiteout, I had slowed to about twenty miles per hour, and now two hulking vehicles were bearing down on the high-rider. I squinted into the rearview mirror and determined that the vehicles were army trucks.

Had war been declared on Christmas Eve?

Behind the trucks were two blurry rows of more trucks, the headlights blinking. A part of me wanted to block the army's passage, to postpone lost lives on all sides, but I pulled over and let them plow forward.

A few minutes later, the military had completely disappeared into the swirling clouds of snow.

I resumed my mission, driving down the center of the interstate, both hands gripping the wheel. And I quit wondering about dreams, because I had a shivering vision of how this holy night would end.

Near Iowa City, I exited and drove into the unplowed countryside, steering a middle course between the fields, guessing where the gravel was. The high-rider rode high above the drifts, as if it could traverse anything, and then I swerved where a driveway should have been, and hit the brakes and slid to a stop.

"What happened to the entrance to our farm?"

Pine trees shimmered in the headlights, two long rows of balsam fir.

"So it's true," I whispered, finally accepting it.

During the past several years, people had tried to tell me that the farm had been transformed. The house, barn, and silos were gone. Replaced by Christmas trees. At least forty acres of evergreens.

Dumbfounded, I rolled down the window and stared at the forest in the cornfield, wondering: who did this?

The wind swirled and the snow kissed my face. For a long while, I just sat there squinting at the trees. I wanted to drive farther up to where the house once stood, where the simple wood structure had sheltered such powerful and fragile hearts, but it didn't seem appropriate to trespass on Christmas Eve. So I drove away from the place that had made me Danny Gospel and over to the Williams farm that was now apparently mine, even though I didn't really want it.

Golden light poured out of the windows of the Williams house, and colorful strings of Christmas lights were blinking all around. I got out of the Cadillac and climbed the stairs to the porch and knocked on the door.

No answer.

The house was silent.

I knocked again. "Anybody home?"

Silence. Just the wind around the property.

I reached out and rattled the doorknob. It was locked.

"Well, that's that. Oh, wait a second."

I fished the key out from my suit pocket, and with a trembling hand unlocked the door.

"Anybody home?"

A fire was crackling in the fireplace in the living room. I shuffled over there and noticed a photograph on the mantel. It was a picture of the Gospel Family. There was Father standing tall but slumped, with me at his side as if holding him up; and Grandmother sitting on a stool, strumming the sweetest guitar; and Jonathan with his banjo, strutting near the torches; and Holly fiddling the violin, smiling at the camera, her eyes already full of Heaven; and Mother, bent gracefully over the harp, inviting the whole crowd to the Higher Ground.

I turned from the fireplace and looked across the living room. Near the north window stood a towering Christmas tree. Angel-topped, glittering, and surrounded by lavishly wrapped gifts, the tree was like a dream. And the gifts around the tree were so large, like the wishes of a child, and I knew exactly what they were. But I couldn't bear to open the gifts yet. Instead, I sat in a comfortable rocking chair and closed my eyes and dream-remembered the time that the Gospel kids snuck out of the house on Christmas Eve. While our parents and Grammy Dorrie were snoring up a storm, Jon and I and Holly tiptoed down the stairs and out the front door. We were aged thirteen, ten, and seven. Like Magi in training, but with no help from the stars, we trudged through the snowy darkness to the Williams farm to witness the miracle of talking pigs.

"Animals can talk every night of the year," Holly said, "because every night is Christmas Eve. But tonight is even more Christmas and more Eve than the other nights. Understand?"

"Nope," Jon said, trudging ahead of us.

I held Holly's hand. "What do you think the pigs will say?"

She picked up the pace, tugging me forward. "The pigs won't waste any words tonight. They won't be talking about their slop. The pigs will be praying."

Jack Williams' farmhouse was all lit up. Shelby was visiting from New Orleans, and the two brothers were keeping late hours. We snuck among the shadows to get into the hog shed, and when we closed the door behind us, there was no sound in the darkness except for our nervous breathing and the peaceful sleeping of the beasts.

Holly pushed a little button on her watch. A green glow exposed her hopeful face. "One more minute," she said.

"Okay, now less than a minute. Be patient. The miracle will happen in fifty-two seconds. It won't be long now!"

"Shhh," Jon said. "We don't want the Williams brothers to shoot us."

"Jack wouldn't hurt a mosquito," I said.

Jon laughed. "A mosquito? In winter? You're right, Danny. The mosquitoes are safe tonight."

"Shush," Holly said. "Get down on your knees."

We kneeled in the half-frozen mud beside the barely visible beasts.

Holly whispered, "It is now officially midnight on Christmas Eve. This is it."

We waited in the cold uncomfortable silence while the animals continued to dream whatever it is that animals dream.

Jon and I loved Holly enough to stay kneeling for at least an hour, waiting for her miracle, but it wasn't that long before we heard voices. They began with a single note, as if warming up.

Holly exclaimed, "It's happening!"

The voices were deep and strong, and coming from the house.

Jack and Shelby were singing. "*God rest ye merry gentlemen, let nothing you dismay. For Jesus Christ our Savior was born on Christmas Day. To save us all from Satan's power when we had gone astray. Oh, tidings of comfort and joy, comfort and joy. Oh, tidings of comfort and joy.*"

The pigs did not awaken to sing along. And Holly became worried. She jumped to her feet. "Lift me over the railing."

Jon stood. "No. That's dangerous. Be still."

Holly ignored him. "Danny, help me. The pigs won't pray when there's a barrier between us. Please lift me over the railing."

I stayed kneeling in the stink, wanting Holly to be happy, yet knowing that pigs are unpredictable and can attack. There was no way I was going to risk Holly's safety for a miracle that she didn't need.

More sounds came from the house. Jack and Shelby were opening presents.

Jon said, "Sounds like the clinking of bottles. I wonder what they're drinking in there. I've half a mind to find out."

"Lift me over the railing, Danny," Holly pleaded. "The pigs need to be reminded to pray. We have to help them to pray so they can help us."

Jon strode over to the door and opened it. "Let's go. Midnight is over."

Holly was on the verge of sobbing. "Danny, you know what I'm talking about. If we help the animals pray, then they'll help us."

Jon said, "Pigs poop. That's what they do, Holly. They make a mess. They don't worship God. C'mon, let's go home." And he walked out into the falling snow with every intention of circling around to the house to party with the brothers.

Holly grabbed my hand. "Danny. Don't leave me here alone."

"I won't. Don't worry."

The Williams brothers laughed heartily. They must have been exchanging gag gifts. Who knows what kind of bizarre presents Shelby had brought to Iowa from Louisiana.

"I'll go in the pen," I said to Holly. "You kneel down and pray, and I'll explain to the pigs what's going on. Okay?"

She wiped her eyes. "Okay."

I climbed onto the railing, very carefully, not wanting to cause a stampede or a feeding frenzy. Death by pigs is not a good way to go, especially on the holiest night of the year. I was being ever so careful, and then I slipped and fell into the herd.

Snort! Snort! Snort!

It was not a joyful noise. But Holly heard a kind of prayer. She honestly believed the animals were singing to God.

She said, "Good piggies! Praise him in the highest! Danny, sing with them!"

I sang, "*Away in a manger . . .*" until I was almost trampled to death, kicked in the head and ribs and guts, and eventually lifted up by Jon.

The fireplace crackled, and I opened my eyes. The scent of balsam fir hung deliciously in the air and my head swirled, verging on other dream-memories. Catching my attention in the room was a folded letter taped to a gift by the tree. My name was written large: "DANNY." I stood and went to retrieve the letter, and sat back down in the recliner and read the words of my brother.

Dear Danny,

Merry Christmas! I hope you enjoy the presents. I found some of them scattered around Iowa, and one of them I tracked down in a pawn shop in Massachusetts. Praise God, I found everything.

Danny, I did some of the paper work for your inheritance

of the Williams farm. That property also includes our old property. Jack had bought our farm after the previous owner, a corporation in Chicago, went bankrupt. Jack was so angry about the corporation tearing down our buildings that he went a little crazy and planted Christmas trees. I was flabbergasted to discover this, but upon reflection I think it was a wonderful thing to do. Father and Holly, especially, would love the growing forest.

Danny, you now own the Gospel family farm.

Your old friends the Samsonov brothers still live three farms over to the west, working mainly with corn and hogs; and they also raise Saint Bernards. Mud Eye and Slopper said you're free to borrow some of their equipment next year, because they always borrow some of Jack's equipment. I hired the Samsonovs to decorate your new house. Did they put up the lights?

Danny, I hope this letter finds you well. When I return from my honeymoon, I'll drive over to your farm so we can discuss various issues.

> I remain, your devoted brother,
> Jonathan

"So I really am home," I whispered to the Christmas tree.

I felt like laughing and crying, and it was all too much to process. I dropped my brother's letter to the floor and thought about his wedding. . . . It was a glorious wedding. My big brother found a lovely wife, a better half. But Jon doesn't have a farm. Imagine that, a grown man in Iowa with no farm. Look at me, I have two farms! And a house, and a forest. I have everything a man could ever want. Except for a better half.

I remembered a once-upon-a-time night by the reservoir.

The winter stars were burning so close to the earth. And Rachel was enfolded in my arms.

She said, "Let's go together, Danny. You'll love the city. There are so many bookstores, galleries, museums, cafés, parks, colleges, and churches. You'll be inspired to write the songs that could never find a voice in Iowa."

The kiss I gave her in response was warm, and my words were not. "I can't go with you, Rachel. New York would kill me."

"I love you," she said, shivering, "but I need more of a world than this place. Please, Danny, come with me."

The sky was throbbing and throbbing with love-struck stars. And I wondered: why can't Rachel see that Iowa is just as much Heaven as anywhere else?

I held her, knowing that I'd already lost her, and whispered, "I thought you were done with the city, because of what it did to your parents. Why would you ever go back?"

Rachel closed her eyes, and shivered again.

The Williams' living room—my living room—was alive with the same light that was gracing millions of homes that holy evening. Depending on time zones, some families were just starting to unwrap their Christmas presents, while others were finishing and cleaning up, and still other families were singing in church.

Quietly, the song of the Dream Tower came back to me:

"If you sing your life, you pray it twice, through the dark days and the sun-filled nights. All of creation groans.

*And everywhere there's a reverie. All of creation groans.
And everywhere there's a reverie."*

Now it was time to open my presents.

I stood and approached the glittering tree. I'd received
many gifts in my life, but none so painful. My hands trembled while I slowly unwrapped the first present. It was
Grammy's guitar. The strings were perfectly tuned as I
played a few chords and whisper-sang, *"How sweet the
sound, that saved a wretch like me."* The next present was
Jon's banjo. I smiled and plucked a few notes, the tears
streaming down my face. And then I placed the banjo back
under the branches and unwrapped another gift. It was
Holly's fiddle, covered with feathers of all colors. I felt like
my sister was glancing down from the heavenly choir, and
the facial expression of the angel atop the tree suggested
that everything was working out according to the Christmas
plan, even though my heart was breaking into pieces. The
next present was Mother's harp. I began strum-running my
hands over the strings to make waves of ascending notes.
The image of Mother falling was ever in my mind, but this
was a way of lifting her back into the sky. *"How sweet the
sound, that saved . . ."*

My eyes wandered to the base of the tree. There was
one more gift, a tiny green package with a red bow. I knelt
to pick up what I thought was probably one of Father's
crosses. I shook the package and heard the jingle of metal
on metal. "Yes," I whispered, unwrapping the gift. "I'll
carry this for you."

And the telephone rang.

I wondered: who could that be? Shelby? Jon? Grease?
Mud Eye or Slopper? Who else knows I'm here?

The telephone rang and rang, and I hurried into the kitchen to answer.

"Hello?"

"Hi, Danny."

"Rachel!"

"It's me."

"It's really you?"

"It's really me."

"Rachel! Where are you?"

"Listen, Danny. I can't talk long."

"Where are you? I need to see you!"

"Danny. Did you get my messages on your machine? I explained—"

"I didn't get them. What's going on, Rachel? Are you okay?"

"I wanted to say I'm sorry."

"I'm sorry, too."

"Danny, you didn't do anything wrong. What are you sorry about?"

"New York . . . our birthday."

"It was horrible, that's for sure. But I want to wish you a Merry Christmas. And I left some messages on your machine that explained . . ."

"Explained what? Tell me."

"You need to hear the messages first."

"Rachel, just tell me. Please."

"I'm very nervous, Danny. Everything has changed."

"I've changed, too."

"Please listen, Danny. I'm sorry to have hurt you. I wasn't thinking clearly. But you need to know this, Danny.

262 — David Athey

It wasn't a real kiss. I didn't even like Will Bentley. The only reason I kissed him was to set you free."

"I didn't want to be free."

"I know, Danny."

There was a long pause full of sighs and tears. And I heard sirens, but I wasn't sure if they were near the farm or where Rachel was.

I said, "I need to see you again."

She sobbed and said nothing. The sirens were getting louder.

"Rachel, where are you?"

Her words were fading and disappearing, "Danny . . . you need to be . . . free . . . and—"

And the line went dead.

"Rachel! Are you there? Rachel!"

I immediately dialed the code to find out the number where she was calling from, and a disembodied voice said: "We're sorry. The last number that called this address is unlisted."

I shouted at the disembodied voice, "Tell me where Rachel is! Tell me!"

Disembodied silence.

So many thoughts passed through my mind in the next instant, along with things that weren't even thoughts, and suddenly the phone was on the floor and my feet were shuffling out of the kitchen and out of the house. The wind was stronger than it had been earlier in the night, nearly howling as it built up drifts. I rushed over to the Cadillac and reached inside and gathered up my spiral notebooks; and then I tromped through the snow to the storage shed. There was the rusty red pickup. I climbed inside and placed the notebooks in the passenger seat and then sat frozen at the wheel. I took a deep cold breath and turned the key, giving fire to the engine. The old Chevy coughed and sputtered and spun away from the shed, plowing through the drifts as if nothing could stop it. The truck roared up the driveway to the county road.

I didn't hear any sirens, and hopefully that meant I could drive to my trailer without getting caught. Regardless of the risk, I had to hear all of the messages on my answering machine. I had to know what Rachel was talking about. Everything had changed in our lives. We both knew that. But what did that mean? What kind of an "us" were we now?

The messages would tell me.

I remembered how Rachel had scooped up Grammy's guitar a few minutes before the auction and led me down to the cellar, where we sat on overturned rusted buckets. Rachel strummed the guitar—I didn't even know she could play—and sang in a bluesy voice, *"Praise the Lord. Praise God in his sanctuary; praise him in his mighty heavens. Praise him for his acts of power; praise him for his surpassing greatness."*

Rachel sang Psalm 150, the final psalm in the Bible, as if it would be the last thing sung on earth. *"Praise him with the sounding of the trumpet, praise him with the harp and lyre."*

The Gospel Family had tried to obey those commands to praise. Despite our problems, weaknesses, and sins, we'd lifted up our music to the Lord.

"Praise him," I sang in the truck while I plowed toward the interstate, *"praise him with tambourine and dancing,*

264 — David Athey

praise him with the strings and the flute, praise him with the clash of cymbals, praise him with resounding cymbals. Let everything that has breath praise the Lord. Praise the Lord."

Something caught my attention in the rearview mirror. Something back there in the snow was kicking up a cloud and stampeding toward the truck.

"What on earth? Not again."

I tried to accelerate but had trouble finding traction. The wheels spun and the truck swerved while the herd of swine followed me toward the interstate. I could hear a faint snorting and squealing in the wind while I finally got the Chevy to gain speed toward the ramp. I thought: just get on the freeway and that will be the end of them. Pigs can't run sixty miles per hour.

The truck missed the entrance and plummeted down the embankment and turned sideways. The Chevy rolled and the notebooks in the passenger seat flapped and fluttered into the air. The pickup rolled again and hit a tree, and my rib cage was crushed by the steering wheel. My mouth filled with blood and everything went black.

In a blinding light, I blinked and tried to move, but I was strapped to the bed and plugged into all sorts of medical devices. I blinked again. A man in shades stood over me, staring down.

It was impossible to turn away. All I could do was move my eyes. To my right was a glass door. To my left was a window. The blinds were open and the sky was wild with yellow, green, and purple. Arcs and streamers and search-light beams.

The aurora borealis.

The man in shades looked down. "Daniel Gospel?"

"Yeah?"

"Is that your real name?"

"Well . . . it depends on who's asking."

"I am asking for your real name."

"Why?"

"Are you refusing to cooperate?"

"Cooperate with whom?"

"Listen, Daniel. Things could get less comfortable. There are other rooms."

I swallowed hard, the taste of blood strong in my mouth. "Where am I?"

The man in shades leaned toward my face. "You are under observation."

His words made me laugh. "Ouch!" The pain in my chest was excruciating.

"Your heart is damaged," the man said. "Don't laugh."

I nodded. "I won't laugh if you don't." Then I told him my real name. "Daniel David McGillicuddy."

The man adjusted his shades and smiled. "Very good." And he stepped away from the bed and walked out of the room, his heels clicking like tap shoes.

My eyes returned to the aurora. The colors swayed like curtains opening into one another. I strained at my restraints. They would not give. So I rested for a while, saving my strength.

An hour or so later, the man in shades clicked back up the corridor, his steps echoing louder and louder. He reentered the room and locked the door behind him with an old-fashioned key. I tried to remember what that was called—a skeleton key? In his other hand, he held a blue spiral notebook. "Danny, do you recognize this?"

"Yes."

He opened to the place where I'd stopped writing my life story. "Danny. Where are the rest of the words?"

"What do you mean?"

He dropped the notebook onto my chest. The pain was like fire. "Your confession," he said in a scolding voice, "is unfinished."

I swallowed some blood.

He reached into his pocket and then placed a gold pen upon the notebook. "Finish your confession."

I wriggled my fingers. Wriggled and wriggled, but the man didn't seem to get it. "You have my arms strapped down."

"Oh. Yes. Here." He fiddled with the restraint and set my writing hand free, and adjusted the bed so that I could almost sit up. "Finish your life, Daniel. And I want you to clarify something. What was the meaning of the poem that you shared at the Foxhead Tavern?"

I snuck a peek out the window at the aurora. "You want me to explain poetry? It's simple. Heaven kisses you. And you sing."

The man grinned. His teeth were so white. "Daniel David McGillicuddy. Are you claiming to have been kissed by an angel?"

"No. Not exactly. But even so, is that against the law?"

"Yes. Now tell me about Gloria."

"What do you want to know?"

"Do you and Gloria have a serious relationship?"

"I'm not sure. That's up to God."

The man in shades was relentless. "Tell me about your crimes."

"My crimes?"

"Yes. You need to confess them."

"I have been. The last notebook is almost full."

The man smirked. "Daniel. You are accused of stealing and tampering with the mail. You are suspected of sending out anthrax. And you are being held on suspicion of murder."

"What?"

"Murder. And terrorism."

"That's crazy. I've never hurt anyone. Not on purpose."

The man paused, adjusted his shades, and continued. "A clear confession might help you avoid the death penalty."

I laughed, and grimaced from the pain in my chest. "You're making this up."

The man shook his head. "There was a trace of anthrax on a piece of mail in your trailer."

"So? There were infinitesimal traces of anthrax all over the place. The mail carriers were aware of that. Some people wore gloves for a while, but I wasn't afraid."

The man pointed at the blue notebook. "Confess, Danny. Avoid the death penalty. Explain why you messed with the mail. Write it all down."

I took a deep breath and tasted more blood. "Listen," I said. "Before I write it, let me just tell you what happened on 9/11. Okay?"

The man did not respond.

"I kept trying to call Rachel, but the phone was dead. So I turned on the TV and saw the twin towers burning. There

268 — David Athey

were people in the windows, waving shirts and towels, begging to be saved. Where were the fire ladders, or helicopters? Where were the angels? Suddenly the television caught the face of a young woman, leaping. There was sunlight on her face, hazy through the smoke, and the sunlight clung to her skin as she fell. She could have been . . . anyone. I prayed with all my might that she would survive."

The man in shades was unmoved. "What does this have to do with the mail?"

"Stealing the mail was my way to help."

"That sounds insane."

"After the towers fell, I went to the post office. Everyone was in shock. Nobody noticed when I put a bundle of mail in the back of my pickup. I took that bundle home and dumped it on the floor. In the middle of my living room, the envelopes were piled up like debris. And I sifted through, searching."

The man leaned down and whispered into my ear. "Searching for what?"

"Bills, invoices, stuff like that. If I couldn't save anybody in New York, at least I could pay the bills in Iowa City. Mortgages, electricity, water, tuition, rent, everything. I got to be a hero until my nest egg was gone."

"Your nest egg?"

"I'd been saving every penny, thinking I could buy back the family farm. That was my big dream: to start another Gospel Family."

The man in shades backed off. "Your claim is that you only tampered with the mail to help people."

"Yes. Now, may I please borrow a phone and make a call? Or better yet, can I please go home and listen to my messages?"

The man shook his head and pointed at my heart. "Your messages have been erased. Now you need to finish your confession. Don't leave out a thing. Give us the whole story."

I sighed and swallowed and nearly choked on the blood. "I can only tell you what God allows me to know."

The man nodded. "Your cooperation, if it's complete, will be rewarded. By the way, Merry Christmas."

"Yes," I said, grimacing. "Merry Christmas."

The interrogation was over. The man in shades walked out, locked the door with his skeleton key, and left me alone. His heels clicked down the hallway, echoing as if the hallway went on forever and ever. The lights in my room darkened. And the night became silent.

My eyes returned to the window, and I was disappointed to see that the aurora had vanished. But the heavens were throbbing with stars and planets and galaxies.

I wondered: how does anyone ever finish a confession?

Exhausted, I hugged the spiral notebook to my aching chest and soon spun into dreams.

Eve . . . Oasis . . . Psalm . . . Grace . . . Angel . . . Iowa . . . Bride . . . Gospel . . . Family.

Some time later, perhaps a long time later, I was awakened by a light in the hallway. A woman, strangely familiar and perfectly lovely, stood shimmering outside the glass door.

She was dressed in white, and she began to sing a song that was old and new and beautiful. It was like a Spiritual, but without any sorrow.

"*Let's fly away*," she sang.

about the author

DAVID ATHEY has taught creative writing at Buena Vista University, the Dreyfoos School of the Arts, and Palm Beach Atlantic University. Athey's poems, stories, essays, and reviews have appeared in more than sixty literary journals, including *The Iowa Review, Harvard Review,* and *California Quarterly.*

Looking for More Good Books to Read?

You can find out what is new and exciting with previews, descriptions, and reviews by signing up for Bethany House newsletters at

www.bethanynewsletters.com

We will send you updates for as many authors or categories as you desire so you get only the information you really want.

Sign up today!